ThymeTable Mill

Celia H. Miles

ISBN 0-7414-2525-4

Cover artist: Emilie Stevens, water-colorist, lives in Durham, NC, and can be reached at Emilie_inc@mindspring.com.

Author photo by Mona Rae Miracle.

Published by:

INFINITY PUBLISHING.COM

1094 New DeHaven Street, Suite 100
West Conshohocken, PA 19428-2713
Info@buybooksontheweb.com
www.buybooksontheweb.com
Toll-free (877) BUY BOOK
Local Phone (610) 941-9999
Fax (610) 941-9959

Printed in the United States of America

Printed on Recycled Paper

Published June 2005

Dedicated to all those who love old mills–
their romance and their reality

with

Thanks to the following mill owners whose mills Cary visits:
Tanna Timbes–Francis Mill
Kenny Campbell–Old Traphill Mill
Jack Dellinger–Dellinger Mill
the Horky family–Millhouse Lodge
John and Jane Lovetts–Falls Mill
and all the others whose mills I've visited and photographed.

and

Thanks to all my fellow writers, especially The Plotters, who have encouraged, read, critiqued, and edited the manuscript, as well as friend John Duvall for his valuable contribution to Chapter 15 and husband Louis who has been ever constant in finding mills, here and abroad.

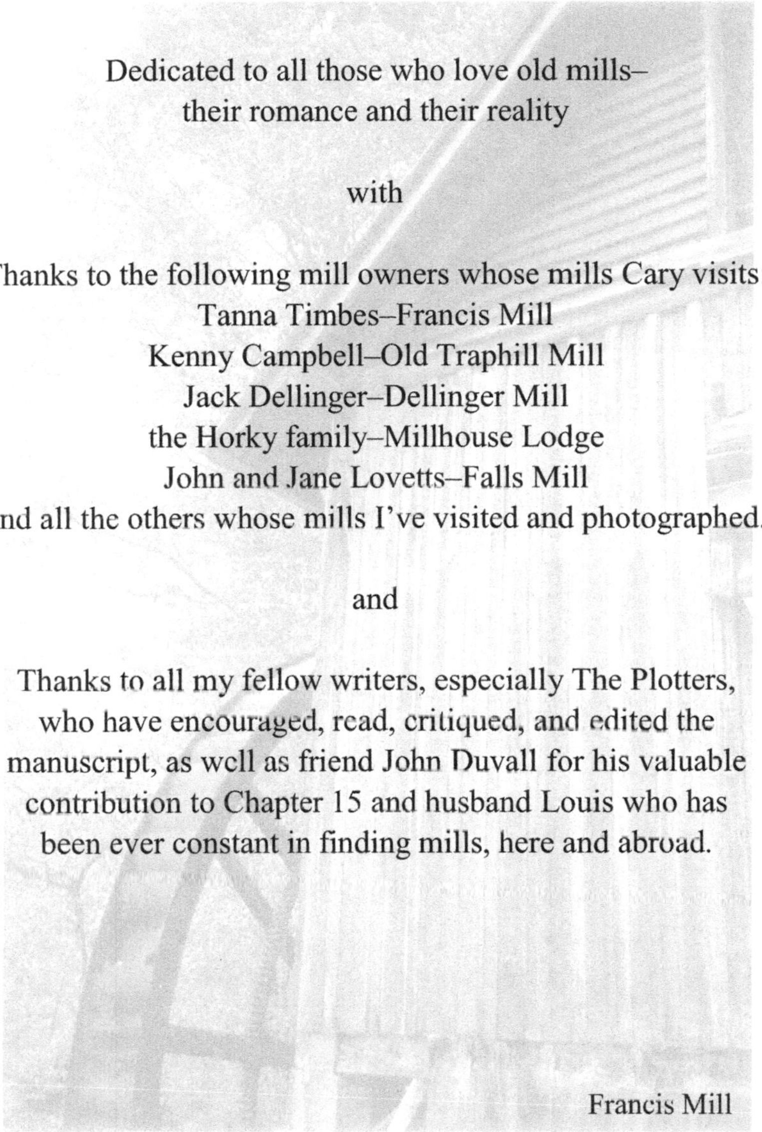

Francis Mill

Chapter 1 "The Poetry of the Earth"

After Cary poured the red-speckled batter into the waiting muffin tin and deposited it in the oven, she sat down across from Mary. She lifted the top of the tea pot and peeked inside, then replenished her cup. She'd almost given up coffee entirely but hadn't convinced her friend to consider doing the same. "Don't you love this February sunshine?" she mused.

Her photographer's eye noted the bent of the sunlight through the window, the splatter of muted shadows left by the thin, European style white curtains. How many times had she attempted to capture the lovely but elusive scene? How many photographs had she torn up and discarded? With some confidence she knew she'd keep trying until one morning the "aha" moment would arrive.

The fragrance of cranberry muffins, coffee, tea, and an essence of mixed herbs created a warmth in the bright kitchen that both women savored. They occasionally breathed deeply and sighed with contentment. At Cary's feet, their beagle occasionally broke his soft breathing with a snort and a twitch of his nose. She looked out the window. From the back of the white farmhouse she could see beyond the yard, now browned by winter, beyond the small stream, and up the hillside. Its few trees hosted a scattering of determined leaves but she saw beauty in the jutting stones and meandering fence. Stalks of mullein stood spiky-tall. "The poetry of the earth is never dead," she murmured and grinned at Mary's questioning eyebrows. "Don't ask me who wrote it. It just came to me." She was apt to quote poetry, a line or two, at a moment's notice.

"Probably one of the Romantic poets," Mary noted. "It usually is." She flung her arms wide and exclaimed dramatically: "O world! O life! O time!"

Cary laughed. "Now, that's Shelley, for sure. Today's a Wordsworth day. Look at that sunshine. Idyllic." She paused, then raised her voice to sound both gruff and sonorous: "Come forth into the light of things. Let Nature be your teacher!"

"Poetry aside, February's definitely not my favorite month," Mary grunted. "If it's sunshiny like this one day, it's icy winds the next...unpredictable to the max."

"And you like predictability?" Cary teased. "Are you going south with Jon or not? Is Jon going anywhere? What's happening with you two?"

"Who knows?" Mary seemed disinclined to talk about, even to think about, the relationship between ex-husband Jon and herself. "I don't trust Jon, can't trust him. If ever a man had a roaming instinct, it's Jon. He's been here now, what, more than a month, you know that..."

"Since you two ate dinner with us three or four days ago, I do know that," Cary said. "But?"

Mary shrugged. "But who knows? I'm not the young impressionable thing I was. True, I like having him around. He's very likeable, even helpful now as he never was twenty years ago. And I give him credit. He has learned to stay out from under my feet–and out of my workroom when I'm on the computer." More than three decades earlier, Mary and Jon Surrett had been among the typical "hippies" (though none thought themselves typical of anything) who found their way to what they expected to be a simple lifestyle, a back-to-the-land existence. In The Cove, they and some friends tried their hands at farming and communal living. When in a fairly short time, the small group disbanded, a few pooled their resources, bought the acreage, and stayed on. Somehow, they had never given their settlement a more specific name. It remained The Cove. Though she liked the out-of-doors, Mary soon realized that more than wishful thinking and youthful fellowship was required for comfortable survival. Her son Johnny provided a major incentive for developing a steady income, along with the not unexpected departure of Jon. After several years of low-paying secretarial work, she put her education and natural facility for language to work, gathering clients who needed help with articles for the foreign market. She now worked from her home, translating technical documents. She liked her independence and realized that a stable home with its attendant responsibilities was not for Jon. He had never completely disappeared from her life, only from any expectations on her part.

"He seems happy enough," Cary said. "For the time being."

For long moments the two women, separated in age by almost thirty years, sat in companionable silence. Neither would push for confidences or revelations not readily shared. Their mutual understanding of that arrangement had made them friends and kept them friends.

"Agnes is up and out feeding her goats." Mary changed the subject. "I tried to get her to stay in, but she's as feisty as a spring chicken." Mary sipped her strong coffee, watching Cary stir the muffin mix. She breathed a satisfied sound. "That's what she says. And she didn't want me to remind her she's way past the pullet stage."

Alice and Agnes Grayson, two sisters now in their seventies, lived just up the road from ThymeTable Farm; they lived on pensions from their school teaching days in Chicago and from the sale of products from their beloved small goat herd. Their fresh goat cheese sold out as soon as the upscale local market received it; in fact, devotees put their names on the list so most of the cheese sold barely reached the dairy case. Though growing frailer and more bent with each month, the sisters resisted their neighbors' advice to hire a full-time helper for their Grayson Goats farm.

"Spence will stop by there on his way back from the herb meeting," Cary said, with a smile. She hadn't been a wife long enough to adopt a blase attitude toward her handsome husband. Her smile tended to appear with the mention of his name.

"You're grinning like a Cheshire cat," Mary said. "How long is this honeymoon in paradise going to last?"

Mary's pretense at brusqueness didn't fool Cary for an instant. She simply put the cup down and laughed. "How did you know what I was thinking?"

ThymeTable Farm, however, was not Eden, but a "working" herb farm; they were not in paradise, only close to it, in western North Carolina. Cary had never expected when she arrived to rent Rosemary Cottage that along with healing from an abusive relationship, she would fall almost instantly in love with Spence Bradford, her landlord. Over a period of months, the attraction and courtship had not been without its ups and downs, misunderstandings and reconciliations. At first, Mary had been protective toward Spence, a relative newcomer to The Cove, her friend and close neighbor. She did not want him to risk being hurt--as he had been by a fickle Darla, who had departed some months before Cary's arrival. When Darla reappeared, hopeful of convincing Spence to develop the property into a condominium golf course complex, Cary had declared her love and put the flamboyant Darla to flight. Cary and Spence had been married over two years and now she wanted a baby. And so did Spence and they did everything young couples do to speed the prospect along. Cary blushed, again holding the cup before her lips.

"I've been there," Mary informed her, calmly. "Had my honeymoon time–a long time ago. I recognize the signs when I see them, just like you're learning to read the signs in nature."

"I can't argue with that," Cary said, feeling like a sage philosopher, now that she and Spence had stopped sparring ("sparking" like firecrackers, Mary had teased) and settled into marriage.

Winchester, who had only opened his eyes lazily when Mary breezed in, raised his head, questioning. Mary bent to rub the beagle's ears. "I swear," she said, "this dog knows within a few minutes when muffins are coming out of that oven."

"Yeah, I may enter him into one of those amazing animals television shows," Cary responded. "He's got impeccable muffin timing." Winchester had appeared on their front porch several weeks earlier, his front paw raw and infected, his ribs showing, his tail tucked between his hind legs, his head bowed, submissive. Cary took one look at his soulful eyes and surrendered. She threw a warm thin blanket over his wet and bedraggled body and carried him into the kitchen. Gradually he assumed that the kitchen was his kingdom and he its master.

Cary and Spence had posted notices in local stores and announced the beagle's presence on the radio station. When one guy, smelling of beer and tomato sauce, showed up and tried to claim him, the beagle snarled and a ripple of hackles spread down his back.

"Are you sure this is your lost dog?" Spence wanted to be fair and give the man a chance. "Go ahead, check him out."

Rather than retreat as the guy swaggered toward him, Winchester stood his ground, as if protecting Cary. She spoke up, "There's a distinctive marking on his left leg. Can you tell us what it is?"

"Uh, what mark?" The man had thrown his cigarette onto the grass and ground it out with his heel. He said he'd raised the dog from a pup and, yeah, he remembered there was a spot, a kinda round dark circle, uh, on the leg. "Them beagles is worth a lot of money," he said.

Cary had smiled sweetly and shook her head. "I'm sorry, but he can't be your dog," she said. "We'll let you know if another beagle shows up around here if you'll leave your phone number."

With a few muttered swear words and an angry look at the stiff-spined beagle, the man turned and slammed the door to his new pickup. Only when he'd wheeled his vehicle around and disappeared in the curve of the road did Winchester relax. Spence glanced at Cary and squatted to pet Winchester. "Honey, I don't remember any dark circle. Which leg?"

"There isn't one." She laughed. "Now, Spence, don't look at me like that. I didn't lie. The distinctive marking is the absence of any. He's the one who said dark circle." She petted the docile animal. "Not to worry, Winnie, I wasn't about to let that man have you," she murmured. "Expensive, indeed!"

Spence grinned. The evening of Winchester's arrival, the two of them sat on the sofa, the meek dog, bathed and fed, between them, and watched a program on British cathedrals. "Hey, we can name him Salisbury," Spence said. That didn't quite suit, and they lazily drifted through the names of cathedrals--Ely, Gloucester, Lincoln--until Winchester fit him exactly. Now he answered to Winchester, Winnie, WinBoy; he answered to anything Cary called him, even Muffin.

"He's a muffin dog, for sure," Cary now said to her friend. She moved the salt and pepper shakers around on the table, then propped her chin on her hands.

"Okay, something's bothering you today. Tell me when you're ready."

The door burst open. Spence said, "I've called 911 and they're on the way. Agnes has fallen. She's unconscious–"

The women jumped to their feet. "Let's go!" Mary was in her jacket in an instant. Cary ran for the closet and jerked a coat from its hanger.

"But breathing," Spence finished. "The engine's running in my truck." As they dashed for the door, Winchester, on his feet, barked his special bark and Spence smelled the muffins. Thanks, Winnie," he said, opening the oven door. "You'll get a bite later. Gotta go." He deposited the pan on the top of the stove and turned off the oven. The women were already in Mary's van.

A few yards from the old lilac bush that marked the boundary of the yard, Alice knelt beside her sister, gripping a limp hand. Spence had covered the wiry Agnes with quilts, but he hadn't dared move her. Immediately Mary went from the prone woman to the house. "I'll get another quilt, warm it up. The ambulance should be here any moment."

Cary hunkered beside Alice, wrapped her arms around her shoulders and the older woman started shaking uncontrollably. Her face was contorted with anguish but she was dry-eyed. "She insisted on coming out here to check on the Nubian," she whispered. "When she didn't come right back we looked out the window. I don't think anything's broken...I mean, we didn't see any broken bones. And," she said desperately, "she's still breathing." Beyond the fence, the small band of goats looked on with interest, chewing and occasionally moving restlessly but not leaving the fence. They reminded Cary of stunned relatives not yet recognizing the reality of disaster or death.

The silence in The Cove seemed to descend like a weight. Spence drove up, parked to the side of the drive, then moved Mary's van so the emergency medical crew could get as close as possible to Agnes. He strode out to the road to watch, just as he saw the blinking light of the ambulance. Luckily the farm was less than ten minutes from the nearest fire and rescue station.

In the early afternoon, when the doctor entered the waiting room, the four rose instantly to their feet. He spoke with quiet assurance: there was nothing they could do at this point; the patient was comfortable, sedated. Agnes had a broken wrist and had, he said, suffered a stroke. For a few seconds she had revived and attempted to mumble a few words. Whether she would regain full use of her speech was uncertain; they could only wait. "She's being monitored constantly," Dr. Stoddard said. "We'll call immediately if there's any change." He peered at Alice. "Are you all right?

You need to lie down, take it easy. I could call for a wheelchair for when you leave."

"No, I'm fine. Just tired," Alice said. Though they tried half-heartedly to persuade Alice to return to The Cove, they remained in the Intensive Care waiting room for hours after the doctor hurried away. Every few minutes one or the other would wander down the hall to peek into Agnes' room. When Spence finally said he'd better go see to the goats, Alice nodded.

"They'll miss us," she said, and then put her coat on. They trooped from the room to the elevator, but there Alice stopped. "No. I'll stay. I can't leave her here alone." Her voice faltered a little.

"Of course not," Mary said. "What were we thinking? We're all too tired to think. You go on and get some rest, Alice. I'll stay here." She hugged the older woman. "No arguments. Jon will come as soon as he knows."

"Come on." Spence put a gruffness into his voice. "Do I have to carry you out of here? We can come back later--and Mary will call if there's any change."

Alice put her head against Cary's shoulder as they waited for the elevator.

Spence lay the dish towel on the counter and began to put out the tea pot and cups for their late afternoon tea time. Cary, busy with Winchester's dish, paused to admire her husband of two years, five months, one week and three days. When they'd met, as she was stumbling over his thyme patch, her heart had given a particular little lurch, just like a heroine in a romance novel, and it did the same now. Worried as she was about Agnes, she smiled and hummed a tune before singing, "Will you still need me, will you still feed me when I'm sixty-four...?"

"You and your Beatles craze," Spence said. "Your brother didn't know what he was getting us into when they cleaned out their attic and gave his collection to you!" He pulled Cary to her feet. "And I never pictured your brother as a Beatles fan." Spence kissed her soundly and then held her close. “Yes, I’ll still need you and feed you when you’re sixty-four...and all the years between now and then.”

“Let’s play the Sgt. Peppers album right now.” Cary snuggled against him; they made a perfect fit. “Good old Phillip.”

Her brother Phillip, a few years older, had been Cary’s protector and adviser always. He had “bossed” her when he was a teen and she a child and he tended to continue that role. Phillip and his lovely wife Alecia were in most ways opposites of Spence and Cary. They liked city life or at least a town big enough to offer cultural activities and commercial opportunities for sophisticated wheelings and dealings with the power brokers. Phillip developed tracts of land and, when Cary had come to Rosemary’s Cottage at ThymeTable, he had hoped the farm and the surrounding area might be available for converting to condos and golf courses. In spite of their differing opinions on land development, money, and lifestyle, brother and sister remained on good terms generally, simply because they recognized their differences and softened their political stances, thus making their parents happy. Now, those parents waited patiently for news of a grandchild. Alecia, svelte and apparently satisfied with her childless state, seemed in no hurry. Cary, on the other hand, wanted a child. She looked at Spence and wanted his child, their child. When, only a few years earlier, girlfriends in her hometown had confessed a similar desire, Cary couldn’t begin to understand it. Now she could. In her logical, thinking moments she was faintly embarrassed about this intense craving for a child. After all, she was not yet twenty-seven; she was not yet racing with her biological time clock. She was young, she had plenty of time, years and years yet. Somehow that did not appease her when the longing to hold Spence’s child swept over her. And she didn’t want to start on some regimen, seeing doctors, noting temperatures, times and hours of most likely conception time. She bit her lip. She was being a little silly, that she knew.

"Let's dance," she whispered, and Spence released her to go put on the Beatles recording.

"What'cha thinking, dearest?" Spence held her to him and they moved, not necessarily in time to the music.

Three kisses later, Cary assured him she was thinking of him, of her lovable herb farmer.

"And...is that all?" he whispered suggestively, nibbling her ear tenderly.

"Not quite," she said and they waltzed with sedate married decorum toward the bedroom.

"It's long past dinner time," Spence said, some time later. "How about I create a veggie and barley soup for us? I, for one, am hungry."

"You're always hungry. Just open a can of something. I'll make a salad. We may have to return to the hospital tonight. If Alice wants to go back." Cary pulled on her favorite fleecy robe and rabbit slippers. She noticed that Spence stopped to sort bills and catalogs at the large roll- top desk that served as general office for the farm. He kept meticulous records and a most orderly and organized desk. When he saw her questioning gaze, he swept one stack of material into the trash basket and went toward the kitchen.

Mary called a short time later, reporting that Alice had finally eaten a little and would try to sleep. "I gave her a healthy cup of ThymeTable's special tea," she said. "Jon's staying at the hospital a little longer. No change. See you in the morning."

After they'd done the dishes they settled in the den of the farmhouse, where Spence could work on the books and Cary could study her herb encyclopedia, keying notes of interest into her laptop. "I must call Justin," Cary said. "Mary didn't mention that she'd been in touch. He'd never forgive us if we didn't call, if we waited-- too late."

She could not bring herself to utter the words "if she doesn't pull through," because at heart she was an optimist, sometimes, as her brother pointed out, to the point of being ridiculously naive. She preferred to recall the line of one of

Shelley's poems about "one wandering thought poisoning the day." Why allow worry, useless and non-focused worry, to pollute the present moment when disaster, sickness, death could indeed poison the future. She and Mary had bouts of philosophizing about attitudes. "If I worry now about something I can do nothing about," Cary said, "then I am ruining the beauty of now, I'm kind of blighting the sunshine with a cloud I have created. I know that the real cloud may come, will come, and darken the day, but by worrying I have darkened now and changed absolutely nothing."

Mary, more pragmatic, had shrugged. And wondered just how one prevented worry from occurring. "Oh," Cary said, "I think one should do something about anything that can be changed, I don't mean to exist like an ostrich. I guess what I abhor is people who claim to worry about every thing, big and little, as if their worrying about it absolves them from doing anything."

Mary had pointed out that one could both worry and do something; they weren't mutually exclusive behaviors. "I know," Cary had said. "So now I should worry that I'm worrying too much?" Mary grinned. Cary was not the type to worry that tomorrow's rain would delay her photography outing or that the new outfit she'd bought wouldn't be quite right for Alecia's country club party.

"Don't worry about it," Spence said absently. "Call him tomorrow."

"I'm dialing right now," Cary responded and Spence took a moment to ascertain that she was doing just that. "Would you rather talk to him?"

"Not at all," Spence said. He put the papers aside and stood. "In fact, I'll take Winchester for his walk."

Spence wasn't exactly jealous of Justin, Cary knew. But since the young doctor had once been a competitor for Cary's affections, he didn't view him now as he once had. Justin's father Robert had died soon after Cary's arrival at ThymeTable and Justin declared he'd never want to live out in the country. His residency was almost finished. He was engaged to a friend of Cary's and Cary prided herself on introducing them and playing cupid. Meanwhile the home place now sat empty while Justin and Denise decided about marriage and where he would practice. Her jewelry design business flourished in Virginia, and at least once weekly she called Cary to chat and ask if she were pregnant yet.

Chapter 2 "No Place for Sissies"

While Cary read about the medicinal properties of elderberries, she was imagining blue baby clothes, then pink blankets, then she took the dream child by the hand, dressed in yellow so she could later impose baby boy or baby girl behaviors on it. She hardly noticed Spence's sigh and his "Oh brother." A few moments later she couldn't ignore his scraping back of the chair and pushing the account books far away.

"What is it?" Cary asked. "What's wrong, Spence?"

"Bills, bills, bills," he grunted. "We lost money in the last months. That holiday herb fair in east Tennessee was a bust."

"Well, the rain didn't help," Cary said. "The park was almost washed away. And then we had to stay those extra nights because of the awful road conditions."

"Plus all the extra work of taking down the big tent in the rain," Spence agreed. "At first it was too cold in a tent, even with space heaters, and then..."

Cary closed the book and stood up. "We were lucky the lightning didn't strike us." She shivered a little, remembering the icy torrential rains, the wicked streaks of lightning, the news that only a few miles away two houses had been hit and burned. "Want some tea?"

"Coffee, please."

"It must be bad, then," she said. "Coffee it is, but decaf." Just a few days before, when Mary in a shop in Mars Hill ordered coffee, the owner declared she never served diet soda or decaffeinated coffee. "Full of rat poison, both of them," she stated. Mary nicely asked for water. Cary couldn't quite believe that proclamation, since many of her friends drank both and suffered no ill effects. She knew caffeine after a certain hour of the day kept her awake, but poison?

Spence again pulled the slips of paper and the checkbook toward him, his expression worried. When he'd left the financial world for the life of an herb farmer, he didn't expect to become wealthy--and he hadn't--but he liked to pay his bills on time--and he did, but barely recently. His bank account had not fully recovered from its thorough cleaning out by Darla. He glanced at Cary. Better poor--which they weren't--and happy with her than any alternative he could think of. His hands were hardened with outdoor work, his body lean and tough, and his heart soft as mush.

While they sipped coffee and tea, he reviewed their recent expenses. They weren't in drastic trouble but certainly a new greenhouse was out of the question as was replacing a couple of other pieces of equipment.

"What we need is something to revitalize us," he said. "And I don't mean caffeine. Something to bring in money at some point but more important, a new venture. We can't go much further with the herb business without major investments–of time and money. And somehow I'm reluctant to invest much more. I like the manageable size of our ThymeTable patches."

Cary heard what he said and nodded. "Me, too." Of course, they had to make enough money to live but she too resisted the idea of a huge commerical farm. ThymeTable had its tractor, of course, and its greenhouse fans, but the noise level was low and the serenity level high. No leaf blowers polluted the air with obnoxious sound. They managed with their personal vehicles plus one truck for hauling and deliveries. She thought for a moment. "One thing I can do is to slow down on my photography expenses." Her hobby had become almost more than an avocation. Her photography instructor believed her capable of turning professional, but she preferred to enjoy her camera work rather than to earn a living with it. She had started out taking mostly scenes in nature, flowers, close-ups of patterns: leaves on water, moss on stone, fungi on trees. And she still loved those delicate textures. Recently, however, she'd become enamored with old, weathered, abandoned, neglected farm structures: barns, fences, corn cribs, tobacco sheds, and, to her delight, old grist mills. The mill at Cade's Cove in eastern Tennessee and Mingus Mill, outside Cherokee, both in the Great Smoky National Park, had been her introduction to water-powered mills, and now she looked for them, asked about them, kept articles mentioning them–and intended to photograph them all! Still, she supposed, she could curtail her photography excursions if need be.

"Not a bad idea for a few months." Spence smiled, then said, "Just kidding. I don't think your film will bankrupt us, but entering all those contests might!"

Cary knew he was teasing to a large degree. Her habit of entering contests–her ceaseless optimism–was actually a source of pride to Spence. She won often enough to pay, as he pointed out, "almost a tenth of the costs!"

"And should I, we, stop trying for a baby?" She willed her voice into neutral.

"Looks like Mother Nature is taking care of that, so far," her husband said. "But, to be honest, it's not the best time." He stroked her hand. "I'll take on some of the work around the goats, and that means less time to get the south field ready. You know we talked about putting in an acre or two of dill, but I think not, not this year."

"And that means..." It would mean less ready cash from passersby who stopped at the vegetable stand a few miles down on the highway for their fresh organic produce. During the canning and pickling season, dill might be quite profitable. "Alice and Agnes come first," she said. "We'll have to keep their cheese production going."

"That's my baby," Spence said. "Oops. A slip." His grin erased the tired lines from his face. "You are woman–you are strong."

The sharp tones of the telephone jarred them from the moment of contented silence. Cary was remembering--and surely Spence was--the night he and Johnny had rescued her from her hours of "imprisonment" in the wedge of a stack of boulders higher on the mountain. At some point, as the rescue proceeded, Spence had called her a "brave girl." Retaining her sense of humor and independence even in her chagrin and pain, she had reproved his word choice, declaring, "I am woman."

"Hi, it's Justin."

"Oh, hi." Cary couldn't keep just a touch of disapproval from sneaking into her voice.

In the past ten days, Agnes had shown no improvement; she didn't regain consciousness, and each time Cary saw her, she seemed to have shrunk. Neither sister was tall or robust but they had the sinewy strength that came from healthy eating and daily manual labor. And they had a vitality that came from, they said, realizing they had found in their retirement a place profoundly their own. From inner-city teachers they had metamorphosed into natural farmers; they blessed the day they'd accidentally heard about the community being formed outside Asheville and had joined forces with Mary, Jon, Don Abbott (whose farm Spence had later bought), Robert and his young son, and others. When ultimately only the "core" remained, buying out those who'd found rural existence too demanding, they had over the decades become good and loyal friends.

Since Agnes' hospitalization, Justin had been unable to get away from his work to come visit. He'd called and explained, and, true, his demanding work schedule justified his absence, but still, the Grayson sisters had watched him grow from a tow-headed motherless child to a handsome blond physician. That he hadn't somehow, somehow found a way to escape the heavy workload of a new doctor Cary couldn't quite accept.

"How is she? It's too late to call Alice and I just got in. Listen," he went on, "I'm trying to arrange a few days off so I can come down. Denise too."

"We'll be glad to see you, Alice especially. She goes to the hospital every day and it's taking a toll on her health, but we can't fault her for going–or stop her, even if we tried."

To his questions Cary told him more about Agnes' condition, that soon they'd have to move her to a nursing home. A certain bitterness must have crept into her voice because Justin said, "That's going to be hard. Our health care system leaves a lot to be desired. Maybe I can help..."

"If you have any influence with facilities around here, maybe you can," Cary said. "Some of the places you wouldn't want to send anyone to and most are full, overflowing." Her long sigh told him how discouraged she was.

"I'll be there as soon as the medical center here gives the okay," he said. "Denise is looking forward to getting away, too. She's had a fight–kind of–with the owner of the space she leases and he's threatening to not renew. I'll let her tell you about it." After he said goodbye and "hello to Spence," Denise came on.

Cary wanted to know all about her problems. "Did that red hair of yours get you in trouble?" Since their college days, they had referred to Denise's quick temper as her red hair. After a reckless episode and a reprimand, their dorm mother had quite succinctly stated, "That red hair of yours will get you into trouble, young lady." Since then, rather than consider her vivacious temperament and tendency to take chances, the girls had always blamed Denise's red hair for difficulties she found herself in.

"It has," Denise said with a laugh. "Jonesy's little granddaughter wants a place to play–a place for a dance studio and she's determined to have my studio." There was no immediate danger; the lease had months to run but it was irritating, Denise told her, especially since the location was excellent. "Sometimes I get tired of all the hassle Mr. Jones throws at me. This granddaughter is barely twenty-two and she wants to teach dance–in this and only this space."

"Problems in all directions," Cary reported to Spence who semi-dozed over a stack of catalogs. "They'll be down in a few days."

"About time," grunted Spence. Cary kissed his forehead. He yawned. "We'll open up Justin's house and let it air out. It'll be musty after these months."

"You're sweet," she said. "Mary and I will see to the linen and all that stuff."

"Let's take that hound of yours out for his walk," Spence said. Winchester raised his head and saw that Cary was standing up. He yawned himself upward and padded toward the door.

"And we can check on Alice," Cary said. "Her light's out but I'll poke my head in for a minute."

Cary was sitting with Alice when they heard a vehicle crunch into the drive. Justin went directly to Alice and enveloped her in a warm hug. Her eyes took in his health, his good looks, his doctorly demeanor. She said what he and surely every young physician heard too many times. "My, you still don't look old enough to be a doctor. If I didn't know better, I'd think you were nineteen!"

"Hmm, and that would make you, let's see, about forty five–if I didn't know better." Justin held the old woman at arm's length. She was thinner than ever, tired, but smiling. "Still got your own teeth, I see!"

"Rascal! I've still got my mind, too. And some special cheese for you and your girl." Alice and Denise hugged briefly. "Are you feeding him properly?" she asked, with a twinkle in her eyes.

"Hospital cafeteria food, Alice, that's what he gets most of the time. He still eats meat, and that I don't cook." Denise went out to the front porch and lugged in two large picnic baskets. "We picked up a few things for you, Alice, and I made some of these goodies," she announced with pride.

"Can you believe she's learning to cook, to bake? Following in your footsteps, Cary." Justin took the baskets and with a flourish removed the cloths to reveal loaves and cookies, dips, along with gourmet boxes of chocolates and bottles of fancy sauces. The packaging, complete with ribbons and colorful pink and purple tissue paper, revealed Denise's flair for color and design.

"We'll eat well and often," Denise said. "And you and Spence must come up and join us. We've got our own food and a big thermos of soup in the car."

"But first, what do you think...?" Alice wanted Justin's appraisal of Agnes' situation. The couple had stopped by the hospital before driving on to The Cove.

Carefully but with the candor Alice would expect, Justin spoke of her sister's condition. He could not be wholly optimistic. When he ended, he kissed Alice on the cheek, and she said quietly, "Old age is no place for sissies, that's for sure." She then drew herself upright and added, "But we go on. Thank you, Justin, for not treating me like a child."

Within the hour, quite a picnic had been spread on the dining room table at Justin's house. It was the first meal he'd eaten there since his father's death three years earlier. As they sat and held hands, saying a silent grace or honoring those who did, a wave of desolation seemed to sweep over them, awareness of Robert's gentle spirit, awareness of the fragility of Agnes' life. For a few moments they hesitated to reach for their soup spoons, to begin the clink and clatter of eating.

"To life," said Spence quietly. "To survival and good friends and this good place."

They raised their glasses of water and toasted their friendship. Each person added a word or two. "To my dearest Alice and Agnes," Justin said. "My surrogate grandmothers."

"To green things and new beginnings," Cary said.

"To goats and creativity," Denise announced, with a grin.

"To this good place," Alice whispered, "and all of us." Then, "We've got company."

The door opened and Mary and Jon entered, followed by their son Johnny and his girlfriend, Suzanne. They had eaten, but Mary immediately put the tea kettle on and Johnny threw more logs on the open fire. Two hours later, after

Spence had taken the sleepy Alice home, they sat back and continued catching up on the news. Justin talked of his long hours, the challenges of providing good care in a timely manner, and strategies inherent in being the youngest physician in the practice. Clearly he enjoyed his new prestige while proclaiming his sense of inadequacy in dealing with all the paperwork.

After a while he shrugged and said, "No more talk of work. I'm on leave for these next few hours."

They turned to Denise. She entertained them with stories of her verbal battles with her landlord who, she declared, was determined to oust her from her studio while making it seem she wanted to leave. "I think he's paying those motorcycle guys to park outside," she said, "and the city not to pick up the garbage cans until they're overflowing!"

They laughed, but Cary recognized frustration behind the stories. Denise sighed, "And he just might win. I am tired of feeling like an unwanted guest."

"You're paying darn well for the space," Justin reminded her. Occasionally Cary noticed Justin's eyes darting around the room. Assessing it for possible sale, she wondered, or reclaiming it as his home? Had she asked, she wasn't sure Justin himself could have answered with certainty.

"You need a break, Cary." The excitement of Justin and Denise's visit had dissipated, and Cary seemed glum and edgy. Spence watched her pace through the kitchen, her face tense. "Take Mary up on her offer. Go explore somewhere."

"There's really nothing I can do around ThymeTable in this weather," Cary said, "but–"

"But you can find that special little mill you've been talking about, up toward Bakersville, the one on the Register of Historic Places." He raised his eyebrows. "Even I can see the light would be good, no rain, no snow. Crisp and cold and no heavy foliage obscuring the view."

"Spoken like a pro," she said.

"Just the husband of a good photographer," Spence said. "A good photographer who could be even better if she'd forget all the chores around here and indulge herself. Go, I say."

"I will, then." Cary paused, stooped to rub Winchester's back. Then with a slight frown she walked to the window, pivoted, walked to the door as if to check that the living room was still there.

"Good thing there's nothing in the oven or it'd fall for sure, with all this pacing. Honey, what's wrong? Agnes? Me?"

"Hormone time, I guess. Spence, how do you feel about adopting?"

"My god, Cary, will you give it a rest! I've told you–" Spence stopped himself, aware that he sounded too abrupt. He patted his lap. "Not you, Winnie," he said when the dog's ears perked up at the sound of a lap being patted. "Come here, darling. Let's wait a while longer before we consider our options. I want a child, our child, but for now, I want my wife. I'm happy as we are."

"But what if I, what if I–" Cary, now on his lap, didn't want to finish the thought. Spence tucked her head against his chest. She smelled of rosemary.

"What, Cary? What's really bothering you? We can go for check ups if you want, see if there's..."

When she broke into ragged sobs and shivered, Spence hugged her more tightly. In a moment he said, "Oh, you think–" His eyes darkened.

Both were remembering what had brought Cary to ThymeTable, that she rented his Rosemary Cottage to recover from an abusive boyfriend.

"What if, if the fall did something to my insides? What if I can't ever have your baby?" She pulled back and looked at him. Her eyes brimmed with tears. She always called the accident "the fall," not quite admitting what everyone knew--that Lanny had pushed her down the stairs. He had rushed down and would have jerked her upright had not the sight of her white face and twisted ankle stopped him.

"Shhh, we'll go in next week and have a talk with your gynecologist–and with my doctor, too," Spence said. "That we can do. Then we'll see." He traced her lips with his fingers and kissed her gently. "Damn that guy," he said. Then, "Go call Mary and I'll make you a loaf of my special brown bread to take with you." He lifted her from his lap. "I know how you are, paying no attention to mealtimes when you're on a photo trek."

Dellinger Mill, outside the small town of Bakersville, was easy to find and a delight to photograph. A sign listed the millers, starting with Reuben in 1867, Dave from 1874 until 1936 and Marve from 1902 until 1955. After a long moment of silence, Cary breathed, "Wow, that is some family tradition...and still going." They had seen a truck in the parking area across the highway, and now the owner stepped from the mill to greet them. He wasn't there usually at this time of year, he said, but he loved the place. As a boy, he had helped the "dress the stones" when his father operated the mill for the community. Now retired from his computer programming career (which included working with NASA's Apollo space mission), he spent many hours there, "just puttering around, always something to do." He pointed out the lengthy restoration work required to put the mill back in operating condition, after it had been idle for almost two decades. "This is the 'new mill' that my grandfather built after the original one upstream was lost in a flood in 1901," he told them. "And it was on television, the restoration, on the Home and Garden channel, in 2000." After an hour or so, Mary blew on her cold hands and returned to the car and the thermos of hot tea. She had brought a short article to work on, seeing that Cary was enthralled with the mill and never rushed her "shooting."

Carrying both cameras, Cary snapped photo after photo; she pulled herself up into a small holly tree to gain a different perspective, she lay on the floor for a sideways closeup of the set of grindstones, and she leaned precariously over the upper floor. "I learned very early," she told him, "that pros aren't content with even a dozen shots at a scene or even a roll." She was not indiscriminate, but to the watching miller she seemed to simply snap–from angles he'd never considered.

"I read somewhere," she said as she crawled out from under the dripping raceway, "that four hundred shots aren't uncommon–to get the one that a major magazine might buy. Not that I'm aiming for a major magazine." She wiped rivulets of water from her brown hair and jacket. "I also now know never to leave home without a couple of extra towels and cloths."

As they left, Mr. Dellinger had half a loaf of Spence's bread and they had a two-pound bag of corn meal. "I always have some in my truck. As you say, never leave home without it," he said, shaking Cary's hand. "Neat little car," he nodded toward the MG. "We don't see many of these around here." Mary rolled down the car's window to say goodby. "Come back anytime, ladies. The mill's real pretty in the spring and fall. It's kind of bare right now."

Mary laughed as they pulled onto the two lane road. "Bare is beautiful, huh?"

"I'm glad I brought two cameras. The black and white images should be great."

"Feel better now?"

"I didn't know it was so obvious, Mary. And yes, I do. I've been in a real slump lately. This cold air woke me up."

"It must be ten degrees colder up here," Mary said. "Next stop–the herb place near Weaverville? Or the mill on Reems Creek?"

Cary nodded to the second option, closed her eyes, and after a few moments, sighed so heavily that Mary said, "What?"

"Mr. Dellinger and I talked a lot about his mill and finally I just asked outright about the cost...Lordy, Mary, it was at least $50,000 to get it fixed up. Whew!" Cary was serious, but her sideways grin told Mary she was aware she'd picked up Mrs. Alison's favorite expression and tone.

"A lot of money," Mary said, some amazement in her voice, partly at the amount of money and partly that Cary would ask. "But he did say it was in pretty bad shape when they started."

The women rode back toward Asheville in easy silence. Cary took the time to jot down notes about the mill and her shooting info. After another thirty minutes of photographing the outside of a large old mill, now a restaurant, outside Weaverville, Cary shivered as the sun began to set. She was happy to return to her car and head toward ThymeTable, but she announced, "We'll have to come back here when the light's different."

"You love these old mills, don't you?" Mary asked while Cary jotted down a few notes about the mill. Mary joked about her little green notebook but Cary had been convinced in one of her photo workshops that keeping field notes was essential. "For contests and for submissions to photography magazines, they're helpful, sometimes required." The pro photographer had assured the students that he never relied on his memory and they shouldn't either.

"I do. I'm about as technologically challenged as it's possible to be, but seeing a grist mill is a thrill every time." Cary turned down the music, a Lucinda Williams CD, and finished her notations. "A connection to the past, maybe? I don't think I ever paid attention in Virginia. I don't know why, but the sight of a dilapidated mill wheel saddens me and seeing one being rescued, like the Dellinger Mill–restores my faith in something!"

"Articulate, aren't you?" Mary smiled at her friend. "Hey, with your photos and my technical writing skills.....who knows what we could do, maybe write a book!"

"Yeah, sure," Cary said, her voice distant.

"What? Where did you go, all of a sudden?"

"Oh, just thinking. Spence has also been down lately. Not just because of me moping around. I guess it's partly

Agnes, but he says we shouldn't count on a new fan for the second greenhouse or repainting the outbuildings."

"What about asking Jon?" Mary said.

"No way," interrupted Cary. "Jon did enough with the conservancy deal. Even if he had–" She stopped.

"I know, I know," Mary said. "Even if he had more capital, which I doubt, you wouldn't ask. Okay."

"Jon saved the day for us then, but we can't rely–can't expect him to be Mr. Moneybags."

"And he certainly doesn't see himself in the savior role." Mary signaled and turned onto the road to Thyme-Table. "Jon's more the prodigal type. He's looking restless already and he's only been back a few weeks."

It had been Jon's lucky infusion of money that prevented The Cove from perhaps becoming a victim of developers. When the farm most needed it, Jon had unexpectedly received a large sum from an overdue gambling debt. He had proposed turning the land into a conservancy if that were required to save it. It had not been necessary to finalize that arrangement; the developers had backed off and payments had been made. Still the threat existed. Jon would do anything he could to prevent Mary and the others from losing their land, but he wasn't exactly a dependable type. He and Mary had managed an amicable divorce many years earlier; they remained "friends" according to Mary, cordial and considerate as far as anyone could tell. Mary's self-sufficiency and reticence didn't encourage questions about the relationship beyond that.

Soon after Cary and Spence were married, Jon had shouldered his backpack and departed once again. He sent a couple of postcards from Idaho and then this January, not quite as rotund as before and slightly stooped, he'd reappeared and moved into Mary's house, the house they'd essentially transformed over twenty years before. Dropping by occasionally, Cary saw that he slept in the small spare bedroom–or that his pants hung on the bedpost and his socks decorated the floor. She saw that he prepared his own breakfast and sometimes brought home the evening meal for

Mary and himself. Mary was not a cook and she styled her eating habits as "haphazardly healthily." Cary teased that she would be content with tofu and water...well, coffee. She spent hours every day at her office, at work, translating technical documents, sometimes writing up brief reports or editing them for clients in Maine, Michigan, New Mexico, and New York. "Distance doesn't matter in my work," she told Cary. "I like to be able to do my thing 'far from the madding crowd.'" Always she had work piled up, more deadlines to meet than she'd expected. Sometimes she worked through the night, finishing as Cary was just getting up. She was the one person Cary knew whose body rhythms or internal clock seemed totally unconnected to the sunrise/sunset farm routine. "Even when we had chickens and a big rooster woke me up every morning," Johnny once said, "his crowing never fazed Mom." Cary, whose ideal getting up hour would be eight o'clock, envied her that she could wake up and be alert at eleven o'clock–a.m. or p.m.

Chapter 3 "To Everything... a Season"

His arrival at The Cove and the Bradfords' kitchen could not be called dramatic but it was certainly unexpected. He was drinking the farm's special Tea to Sleep By when the two women, still exhilarated by their mill visits, opened the kitchen door. Cary sniffed appreciatively the fumes of basil and thyme. Johnny was watching him, Winchester was watching him, this elderly stranger in overalls and dark blue flannel shirt.

"Whoa." Mary stopped abruptly. Cary bumped into her.

"Hi, Johnny," Cary said. "Whom have we here?" For a sinking moment she thought the man might be Winchester's owner, come to claim him, but the beagle had been with them almost six months, and he showed only a routine interest in the newcomer.

"Whom...?" Johnny grinned and drawled, "This here's Mr. Jabbers, at least I reckon that's whom he is." Johnny couldn't resist teasing Cary sometimes about her grammar and her poetry-spouting. When he did so, he slowed his normal speech to a molasses-crawl, what his mother called his "deep southern sweet" sound.

"Rawlston Jabbers, ladies." The old man stood up and extended his hand, still cold, blue veined and boney. "This young fella," he nodded toward Johnny, "picked me up down on the highway, out by the BP station. Offered me a ride and 'fore I knew it, offered me a chair and a cup of tea.

Delicious." He smacked his chapped lips. "We just got here."

Mary caught her son's eye and gave him silent instructions. Johnny rose, peered into the tea pot, and added more hot water. He set out two mugs, rummaged in the cabinet for cookies, anything to avoid the questions he knew the women were formulating. "Good day?" he asked. "Good shooting?" He'd been a college boy long enough to know that asking a question could often forestall a more probing one from a professor.

"The mill outside Bakersville was great," Cary answered. "And we stopped by the Weaverville Milling Company to photograph that mill." She took her cameras into the other room, shed her coat, splashed water on her face, and returned to find Johnny still opening cupboard doors and checking various jars and tins. Mary sat silent and speculative.

"We don't have any homemade cookies, Johnny," Cary said. "You'll have to make do with that box of chocolate chips, behind the cereal." She placed spoons and napkins before them and pulled out the chair to sit opposite Mr. Jabbers.

"You're welcome, of course, to tea. It's too cold to be wandering on the highway. But–"

She saw a man surely in his seventies or eighties, tired eyes with a dash of mischief, a newly shaven jaw line with a couple of tiny nicks showing. He had a full shock of gray hair, not particularly well cut. He certainly didn't look dangerous but there was something about him...his blue eyes kept shifting from one person to another. Yet Winchester had now snuggled up close to his heavy work boots. Though muddied slightly the boots had the stiff sheen of newness.

"Where are you from?" Mary asked, settling in next to Cary. She thought a blunt question was in order. Johnny sat out of a direct line of his mother's vision.

"Over in Yancey County. Maybe thirty, forty mile from here. I'll tell you ladies the truth, now." The old man rubbed his jaw and took his time.

"He wouldn't tell me nothing," Johnny interrupted. "Not a thing, 'cept he was feeling dizzy, so I made tea in a hurry." Johnny pushed the cookies toward Mr. Jabbers, who waited until both women took one, then he chose one. They concentrated on chewing the cookies. After Mr. Jabbers finished and brushed a crumb from his overalls, he closed his eyes. Johnny gave a mighty sigh as if wondering when the story would emerge. Mr. Jabbers turned from one to the other, blinked, and began his tale.

"My sister and...me, we headed for Florida, got some nieces down there in the Panhandle. They wanted us to come spend a month or two. Well, VeEmma was right hateful about the trip, her doing all the driving, her paying all the expenses." He demolished another cookie and at a glance from Cary, Johnny rose and went to the refrigerator and found a container of leftover soup.

"Well, one thing led to another. I told her I'd pay up with my next pension check, but that woman kept on and on. That's one reason we don't live together, she talks all the time. She'd talk to the devil if he'd listen. Me, I'd rather not say much." He stopped again, watching Johnny stir the soup.

"Go on," Mary prodded him.

"That VeEmma, she wouldn't shut up and us not more'n started. Finally I said, stop this here truck–she drives one of them little foreign trucks, not big enough for nothing. I said, stop right here at this station. I'm going back home. Well, she didn't stop at that place but by the time we got to this county, she'd said enough and I had too. Told her to pull over. I jumped out and she took off. Roared on down the highway."

"No suitcase with him, just this little kid's back pack," Johnny said. He placed the bowl of steaming barley soup before the man, cut some bread, buttered it, and shoved it on a plate. "Eat this, before you faint again."

At the women's startled looks, Mr. Jabbers said, "I'm fine now, just a little trouble with my blood sugar." He handled the spoon with delicacy though obviously he was hungry.

Mr. Jabbers appeared reluctant to keep talking about his situation. He didn't want to go to Florida, he told them; and his nieces would be glad to see VeEmma get there alone. He would find his way back to Yancey County in the morning. And, at Cary's insistence, he promised to call his family in Florida so they wouldn't worry. When he saw Mary silently assessing his clothing, he blinked and said, "Bought new clothes, too, for the trip." A few moments later, he announced, "And lost my watch." A slightly pale band on his arm testified to its absence.

Something about the pale old man seemed to say "take care of me" and something in each of the three responded, yet they sat for a while pondering this stranger that Johnny had brought to the farm. Into this silence Spence arrived.

"This is Mr. Jabbers," Cary performed the introductions, "from over in Yancey County."

Spence shook Mr. Jabbers' hand, noted that Mary and her son busied themselves at the stove and sink and that Cary seemed uncertain about what to say next. He said, "Let me wash up and I'll join you for some soup." He left the room, with Winchester trotting behind. A few minutes later, Cary summed up Mr. Jabbers's tale.

"When did your sister and you start out for Florida?" Spence asked. He devoted himself to the soup while Cary quickly grilled a cheese sandwich for him.

"Early this morning. I don't pay much attention to time." Mr. Jabbers held up his watchless arm. "I just kept walking."

"And you picked him up around five this afternoon?" Spence said to Johnny. "Long time out in the cold. You have your family's number in Florida, Mr. Jabbers?" At a nod, he said, "Then you'd better go and call them. Tell them you're okay. That way, when your sister--VeEmma, is it?--gets there she won't worry."

He waited for the man to push back from the table and then steered him into the other room. "We'll give you some privacy," he said. He stood in the doorway until he saw Mr. Jabbers fumble in his pocket and pull out a slip of paper.

Back in the kitchen, they could hear him punching in numbers, and when he began to talk they looked at each other. Cary spoke first. "He can stay here." Spence squeezed her hand and nodded.

"What did you have in mind, Johnny, son?" Mary asked. "You picked him up."

"He could sleep in my old room," Johnny answered. "I'm outta here in a few minutes. Got to see a man about a new computer for Suzanne."

"He seems harmless enough," Mary said. "One night can't hurt. Our place seems the solution And Jon's there, of course." She drummed her fingers on the table.

"Of course," responded Spence. They were silent, perhaps contemplating the fact that Jon did not seem in any hurry to leave The Cove now. His green backpack was gathering dust in the closet. And now, this stranger appeared.

"Is he hiding out from the law?" Cary asked lightly. "Or did Providence send him to help out with the goats?" She looked up as he rejoined them. "Oh, did you reach them, Mr. Jabbers?" The old man seemed a little shaky.

"Could you call me Rawlston?" He sat down and took a cookie. "Nobody calls me Mister." He turned to Cary and took a deep breath. "It's settled. I told them not to expect me. Just as happy...a hen party is what it'll be when Vee gets there. She'd called them on that little cell phone of hers to see if they'd heard from me." He started to take some bills from his pocket to pay for the call but at their protests, he said graciously, "I thank you."

The next morning Cary introduced Rawlston Jabbers to Alice, her goats, and to Justin and Denise. Alice practically ignored him, busy as she was with the feeding and milking. Noting his soft hands and pale face, she dismissed him as a potentially useful farm hand. But after he'd puttered about, getting in her way, and then carrying in milk, putting out feed at her directions, she insisted on giving him one of Agnes' down-filled coats. It was short in the arms and just a bit tight on the shoulders, but warm enough. He took it with a smile of pleasure and a courtly bow of thanks. Denise pronounced the deep purple jacket quite fetching with the overalls.

"It's not perfect, but for now, a solution," Justin said. "We've got to get back to Virginia. I can see that the house needs to be taken care of. Rawlston has said he can stay here for awhile. For some reason, I trust him. And his sister's bound to show up in a few weeks and take him home." Spence, Cary, and Mary had come up to say goodbye to Justin and Denise.

"Meanwhile, the house is lived in. You all won't have to be checking on it about pipes and stuff all the time," Denise said. She looked around the comfortable sitting room with its shelves of books with a certain longing. "I like this place. I could live here."

"Don't be silly, Denise." Justin spoke sharply. "Your work needs exposure. You should be in a city, around creative..." He stopped. "I didn't mean that the way it might have come out. Don't give me that look, Cary!" Justin put his hands up as if warding off a blow–or a glare from Cary. "It's just that we've talked about this. I'm in a practice, getting started. Denise's jewelry is known in Richmond. She's settled--"

"I'm about to be thrown out of my studio, Justin. You know it will happen," Denise said.

"We'll deal with that when it does. Meanwhile, there's doctoring to be done..."

"Car to be paid for, to say nothing of--" Alice said.

"Student loans," offered Rawlston. Alice's eyes widened in surprise. She was used to her sister finishing her sentence, just as she often completed Agnes' comments. They had done it for decades.

Justin shrugged. "That too." He shifted his feet. "All of you can live out here and be content, but I, we can't. Without Dad, this house isn't 'home' to me. Maybe I've been gone too long." He dug into his pocket, handed the old man a ring of keys. "Just give these to somebody," he waved to the assembled group, "when you go back to Yancey. The utilities are drafted from my account, so you don't need to think about that. I, for one, hope you stay through the rest of the winter, through snow season at least, but when your sister comes, just lock up."

Rawlston blinked his fading blue eyes. "Oh, oh, yes, I'll take care of the place." He pocketed the keys and shook Justin's hand.

Mary draped an arm around the old man's thin shoulders. "And we'll help if you need us."

They hugged Justin and Denise, tucked fresh goat cheese and still-warm bread into the Jaguar, and watched them zoom from The Cove.

"That boy drives like a maniac," Alice said, her disapproval tinted with love. She shivered. "Let's go visit Agnes." She turned to Rawlston. "She's at Brentknoll Nursing Center."

"I'll just rest," he said. "I never want to set foot in one a–" He broke off.

Mary frowned. "Something wrong?"

"VcEmma's first husband..." he trailed off. Looked bewildered. They left him in front of the fireplace.

"He seems quite content to stay here and look after Justin's house," Mary said.

"Looks like the cat that got into the cream," Alice mused.

"You think we should investigate?" Spence only half listened, his eyes on ThymcTable's greenhouses; he noted a few places needing attention. "I'll stay here today and do some work at Number 2."

"Oh, not necessarily." Alice answered his question. "I think he's honest. But there's something about him..." Alice lay her head back, wearily. "And it will be good to have another pair of hands around, even if he's not used to working outdoors."

At the hospital the three women found Agnes unresponsive; she could not even return Alice's squeeze of her fragile hand. She was so still and thin they could almost have been looking at a cardboard cutout, covered by a thin blanket. Her breathing was aided by tubes attached to her nostrils. The nurse's aide said with practiced diction, "Pneumonia's a big risk now. She's sedated at the moment, but," she hesitated, then went on, "there's not much difference with or without her drugs." She laid a young hand, with its nails bitten to the quick, on Alice's shoulders and left the room.

Cary wiped a touch of saliva from Agnes' lips, and Alice took a comb from her purse and ran it through her sister's sparse hair. Mary drifted around the room, rearranging the few items on the bedside table and the flowers on the window sill. After awhile, they left Alice alone with her sister and waited in the nearby lobby, assailed by odors and by moans and an occasional outburst from various occupants in wheelchairs who sat in the hallway. Cary bit her lips. Mary went for hot chocolate from a vending machine. She offered the cup to Cary who shook her head. Mary held it to her mouth, allowing the scent to help obliterate the offensive smells. Almost an hour later Alice joined them, saying she'd once again stopped by the head nurse's office. The news was not good. Bedsores a possibility since Agnes was too weak to sit up; pneumonia more probable; general weakness, nothing positive to report except the patient was not as restless and agitated as upon initial admission. The supervisor hardly dared be even cautiously optimistic.

"She as good as implied--" Alice started and then pressed a tissue to her mouth, "She thinks it's just a matter of time, days at the most, almost no brain activity." Alice swayed slightly, and the women guided her to a sofa.

A few minutes later, when Alice had straightened her back and said she was ready to leave the place, Mary led the older woman to the car and helped her into the back seat. "Here, lean on my shoulder. You need a good cry." Seeing that Cary looked as if she'd burst into tears herself, Mary motioned for her to leave. "She'll bring some coffee. Come on, let go. You've been strong long enough." Mary held the weeping Alice for long minutes.

"I may have to decide...Mrs. Carbent, the supervisor, implied I should consider...consider the options for Agnes. She's on life support most...they don't think..." Alice stopped, blew her nose, and sat up. She looked at Mary. "I've got to say it: could I withdraw life support, could I pull the plug on my sister?" Mary had never seen Alice so vulnerable, so tiny and frail; yet once the words were uttered, Alice sighed with relief. Then she shivered and pulled her coat tightly about her. "Let's go home. Where is that Cary?"

Mary smiled briefly at the note of impatience in Alice's voice. "Here she comes. We're on our way."

The next day Mary told Cary that she and Alice had talked for another hour or so after returning home, or Alice had talked while Mary mostly listened. Interspersed with recollections of their childhood and memories of their teaching careers and favorite students and less favorite administrators, Alice had returned several times to the question: could she decide on continued life or death for her sister? "Ultimately," Mary said, "I think she can. She's strong in spirit. She sees death as a transition, not as the final end-all. But she wants at least a few more days before facing that decision."

Alice did not have to decide. Three days later, three visits later, the Agnes they knew was gone in every way except a slightly recognizable body. After the last visit, all the way home, Alice seemed to be consulting with herself, silently, nodding her head several times. Perhaps, Alice said much later, Agnes realized the dilemma and solved it before her sister would have had to. Mary left her number as the emergency one; the call came in the early morning, a little after five. Seeing the light on at the Grayson home, Mary knew she wouldn't have to wake Alice. She found her sitting in the small den, looking at photo albums, scattered about the settee. Alice's eyes held a question, and Mary had only to nod and take the older woman's hand. After a few minutes,

Alice said, "*Gone* is the loneliest word in the English language." A tear escaped from each of her forlorn eyes; then she said, "Please stay here. I want to tell the goats. Then we'll go."

"No service, no minister, no fuss," Alice said. Following her sister's wishes (and her own, so written and declared to their lawyer), she collected Agnes' ashes some days following her death. She had appreciated the cards, flowers, calls from those who bought Grayson cheese and she graciously welcomed friends who lived near The Cove when they called and stopped in to offer sympathy and assistance. However, the sisters had chosen what Alice called "a simple lifestyle followed by a simple deathstyle," and she stuck by their choice of ceremony or lack thereof. Alice told her friends, "This Cove is and has been our community. I've thanked Mrs. Alison and the others down the road for their offer of the church for a memorial, for dinner. But no, we wrote out what we wanted. Dust to dust." She repeated firmly, "No fuss."

Rawlston made himself useful in a quiet, unassuming manner. He sat with Alice in the evening, listening to her favorite organist, Virgil Fox, or to a Mozart concerto, and with a word or two indicated what he especially enjoyed and what he didn't. He said very little, though. When Alice mentioned his lack of conversation, he simply said, "You've heard, 'with a name like Smuckers...'"

"You have to be good," she finished. "So, with a name like Jabbers, you'd think you'd talk all the time."

"Well, with a name like Jabbers, I determined to be quiet."

"It is a strange name, never heard it before in my life," Alice said. "Is it an old western North Carolina name?"

He hesitated, as if thinking hard. "Nope, fairly new in these parts."

“Have you checked with the county or whoever to see if it’s okay?” Mary handed the box back to Alice, once she had closed the car door and was steady on her feet.

“Nobody asked at the crematorium,” Alice said in her school teacher voice. “And nobody needs to know. Justin will be here tomorrow. You know Denise is in Boulder or somewhere at a craft show and can’t make it. Just us.”

“And Rawlston?”

“And Rawlston,” Alice said.

The following day, at sunset, in March air so dry and cold it hurt to breathe deeply, the small group trudged through the clustered goats to the upper end of the pasture. A mulberry tree stood like a sentinel there and three large rocks jutted from the ground. The sisters had often walked up to this spot and gazed down on their home, the collection of outbuildings, the neat fencing, their very special goats. Because the friends adjusted their pace to that of Alice, the walk itself became a time for contemplation, a sacred walk during which they reflected on what Agnes had meant to them.

As if instructed, they formed a semi-circle under the bare tree and stood without speaking, looking outward across the field and valley below. “We don’t have a plan,” began Alice. “We are here, Agnes, to remember you, to honor your life, and,” she paused and seemed to slump for a moment. Then with Mary’s arm at her shoulders and Jon taking the box of ashes from her, she continued, “and, to let you go, to let your spirit find in this transition the peace you found here at The Cove.”

Jon opened the box and each person extended cupped hands, into which he poured with reverence the chalky remains of their friend. “We will remember you here–and in our hearts,” Jon said, his voice faltering a bit. He and Alice stepped beyond the circle and Alice, straight backed, drew back her hand and in a sweeping motion scattered the ashes before her. Jon moved slightly to her left and did the same.

“You made ThymeTable your place and took me in, encouraged me, fed me,” said Spence. “Thank you.”

"Our birth is but a sleep and a forgetting," Cary's tears flowed down her face as she began to quote from Wordsworth, then she murmured, "I'll never forget you, Agnes."

Each person said a few simple words, a tribute to the strength and spirit of their friend as the sun sank behind them. Justin said, "The two of you, Agnes and Alice, you were true friends to Dad, and the mother, double mothers, I needed." He managed a smile. "I should say grandmothers–you taught me a lot. You and those goats."

Alice spoke again when all hands, except Rawlston's were empty. "To every thing there is a season and a time to every purpose..."

"A time to be born and a time to die...a time to weep...a time to heal..." Rawlston paused at their looks of surprise. Then he continued, "A time to silence and a time to speak...." He let the small breeze take the ashes from his hands.

Alice's voice trembled. "We may be misquoting but–a time to love, a time to embrace." The nine moved together for a general embrace.

There was an awkward moment, broken by Johnny, "And now a time to eat." They turned to descend the hillside, noticing that the goats had followed them but had stopped, like respectful mourners, some hundred yards below.

"We should have brought a pot of tea and some cheese," Justin said. "A memorial ritual."

"Agnes would be the first to say, get yourselves inside where it's warm," Mary said. "We're eating at Thyme-Table," Cary announced.

"And we do have fresh goat's cheese," Spence said. In a sudden movement, he bent and picked up the tiny Alice before she could protest. The others smiled at her startled expression, and she gave in with good grace, encircling his neck with her arms.

"Not a word," Spence said. "If I could tote Cary off in the middle of the night, you're easy."

"It's getting to be a habit, Spence, our carrying women off this mountain," Johnny said. Suzanne cast a flirtatious glance at him, and he said, "Don't even think it, girl!" He staggered as if under the weight of Suzanne, and she gave him a good natured shove. With subdued laughter, they trooped into the kitchen at the farm.

Chapter 4 "Like a Passion"

With swiftness typical of western North Carolina, the weather changed and over the next week cold rains drenched The Cove, heavy fog covered mountain tops and lay low in the valleys, and general gloom prevailed.

"This is the time when our ancestors were repairing tools and sharpening hoes," Cary said to Spence. "You've been in a funk for a couple of days. What are you doing?" She had just finished her exercises in the spare room and was breathing hard; she helped herself to a large glass of water and sat down, pushing aside a clump of photography magazines. "You're not upset because we're going in to see the doctors tomorrow?"

Spence had various catalogs spread on the table, and he was lackadaisically drawing something.

"No, no, I'm glad we could get appointments on the same afternoon." He smiled at her expression of concern, and ran his hand along her thigh, trimly encased in spandex. "We need to know, for both our sakes. No, I'm thinking about how to increase our income..."

"We live well enough, darling. We don't want to spoil this farm."

"True." He shrugged but didn't manage to look nonchalant. "Maybe it's more than that, then. I love the herb business but I've been doing it for several years. Right now, getting ready for the season just seems tedious." He crumpled the sheet of paper, a diagram of fields. "We could turn one field into daylilies; they're a big item now, but somehow that idea doesn't excite me."

"Hey, my former Peace Corps man, maybe you need a challenge." Cary pressed her breasts against his shoulders and nuzzled his neck. "A baby would be a challenge!"

"I'm up to it," Spence said. He pushed away from the table. "Maybe it's this weather, right after Agnes' death. I feel bad about feeling bad, thinking of Alice over there by herself."

"Rawlston stops in every day to see her–to see the goats, he says."

"Together the two of them don't weigh enough to stand against a strong wind," Spence said. "At least, there won't be quite as much work in the winter, no milking to be done."

"They could handle it. Don't underestimate either one." Cary stretched and rubbed her flat stomach. "They're thin like wire is thin. Tough, though."

"You're right. Want to take a walk?"

"In this ungodly rain? In the dark?" Cary looked out the window. "Yep, let's go! I'll get our raingear."

"I'll get a couple of flashlights." Spence hurried to the closet.

They walked and walked, in mud, along side their fields, down to the main road, up beyond Justin's house and Alice's; lights glowed in both but they didn't want to talk to anyone, not even to each other. The rain seemed to wash away some cares and worries. Cary at one point stopped and flung her arms to the sky. "Let's see if I can remember some of this. 'I bring fresh showers for the thirsting flowers...'"

"Drowning flowers–if anything was in bloom," Spence interrupted. "I know it's Shelley."

"I...something...'of the lashing hail/And whiten the green plains under, /And then again I dissolve it in rain....'"

"Yes!" Spence stood laughing in the slow steady rain.

"'And laugh as I pass in thunder,'" Cary said. "Miss Smith–she was my sophomore lit teacher--would never believe I remember all this. Let's see. My favorite lines are 'I am the daughter of Earth and Water, / And the nursling of the sky; / I pass through the pores of the ocean and shores, / I change but I cannot die.'" At that moment a cloud scuttled across the moon.

They walked on, Spence chuckling. Then from feeling silly at flinging the poetry into the rain, Cary turned somber. "'I change but I cannot die.' I like that...like Agnes has changed but not gone."

"Being a farmer, being on a farm, makes you think like that, darling. A time for everything, a season...."

After a moment, Cary returned to more earthly thoughts. "Interesting that Rawlston knew that bit from Ecclesiastes."

"Hmm. Not unusual that he'd know his Bible, but I had a feeling he knew more than he said. Did you notice a change in his voice, just for a minute?"

"For a moment, he could have been one of my college professors," Cary agreed. "I like him and trust him, yet I wonder..."

"Leave it alone, for now. He's fine, tells me he checks with his sister. He had Johnny buy a phone card for him for long distance. And he doesn't have any responsibilities that call him back to Yancey."

"Wow, look at that stream now." Cary's thoughts were diverted as her flashlight illuminated the water rushing by. "It's almost out of its banks."

"Yes, we need to work on it some. A little more and it'll spread out and," Spence threw the beams wide, "without much effort it could head for the thyme."

Cary nodded. Another line of poetry kept eluding her.

Halting at their back door, some thirty minutes later, Spence said, "Crazy woman." They were soaked, in spite of their raincoats and hats. He looked at Cary, dripping onto the porch. "If it weren't March, I'd say let's shower out here, but brrrrr, this old man needs hot water and a warm towel."

Cary laughed and began to shed her clothes. "I'm not going inside in these." In two minutes she was naked. Shivering, she kicked the bundle of wet clothes to the side of the porch and headed for the door. "Here's Winchester–ready for a walk! Your turn." She dashed inside.

"I've had an idea," she said a short time later, her eyes glowing. Spence had thrown his wet clothes on the porch, had dried the soaked beagle with a towel, and had showered. They were enjoying cups of hot chocolate with peanut butter cookies. "It came to me–almost came to me–when we were close to the stream. 'The sounding cataract haunted me like a passion.' That's what Wordsworth said. Well," she said again, "I've got an idea. A passion."

"At this time of night?" Spence teased. "Idea or passion?"

"A mill."

"What?"

"A mill. Let's build one. Right here on ThymeTable."

"My god, woman, that cold rain did something to your brain. A mill?"

"We could do it, Spence. Think about it."

"Could we go to bed instead? You're sneezing already–and this is making me sleepy." He set his empty cup aside. "Sleepy and–beside your idea, what was the other thing?"

"But, what do you think about it? A mill on our farm."

"I'm not inclined to think about anything at the moment," Spence said, "except sweeping you off that chair and into bed. Let's think ideas later and passion now."

Cary didn't want to argue with that inclination.

"There seems to be no physical reason that a normal pregnancy isn't a possibility," Dr. Mendales said. "Distinct probability is more like it, given the fine condition you're both in." He studied the folder of test results and then said, "Nowhere is it written that, with normal sexual relations, conception will automatically occur." He attempted a certain levity. "Certainly not within a desired time frame. Put as bluntly as I wish to be, stop trying so hard and see what happens. Are you troubled or worried about something?" He held up a hand when both Cary and Spence started to speak. "I know you assured me you're happy, etc., and you look it.

But sometimes anxiety or some other fear may–I stress *may*–inhibit conception. My advice is to take some time away from the norm, and for goodness' sake, don't expect divine interference–or human either, at this stage of your marriage." He sounded a little impatient.

Cary looked chagrined and Spence appeared relieved and yet solemn. They stood up and Dr. Mendales walked with them to the front desk. There he shook hands with both of them and wished them a good day and good luck. Then he smiled, "That's half of it, you know. Luck."

As they reached the car, Spence sighed as if in great sorrow. "What?" Cary asked. "Did you just think of something we should have told him?"

"Luck, the man says, luck." Spence lifted Cary's chin and gave her a quick kiss. "Not a word about skill, not a word about my artful lovemaking."

Cary giggled a little. "It is good to know, isn't it, that we're fine." She settled the seat belt around her and said, "I've forgiven Lanny, or thought I had, but today I realized that if, if he had caused a problem, I'd certainly take back my forgiveness. I'd have gone after him with a stick!"

"Hey, a whip would have been my weapon of choice," Spence said. "How about lunch somewhere special? To celebrate the great shapes we're in?" He kissed her forehead.

"You know, my choice is the Wildflower."

"And your choice is my command," Spence said. When Cary's parents came to visit, the quiet, well-appointed restaurant was a favorite, not only because of the excellent food but, as Mr. Randall put it, "We can hear ourselves talk."

Over a leisurely meal, they talked of herbs and schedules for festivals. They held hands and mused that seldom did they get away from the farm together. Over dessert and coffee, Cary said, "I think I'll explore some more mill sites, before the leaves come out. There's the Francis Mill in Haywood County, right on the side of the highway, Highway 276. I've read about it."

"Go for it. I've got to see about any damage the rains have done. And I promised Johnny I'd help him with his car this weekend. He wants to get it up on the rack again."

"We're just an old married couple," Cary said. "Life is good." She grinned. "But I still love that idea."

"What idea?"

"A mill for ThymeTable."

Chapter 5 "That Was Solid Power"

"We're off to Haywood County," Cary told Rawlston as together they threw hay to the goats. "Mary and I–to see the Francis Mill. It was built in the late1880s and it's being restored." She dusted her hands on her jeans. "The owner said someone else might be there, a miller who used to know her grandfather." With her hands on her hips she gazed toward the farm. "I just know we could build a mill here on ThymeTable. Wouldn't that be fun? But I can't get Spence interested. His mind is occupied with repairing the damage from all the rain. Mills fascinate me. I wonder if there were millers in my family's background. I could ask Mom." She stopped, with a small frown of embarrassment, realizing she was rattling on. Rawlston smoothed the hair on Mercury, the Nubian who had developed, it seemed, a special fondness for the old man.

"A lot of money and a lot of work." Rawlston said. "Maybe Spence is thinking of that." He leaned on the gate and added, "And a lot of fun."

"No, he's just not thinking of it at all," Cary stated. "I'll run in and say goodbye to Alice."

Rawlston straightened up and rubbed his back. "We're testing a new flavor of cheese. Camomile and a touch of pennyroyal. Strange flavors but she wanted to try it." He stood, shifting his feet as if undecided about something. "Guess I'll go rest a bit." His paleness had vanished; being outside with the animals and in the wind had given him ruddy cheeks that now hosted a stubble of gray. The day before, Cary had joked about his not shaving now that his sister wasn't around. He'd blinked and said with his shaky hands sometimes he nicked himself. "I may grow a beard," he'd said.

When Cary came out of the house a few minutes later, carrying a packet of cheese, Rawlston was still there as if in deep thought. Mercury alternated between nuzzling his hand and nudging his leg, asking for attention she wasn't getting. Seeing Cary, Rawlston called, "Hey, can you give me a lift into town? Johnny's coming out later and I can ride back with him."

"Sure. I thought you were going to rest. Are you okay?" Cary thought he looked distracted, his mind far off.

He nodded. "I'm fine. I'll get my coat and meet you down at Mary's in a few minutes." He patted the goat once more, took out a handkerchief and wiped his hands, careful not to dirty his new overalls.

Sometime earlier, Cary had decreed that new clothes were in order for Rawlston, that he couldn't live in just the one pair of overalls he'd arrived in. When she asked the old man what kind of pants he wanted he said, "Overalls suit me just fine." Spence had been on his way to town and offered to take Rawlston with him, but he blinked and said he was too tired to go traipsing around stores. Spence raised an eyebrow and asked his wife, "Where's the best place to go for overalls?" She reminded him of the Dickey Work Clothes store outside Weaverville. Mary furnished gloves, and Johnny had provided a cap with a tractor logo on it. New shirts had appeared, courtesy of Jon and Spence. Rawlston looked quite spiffy.

"Hi, I'm Tanna." The owner of Francis Mill met the women in the driveway and welcomed them enthusiastically. However, she told them, she had just received a telephone call: she had to dash to visit an aunt who had just been taken to the hospital, so she couldn't stay to show them around. Quickly, though, her love for the mill and her determination to save it became apparent, and Cary felt an immediate affinity for her, perhaps with a twinge of envy that Tanna actually had a mill to work with. And it sat only a few yards from the house, as well as a few yards from the highway. It still sported a Christmas wreath on its second story. A small grant from the Society for the Preservation of Old Mills helped start its restoration, Tanna told them. A Post and Beam Workshop held in the summer of 2004 had restoration expert, Jeffery Finch, in residence, but much work still had to be done. They planned another two-week workshop for the following year. The mill was built by Tanna's great-great grandfather, William Francis, in 1887. "Then," she said, "his son Monteville Pinkney inherited it and then his son Dewey ran it–we called him 'Pappy'–until 1976. My mother Hester Boone inherited it, but my father died and her health was poor, so for almost thirty years, the mill has not operated." She and her husband now intended to restore it to working order.

"So you're the second woman to own it," Cary said. "It's a big responsibility."

"Bigger than Tim–my husband–and I ever anticipated," Tanna said, but she was smiling widely. "If we'd known...but now we know and we'll get it done." She laughed. "With the help of a lot of friends." She told them briefly that a Society for the mill's preservation had been set up and that they would apply for various grants from local and national organizations. "We're great optimists–or fools!"

When Mary said she might write an article on the technology involved in the restoration, Tanna told them to spend as much time as they needed around the mill. She was moving toward her vehicle. "I'm late now. Sorry I can't stay." Just then an old blue pickup truck pulled into the driveway of the house where they stood admiring the mill across the small stream.

"Oh, here he comes," Tanna said. "I called Mr. Noland and told him about you all visiting, about your interest in old mills. He's been under the weather and his daughter wasn't sure he was up to the trip. But he's prevailed, I see."

Tanna beamed at the toothpick of a man who with great caution and much stiffness descended from the cab.

Cary heard him say, "Thanks, Buddy. But you could have taken them curves a little faster. Darn slowpoke!" His smile was gummy but genuine.

Tanna shook his hand, welcomed him, and said, "This is Mr. Noland, from over in Madison County. He can tell you more about milling than I ever could. He's done it himself."

She introduced the women, got into her car, and said to the young man who slid from the truck, "Thanks for bringing him, Buddy. Take care."

Buddy closed Tanna's door, and stood with a cigarette in his hand and a tolerant expression on his face. "Grandpappy is right pleased you're getting the place fixed up," he told her. Tanna pulled onto the highway with a wave and a burst of speed that made the boy shake his head.

In short order the old man announced proudly that he was way over ninety–"ninety-five or something, give or take a year or two--" and could still see like a buzzard. "But," he said, "My hearing leaves a mite to be desired." He gestured to the young man. "Buddy here, he just ignores me most of the time. He's my great-grandson."

"I ignore you when you want me to push this truck beyond seventy," Buddy said. "I'll be over here under this tree. Take your time." He lifted a folding chair from the truck, set it near the old man, and took one for himself. He returned to drape a blanket over the chair. "In case you get cold," he said.

"He's a-studying to be a deputy. His daddy's a preacher but he's goin' to college to lock people up." He gestured to the young man. "Don't that beat all?"

"Let's go look at the mill!" Cary's face was flushed with excitement.

"You're not from around here?" Mr. Noland said.

Cary expected the question; she'd heard it many times, especially when she met older residents of the area. By now she had her answer down pat. "No sir, but I wish I was. It's a great place to live." To forestall another question, she said, "I'm from Virginia, a small town close to Roanoke."

He nodded, as if satisfied that since she didn't sound "right" she had a reason for it.

Mr. Noland walked toward the edge of the yard as they talked. "Tanna said you all growed herbs over in Buncombe County. Ever dealt with ginseng?"

"I know what it is and maybe where some grows, but no. It's not an herb that takes to, uh, domestication."

"Used to dig it myself some as a boy," he said. He paused, looked across the stream, and as in tribute, said, "Pretty little mill."

They crossed a narrow bridge to the mill, Cary immediately assessing various photographic opportunities and Mr. Noland apparently assessing the state of the mill. No one spoke for a few minutes. Cary snapped away while Mary occasionally extended her hand to aid the old man without seeming to do so. He ambled around the perimeter of the mill, peering at the gaping side, noting the crumbling stone foundation and missing wooden steps. "The wheel's been straightened back up," he said. "That project last summer, I reckon."

He paused and swept the structure with a long look, perhaps caught between the present vision and memories. "This here is a big wheel for these parts." He nodded solemnly toward the wheel which, except for one bucket rusted through, seemed in fairly good repair. "Twenty-four foot in diameter, 'bout the same size as on my daddy's mill." He went on, "Everybody looked to that mill on Upper Forkety Branch. It was what you might call an institution." He looked at Buddy as if proud of his declaration.

"Wait, wait," Cary cried. "Can I–do you mind if I tape this? I want to hear it all and remember it all. I've got a tiny recorder in the car. Do you mind?"

The old man looked pleased. "I been interviewed lots of times, Miss, mostly 'bout growing up before the war." He winked at Mary. "That's the big war, the first World War. I don't mind talking a bit, been doing it all my life, nobody listening, till now I'm too old to do anything else." Cary snapped a few more shots, before realizing Mr. Noland was silent, waiting. They re-crossed the stream. With some concern, Mary walked behind the old man but his footing was steady and sure.

He lowered himself into the folding chair on the lawn and Cary ran to the car. "Got a cigarette on you?" he asked Mary.

From several yards away, without looking up, Buddy yelled, "Grandpappy, you know what the doctor said. No smoking and no more Pepsis."

"Dang, ain't that the way of it?" Mr. Noland said. "I can't get away with a thing, with this here up-and-coming sheriff a-watching me." But he grinned at the young man and took a packet of chewing gum from his pants pocket. "Nice morning to be out, ain't it? The sun's warm enough."

He and Mary discussed the weather and brands of chewing gum until Cary returned and began to ask questions. The tape recorder was ultra small, so small Mr. Noland looked as if he didn't believe it was up to the task. He said his family's mill had been washed away in a big flood, "mighta been fifty years ago," and that no one then had the inclination or money to rebuild. "But," he went on, "in my mind's eye I can see that corn mill better than I can remember things that happened last week. Why, if that old mill was setting up there right now, I could walk in there and pour a bushel of corn in the hopper and start the thing rolling." He stared at the distant Smoky Mountains. "It was a gathering place for us boys and menfolk. The wives couldn't fault their men for wasting time, or the mamas their boys, if they was a-waiting on the corn to be ground. Some things you can't rush. We done a lot of horse trading and knife swapping in the meantime." He stopped again, added another stick of gum to his jaw.

"And some drinking, too, I bet," Mary said.

"No siree bob. We was all good church goers, Baptists mostly around there. I bet I didn't see three jars being passed around in my whole growing up there." He grinned.

"That's jars of moonshine, ladies, since you ain't from around here."

"Look what you missed, Grandpappy," interspersed Buddy. He occasionally turned the pages of a thick textbook but obviously was also listening closely.

"Didn't miss a thing, Buddy. And never had but one beer, two beers, in my life. That was enough for me. Not even a beer when I worked for awhile up at that plant in Spruce Pine."

The twinkle in his eyes told the women they were in for a story. "One beer?" Cary said.

At the same time Mary asked, "Why just one? What happened?"

"My family didn't hold with drinking, was dead set against it. Naturally, I was curious and I guess I tried drinking too early in life. Me and some boys, older than me, went to the carnival that come to town ever year. I was maybe ten or eleven and they promised they'd take good care of me. Otherwise my daddy would've kept me at home. Anyway, this carnival set up in the big field next to the school, had all kinds of oddities, two-headed calves, the world's fattest man, even had them Siamese twins...now that was something to behold." He paused to remember the strange sights. The women leaned forward, to encourage him to continue.

"Ain't much more to tell about that one beer," he said. "The boys was having a mighty good time and there's me tagging along. One of'em, Josh Adkins, said, 'Hey, Elbert's not having near the fun we are–and you know why.' Pretty soon they took it their heads to share the beer they kept going back to the Model T to drink. That car was a novelty itself. One of the boys' uncle had let him drive the thing, and him not more than fifteen. Anyway, we hunkered down behind the car and they opened a bottle and give it to me. Now I'd been eatin' this and that, cotton candy, popcorn...they put that bottle–brown, it was, I'll never forget it–in my hands and I just guzzled it down. They egged me on and when I'd finished that bottle, they opened another. 'Bout that time somebody come along, somebody they didn't want to see, and they all stood up and put the beer away and hustled me off in a hurry." He stopped to grin. "Too much of a hurry for my stomach and my head. Things started swimmin' in front of my eyes and I started–pardon my being so honest, ladies–started gagging and puking up a storm. They said I turned green around the gills. They laughed and laughed, except for Ernie, his boots was a mess. They laid me down under a little tree and said they'd be back to check on me. Whew, I never felt so bad in my life." He put a third piece of gum in his mouth. "After a while some lady from the church saw me, looking so puny. She and her husband took me home. Limp as a dishrag. Yep, that was enough beer for me."

Buddy had surely heard the story before but he said, "Did you get a whipping?"

"Nope. Mama told Daddy I'd just eat too much and all the excitement did me in. She musta smelled the beer but she never said a word. Well, she did say when she'd washed my face with a wet rag and covered me up, 'Let that be a lesson to you,' and it was." He seemed to bask in his audience's appreciative smiles and murmurs. Then he said, "Let me rest a minute and we'll get onto the mill business."

Cary asked, "Did your family run the mill as a business or for home use?"

"Well, Miss, you know you couldn't make a livelihood back then just running a corn mill. There was no way. You had to farm or something. We got into tobacco. And many times in the fall of the year my daddy would go to work in the sawmill or be harvesting. So he taught us six boys that we might carry on the job while he was gone. And now I'm the only one left." He cleared his throat and continued. "'Course I know that a lot of people came to the mill many a-time and seen one of us boys there and would think, 'well, I wish your daddy had a-been here, 'cause the meal won't be as good.' He was the expert. People would come from miles around for him to grind their corn."

Mary and Cary settled back on a blanket they'd brought and listened, hardly having to ask a question.

"It was a public business, but they weren't no cash register around. Daddy would start that old mill up at daylight in the wintertime and grind till after dark. But once you got it started, as long as you was grinding one feller's corn it wasn't too important if you got a little more in one sack or the other, but when you switched over to the other feller's you had to be careful not to cheat him. My daddy had a big old box setting next to the hopper and he'd toll his share out."

"What exactly does that mean?" Cary asked, feeling slightly devious since she knew.

"That was his pay, you might say, his toll. People didn't have a lot of cash money so the miller just took his share. It was about a gallon of meal for each bushel of corn ground."

"The miller's family always had bread, I guess," Mary said.

"Daddy and his daddy before him was a deacon and a good-hearted feller, and I imagine he tolled just about two-thirds of the people's corn that come there. Even though I thought we was the poorest people in the world, my daddy knowed they was other people worse off. And when they'd bring in a half bushel or a peck of corn, why he'd just grind it and never take his toll."

"I like your daddy," Cary said.

"We had a big old board there, made out a log. Everybody would set their turn of corn down in line and wait their turn. We had a big pot-bellied stove in there, and people would set around and talk. And if we didn't have a fire there, they'd come on up to the house. We had a great big fireplace...and if any of them was there at dinner time, they would just eat with us. I've seen my mother set plates for three, four, five men who was waiting their turn." He grinned. "Sometimes that meant us boys got the wrong end of the chicken!"

Cary looked puzzled.

"We were lucky to get the part that went over the fence last, young lady! More'n likely we'd end up with cornbread and milk–and the smell of cooking."

Buddy stood up. "I'm off to the convenience store down the road for some coffee. What can I bring you ladies?"

They assured him they had a thermos in the car and would share their bread and cheese and fruit when he returned.

"Double up on the cream, Buddy," his great grandfather instructed.

"Yes, sir."

Cary said, "That's an overshot wheel, isn't it?"

"Well, Miss, you know there's the overshot wheel and the breast wheel and the undershot, depending on where the water hits the buckets–or paddles." With his hands he indicated that with the overshot wheel, the water flowed over the top of the wheel; the breast wheel took water at its midpoint; and water flows under the undershot wheel.

Cary nodded. "I've been reading up on mills," she said. "I think I almost understand how the power is generated."

"Most of the mills back here in the western part of the state operated overshot wheels and that meant a dam or pond had to be maintained. I reckon the average wheel was around fourteen feet in diameter, though there was a bigger wheel, I know, out on Fines Creek and a mighty big one on Morgan's Mill over near Brevard." Cary opened her mouth to ask about them, but Mr. Noland said, "Both of'em's gone now. Fell down. Parts toted off. So I hear."

Gesturing at the metal wheel on the mill, he explained that water was diverted from upstream through a ditch along the side of the stream into a flume ("we called it a chute") pouring over the top of the wheel. Sometimes a stream was dammed up so it provided a more reliable source of power. The flow was controlled so that when the power was not needed, water did not continue to flow and rot the buckets. "That there wheel," he pointed toward the mill, "was delivered in 1914, I remember, because right after that was when Granddaddy had a metal wheel delivered for his mill. It was right before the war made metal scarce. Before that the buckets was wood." He went on to explain that very early settlers had to build primitive "pounding mills" on streams ("saved their womenfolk a lot of pounding") and then larger homesteads might have "tub mills" ("like over in Gatlinburg where they've saved that one") that didn't operate with vertical wheels.

"My head's swimming," Mary said.

"I think I'd better stick to learning about vertical water wheels," Cary agreed.

A few minutes later, Buddy pulled into the gravel driveway. He handed his great grandfather a large cup of hot coffee, along with three jelly-filled doughnuts. "I know Mama said you couldn't have these," he said, "but I knew you wouldn't speak to me all the way home if I didn't bring them."

"Trained this boy right." The old man's grin showed tobacco-stained teeth. He stood up. "Bring your food up to the porch. I know Tanna wouldn't mind if we set there and eat. Her grandpa and my daddy was good friends." Looking around, apparently for a trashcan, he said, "Not good for the birds and such," as he took his gum from his mouth, wrapped it in a tissue and dropped it into his pants pocket.

For the next fifteen minutes the four of them ate in amicable silence, broken by a few comments about the goat cheese. Buddy confessed he'd never eaten goat cheese and never expected to, but he said, "It's not too bad. Wouldn't be my first choice though."

Cary turned the tape recorder back on and encouraged Mr. Noland to continue by asking about the water flow. She was glad she'd been studying about mills.

"We had a little opening and we'd just open that door and there was the things you'd turn the water on with. You took one –kind of a handle– and as you pulled it down that turned the water through. And you took another and pushed it up and that cut the gate off for any water to come out and all of it was going down the flume and hitting that wheel...and if it didn't take right quick, you'd run out there and grab that belt and there it'd go."

"I've photographed several mills," Cary said, "and I think I understand what happens, but could you--"

"There was a shaft going inside to another wheel which was about six foot and then a belt going to a small wheel and then a belt going to a smaller wheel that was about fourteen inches and then that small wheel was turning the rocks–"

"The grindstones?" Cary asked.

Mr. Noland nodded and continued, "And that old mill would grind all day long–free power–it didn't cost you a dime in the world. The only thing you had to do was get that thing set up. That was solid power."

After their lunch, Mr. Noland's voice weakened and he began to tell them about his favorite chickens and pigs. Then his chin dropped and he slept. Buddy said, "Let him rest awhile, then we'll be getting on home. He's like a worm in hot ashes for a few hours and then he tires out." He brought a plastic bag from his truck for their empty cups and paper trash. Cary must have looked approvingly at his behavior, for he grinned. "My mama didn't raise no fools. And my older brother's always saying, 'Pack it in, pick it up, pack it out.' He leads llama treks into the Smokies. Hey, I'd like to come over to your place sometime and see the farm and the goats." He put his chair and book into the vehicle. "I might learn to like that crazy cheese. I bet Mama would like to try it."

Mary wrapped the remaining cheese in wax paper and insisted that he take it with him. In a few minutes Mr. Noland awoke with a start and immediately plopped another stick of gum in his mouth. Reluctantly they prepared to say goodbye. Cary asked the two men to pose by the battered truck. She took a few pictures as they stood, looking proud or embarrassed. Then she joked and talked until she had the perfect glint of grandfatherly pride and youthful love on the faces of the two before snapping several more shots. She promised to send them copies in the next few days. In the late afternoon light she returned to the mill, taking closeups of the weathered boards, the tilt of the wheel, its rusty buckets, stopping only when she realized Mary herself was dozing in the car. She left a thank you note for Tanna, with her telephone number and email address.

Mary added her own note to Tanna about being in touch about the restoration. "She's taken on a big job."

"It's wonderful the mill is still in the family," Cary said.

As they entered the ramp to Interstate 40, Mary, who had been quiet for some moments, blurted, "A new word just popped into my head, and I'm wondering if it applies to you!"

"What word?"

"Quim." Mary smirked at Cary's expression. "Quim."

"Okay, I'll bite. What does this new word, cute as it is, mean? And why me?"

"A quim is a cross between a quirk and a whim." Mary laughed. "Something that could leave you absolutely frozen in your tracks–or enthusiastically doing the wrong thing."

Cary punched her friend lightly on the shoulder. "This interest in old mills is not a 'quim' any longer, and I don't intend to be frozen..." She steered smoothly around a log-laden truck. "You don't really think I'm doing the wrong thing, do you? Really and seriously?"

"No, not really. Your quirk and your whim have already solidified into determination," Mary said. "But I love the word." She saw a strange look flit across Cary's face. "What?"

Cary burst into laughter. "I don't think we'd better use the word without checking out our audience," she said, giggling still. "And I'm not going to tell you why! Let's just say I just remembered a class I took in Middle English."

Mary asked, protested, and tried unsuccessfully to get her friend to say more about the word. "I've never seen it and I'm going to look it up when we get home," she huffed finally.

"Let me know if you find it in your dictionary," Cary said, smiling mysteriously. "My lips are sealed. Let's talk about the mill instead."

They returned to her favorite subject, next to Thyme-Table Farm and Spence.

"This was the best day!" Cary announced for the third time, as they pulled into The Cove. For miles she'd waxed eloquent about Francis Mill and how she wanted a mill, even a small one. Mary admired the youthful enthusiasm but tempered her responses with comments about costs, expertise needed, and generally practical matters.

"I hope Jon doesn't expect me to cook tonight," Mary said. "That man hasn't learned a thing from being around Spence. He expects food to appear magically–"

"Then he's not learned a thing from being around you!" Cary laughed at Mary's exaggerated frown. "Shall I call you if there's something good on the stove? Spence had a lot to do today, chores in town, so he's probably forgotten about food, too. Too bad we're too far away to expect pizza delivery."

"I bet Johnny will bring a couple of pizzas if I call him," his mother said. "That's what I'll do."

"See," Cary said. "And once again, food will magically appear! With pepperoni and olives for us, please." The two women laughed and went to their homes where each found a man dozing in the living room, each very agreeable to pizza.

The evening belonged to Cary who described the mill, played portions of the tape, and exclaimed several times, "We should build a mill on ThymeTable! Spence, we should."

Rawlston, who, with Alice, had come down for dessert, finally said quietly, "It might be better to buy an old mill and move it to The Cove. Easier to start with something to work with than to build from scratch." He fumbled in his shirt pockets, looking for something.

"You mean, move a whole building?" Spence asked. "First, find a mill and then just move the entire thing?"

"Wow," Johnny and his father Jon said at the same time.

Cary and Mary opened their mouths to speak, then closed them, as each seemed to be thinking of the mills they'd visited. In a moment Cary said, "How in the world would we find a mill for sale?"

"Advertise in mill journals," Rawlston said.

"On the Internet," Johnny and Suzanne said.

"Word of mouth," Jon contributed.

"Okay, okay." Spence threw up his hands. "You make it sound as if there are dozens of mills out there."

Cary wrapped her arms around Spence. "I'll start looking..."

"Whoa," Spence said. "I hate to raise the question of funds, but I'd need to do a complete financial analysis. Like, how much are we thinking of? And then what do we know about putting a mill into working order, getting the site prepared, health, safety considerations...all of that?"

"We can deal with all that, darling."

Mary looked at Jon. "Have you got any more land to sell in Mexico?" Her tone was light but the question seemed serious. They waited for some sharp retort from Jon or an enthusiastic yes or no. He turned red and shifted his eyes from his ex-wife's direct gaze.

"What?" demanded Mary. "I don't really expect you to pull money out of your hat and you're in no way obligated to this Cove." She paused and then added, "Financially or otherwise."

"Hey, Mom, take it easy," Johnny said. He was a born peacemaker. Tension dismayed him and throughout his childhood, when Jon was home, Johnny had usually walked out of the room when his parents' discussion deteriorated into quarreling and harsh words. In Suzanne, calm, placid, easygoing, he had apparently found his perfect mate. She reached for his hand and he leaned back to touch her shoulders.

Jon's flush subsided a little and he said, "That money's gone. For now. I invested in some winery stock, new place down in South Carolina."

"Gone? All of it–" Mary's surprise reflected in their faces. It had been a considerable sum, enough to allow Jon to stall the developers' proposal to buy Cove land for a golf club. "Gone?" Mary repeated. "At least you could have helped your son, our son, buy a house for when he gets married." She didn't bother to hide her disgust.

"Leave me out of it," Johnny said. "I haven't asked anything from him–from you, Dad--and I don't expect anything." His tone was calm, not cold, but Jon bristled.

"I haven't heard about a wedding next week or next month. By next year, who knows? The boy's right, he doesn't ask for anything from me. Be just as happy if I left this place." Jon's hands clenched his cup of tea.

A cool wind seemed to have slid through the comfortably warm room. Johnny looked from his father to his mother and said nothing. He shrugged. Suzanne massaged his shoulders.

"There's a mill over in east Tennessee," Rawlston said. His voice was breathy and he coughed a little. Drawing a handkerchief from his overalls pocket he coughed again.

They turned to him, glad to be diverted from the irritation between Jon and Mary.

"Near Elizabeth City, up that way anyhow," Rawlston said. He stood up and walked to where his jacket lay and pulled a crumpled note from its pocket. "Here's the directions if you want to go look at it." He coughed again. "Don't think I'm up to the trip."

To their questions about the mill, how he knew of it, what it might cost, Rawlston was vague, repeating a couple of times, "You'll have to check it out." He didn't know the owner or the condition of the building, only that it was there and maybe for sale. "Somebody said the old owner's kids sold it to a Florida man who liked the idea but not the reality of a mill. That's all I know." He wiped his forehead with a handkerchief and then blew his nose. His fatigue showed.

"Going to town tired you too much, didn't it?" Cary said. On cue, Johnny stood and offered Rawlston and Alice a ride home.

"I know you can walk it, but why should you?" Suzanne said to Rawlston. She took his arm and Johnny pulled Alice to her feet. "It's all of three minutes in the truck." She and Johnny zipped up their jackets and she held Rawlston's for him. "We need to get back to the studying. These long hours and big pizzas are too much for us."

"You young people can't take it like us old guys," Jon said. He winked at the young couple, and Mary gave him a small smile. They seemed to be returning to an even keel.

"Darn, I can't go look at this mill tomorrow," Cary said. She had promised to assist Mark Coleman, her photography instructor and mentor, in a day-long workshop he was conducting at Lake Lure. Mary had a translation project due in two days ("and three days' worth of work to do on it," she said). But they agreed that Jon and Spence would investigate the mill the following day.

"To keep Cary happy," Spence said with a grin.

In the kitchen, Mary whispered, "Smart move, on your part, being busy tomorrow."

"I promised Mark weeks ago..." Cary started, then she noticed Mary's expression. "Oh, you mean?"

"Let Spence–and Jon, for that matter–get involved in your quest. This may be a determining factor. It is a big undertaking, Cary, and not to be gone into lightly." She held up a hand when Cary's eyes darkened in protest. "You do want Spence to want a mill, don't you? Do you really expect him to start such a big project just because you want it?"

"No, no..well, I mean yes...." Cary thought for a moment. "It has to be a two-way deal. You're right. If he does it only to satisfy me, I wouldn't be satisfied." She grinned. "I keep learning. Marriage is complicated. Thanks, Mary."

"Don't look at me." Mary dumped the pizza debris and tied up the garbage bag. "I'm not the one happily practicing it!" The women laughed. Outside they found Jon and Spence settling on an early departure time. They also intended to make a couple of other stops along the way, herb farms Spence wanted to visit.

Standing on their porch, Winchester wagged his tail, ready for his walk. Cary turned to Spence and kissed him.

"Hmm," he said, "was that a comma, a question or an exclamation kiss?"

"Well, it wasn't a period kiss, not a full stop." Cary batted her eyes seductively. "The evening's not over yet."

Winchester looked as if he knew he wouldn't have a long walk tonight.

Chapter 6 "Recycle's My Middle Name"

"What in the world is that? Are those?" Cary watched Spence and Jon unload various metal objects. It was almost dark and the pieces of iron or steel clanked resoundingly as the men dropped them against each other. They had pulled the truck to the storage shed some distance beyond the house, and Winchester's barking alerted her to their return. She'd been home from the workshop for a couple of hours and had been alternating between reading her herb encyclopedia and a book on mills. She could see that the men's pants and shirts were smudged and their boots muddy. Spence's shirt was pulled from his trousers. "You look as if you've been through somebody's attic, somebody's wet attic."

Wiping his hands on his shirt, Spence groaned as he straightened up. When Cary put her hands on her hips in a decidedly wifely gesture of impatience, he finally answered. "These actually came from somebody's basement...the lower level, anyway, of that old mill Rawlston told us about. We rescued the salvageable parts. The building's just about washed away."

Though Spence couldn't see Cary's expression in the shadows, he sensed her disappointment.

"Sorry, honey. But it's almost totally gone. It's sad to see any building get in that shape. A neighbor who's looking after the property came over. The owner in Florida authorized him to sell anything he can."

"Or give it away," Jon said, wiping his face. If Spence looked disheveled, Jon was a muddy wreck. "What a mess the place was, sad, too, to see it in such a condition." He methodically arranged the metal shafts, then continued, "Rescued is the right word, huh, Spence?"

"Yeah, next week a bulldozer will knock the building down and by next spring there'll be a new house on the creek. Now, don't look so sad, honey. Nothing could save the structure. Dry rot, wet rot, a couple of fires–"

"Looks like vandals or transients have camped there and been careless," Jon said.

"Anyway, most of the machinery has long since been sold, stolen, or in mysterious ways disappeared. The guy was glad to see us because we insisted on going down into the depths, mud up to our ankles near the creek and dust in the back of the place." Spence leaned on Cary's shoulders. He smelled both dusty and dank, of dried sweat and dried mud. She raked a strand of cobwebs from his hair.

Jon said, "It's a wonder we didn't roust out a nest or two of copperheads back under that old lumber. Must have been a dozen bushel baskets in there, all without bottoms!"

"It was a mess, all right," Spence said. "These gears and gear shafts must have been overlooked by anybody else. The guy practically gave them to us. When I tried to pay him a little more, he said, 'Recycle's my middle name! Take'm.' They're still usable, though. The sections are all there. We laid it all out on the ground. It all fits. The cogs of this little gear fit right into that one." He pointed to the pieces, hardly distinguishable in the darkness, a note of pride in his voice. "No cracks we could see, nothing missing that can't be rebuilt–assuming we find a mill."

"That means, oh, Spence, that means we'll go ahead!" Cary broke into an impromptu Mexican hat dance, stomping around, whooping. Winchester joined in, barking and running in circles around her feet. The men stared and started laughing. Jon leaned into the truck window and blew the horn. By the time they'd collapsed against the vehicle, chuckling rather than laughing, Mary joined them and Spence enticed Cary to perform her "mill dance" again.

Jon retold the story of the "rescue," greatly expanded, to Mary after they all trooped back to the house. Cary asked if Spence wanted to shower before telling them about the rest of their day, but he and Jon were too eager to describe their adventures and negotiations to take time out to do more than wash their hands and dash water on their faces. They had stopped to eat in Weaverville and thus required only tea, wine, and avid listeners.

"The little building looked forlorn, somehow," Spence said. "And it was small, maybe forty-five by sixty feet. The wheel hasn't been there for over five years. Somebody bought it and took it to some country music theme park up in Kentucky, according to Bert, the guy we dealt with."

"There was an air about the place, something of loss," Jon said. "It was like the building was thinking 'well, all my parts are gone–time for me to cave in,' and bit by bit it fell apart–or was torn apart. Ravaged by time and man." Jon's mystical streak was showing, almost as if he'd entered into the spirit of the building or its spirit had entered him.

They sat quietly for long moments, until finally Mary lifted her cup. "Here's to your rescue of–whatever those things are."

"Nothing else to salvage, is there?" Jon said. "I don't think there's another piece of metal in the building, do you, Spence?"

"Maybe a doorknob. No, the door didn't have a knob, just a bar and string latch. And the roof had most of its tin blown off." Spence looked as downcast as Jon as he described the derelict building. "These old places deserve better."

"Rawlston must have known about the mill from years ago," Cary said. "He'll be upset to think of its condition."

Spence stretched his long legs and propped his feet on the coffee table, a habit that had disconcerted Cary's mother at first, but which Cary found endearing. "We didn't just go to that mill. We must have talked to a dozen people.

Besides the one herb farm, we stopped for coffee at one little place, stopped for a cold drink at a convenience store, stopped by two junky antique barns..."

"So we have some information about other places to go," finished Jon. He patted his shirt pocket from which jutted the top of a small notebook. "And those guys'll spread the word that ThymeTable Farm wants mill equipment. But no more tonight, please. I'm worn down to a nubbin, as one old man said. Can't keep my eyes open." He stood and so did Mary who indicated she'd drive them to her house. Mary had been enthusiastic about the mill and the prospects of continuing the "hunt" but Cary realized that when Mary looked at Jon alone her expression was reticent. All did not seem well with them. But until Mary–or Jon–was ready to divulge the problem, and surely it was more than that he was once again penniless, it would remain theirs.

During the next two weeks an undercurrent of "mill fever" swept over ThymeTable Farm. Cary found web sites that might be helpful; Spence ordered books about mills and made initial contacts with experts and mill owners. Jon scoured local bookstores, without much success, for old books about mills, and Mary even announced that she intended to reread *The Mill on the Floss*. However, their routine tasks went on as usual: they helped Alice with the goats, prepared the various greenhouses with seedlings and the fields for planting, did the general cleaning and clearing that comes with early spring. Beyond the routine, however, stirred a breeze of anticipation.

Cary fretted a little that perhaps Alice was too much alone. However, Rawlston sometimes walked with her up to the mulberry tree, now called Agnes' Place. Her friends discouraged her from making the somewhat steep climb alone, especially since the goats liked to go along and might inadvertently cause Alice to trip or turn an ankle. She resisted their advice at first but common sense prevailed. Her sister's death caused Alice to take long looks at the accumulated material of their lives. She sorted through stacks of memorabilia and sent two packets of family photographs and other mementos ("Papa's spectacles, and Mama's button hook," she said, "for doing up her shoes.") to a small local museum in their home state, Kansas.

"Our nearest cousins are fourth or fifth cousins and probably don't even realize we are–I am–around," she said to Cary one day. "Coomer's Corner has a tiny museum and archives. We never lived there after high school, but they can decide what to do with all this." With determination she shoved high school dance cards, graduation announcements, college yearbooks and diplomas into a carton. "If Spence will take this to the post office for me?"

"Sure, this afternoon or in the morning," Cary said. "Anything I can do to help?"

"Not really. I like going through the boxes and shelves at my own speed," Alice said. "And my speed is slow to nothing. Somehow doing this helps me accept Agnes' death."

Cary took herself off alone a few times to explore and to photograph mills within easy driving time of ThymeTable. In Henderson County she found the Mill House Lodge in Flat Rock; a mill had likely been built in the 1830s on the site and the structure, along with a complex of other buildings, had served the tourist industry for almost fifty years. She enjoyed meeting the new owners who had undertaken a vast dam restoration project. Mill enthusiasts from up north, the Horky family would continue to operate the unique property as a lodge, with cottages and rooms available. In the same county in the Dana community stood the huge Stepp Mill with a tremendous wheel. Her old newspaper clipping said the overshot wheel was thirty-four feet high. Though she wanted to see inside the building, she had not been able to contact anyone about stopping by. The mill had been owned by Larry Justus, a state representative who died in 2003. It was difficult to photograph, but she ploughed through the high undergrowth and tried every angle, along with her own patience, and came away not even halfway satisfied. She knew, though, that she had one excellent shot: a lone crow perched with the stolidity of ownership in the center of an opening where a window had once been, the horizontal lines of the timber contrasting with the sleek and regal bird. Cary vowed to return. Actually, she thought, she vowed to return to each mill she visited.

Whenever possible Cary knocked on doors and asked lots of questions about the mills she photographed and any others people might know about. She learned of several sites where little or nothing remained of a mill except traces of the mill race or cement posts or rock dams. When she could find the sites she tramped around them, recording anything that might be considered archaeological debris. In a strange way, though she missed Mary's company, these expeditions left her content and energized as well as melancholy at the loss of this kind of "community center."

After an all-day visit to Winebarger Mill on Meat Camp Road outside Boone, she tried to articulate some of her feelings to Spence. "The mills weren't built to be beautiful, but they have a charm, not charm like sweetness and proper behavior charm that makes people want to like you. The charm of a workplace. Sort of like your greenhouses. They were built purely to function, to help a rural community survive and be fed. People and animals."

She propped her face up in her hands, elbows on the table. "Like the church fed the spiritual side of the community and the mill fed the physical side."

Spence nodded his understanding and laid aside the manual on mill restoration he had been reading.

"But it was more than the physical, the meal and grits and flour. Mills were focal points in the community, a place where people felt comfortable."

"They were for the men, mostly," Spence observed.

"True. The women were back at the house, barefoot and..." She trailed off.

"Pregnant." Spence took her hand.

Rather than look mournful because she wasn't pregnant, Cary grinned. "I bet those guys carried all the gossip home along with the meal and flour. Mr. Noland made a point of saying no one could accuse the menfolk of 'just a-fooling around' when they were waiting their turns. It must have been cozy–and I guess men need that, just like the women had their quilting parties."

"A lot of sociology in thinking of the old mills," Spence said. "You know, the closest thing to that kind of gathering of the men around here is probably MacDonald's or Hardees in the morning."

"Yes, since we don't have the English pubs," Cary said. "I notice when we've stopped for coffee on the road, those men are talking up a storm. They definitely do not live up to the stereotype of the strong silent male."

"You should know better than to believe stereotypes by now," Spence said. "Especially about the South."

"I do know better."

"Cary," Spence said, "I have been thinking a lot about a mill here on ThymeTable..."

"Oh, don't say you–"

"I want to do it. I just want you to know all the angles. It won't be easy, may be very hard to get a mill here and into operation. It may take years. But I'm for trying. We really have to do something to diversify–I hate to sound so commercial. We need another product, but beyond that, my dear enthusiast, I've come to have quite a regard for these old mills."

"Are we in bad shape financially? We have some resources, my savings, and all the money from my photography–" She stopped and they both chuckled. Cary had sold photographs, had exhibited in a few galleries, was known around town, especially for her close-ups of plants. But Asheville abounded with excellent photographers and they all advised the same thing: don't quit your day job! True, some did make it big, but the majority enjoyed greater acclaim than sales. And those who made a modest living were experts who taught, led workshops, had a steady market niche, or, like her friend Mark, owned a studio offering darkroom instruction and time slots.

"Well," Cary admitted ruefully, "I may be sixty dollars to the good in my photo account!" Her hobby was her major, even her only, real indulgence. Her sister-in-law spent a fortune on clothes; Cary, satisfied with jeans and boots, bought film and books. Spence, too, spent very little on personal items but never skimped on anything related to his herbs. They lived well and simply. They could swing a large loan from their bank but, having been burnt by the savings and loan fiasco, Spence tended toward being conservative in matters of debt. Cary's brother, Phillip, on the other hand, lived on the financial edge, played "with the financial big boys," believed that big loans were the mark of a successful businessman–and he was one of those. He was not likely to go under financially and, in fact, he seemed to enjoy the recurring big waves of fluctuation in his business dealings. He had inherited from their banking father the nerve and verve necessary to undertake huge projects–and the ability to carry them through, losing occasionally and generally coming out on top. Many times he had tried to explain his financial philosophy to Cary, but she (like their mother) remained skeptical, wary of "hunting big game with only limited ammunition." He liked the excitement, the thrill, and so did his wife, Alecia. Or at least, Alecia unfailingly believed he would have sufficient ammo when faced with the charging rhino. Cary didn't like to think of herself as unadventurous, but she knew she was– in terms of investments. She didn't even like to carry a balance on her credit cards while Phillip treated credit cards with a nonchalance she could never achieve. In Spence Cary had found an understanding "money mate" who would take chances but with caution and a backup plan.

"We'll have to borrow some, skimp some, and hope a lot," Spence said. "I have been developing a financial plan to take to the bank. Now, don't get upset, but while you've been out photographing, Jon and I have talked, and he's talked with Mary. They want a share in the responsibility for a mill. I've jotted down a preliminary outline of an agreement. Let's look at it."

For the next hour and a half, he outlined expenses, the sure ones, the likely ones, the unexpected ones. Cary sank lower and lower in spirits. She felt utterly flattened by the overwhelming costs of machinery, moving, site preparation, and, of course, employees. When Spence had finished, literally she had sunk into her chair. "I don't see how we can do it, then," she said. "Even with Jon and Mary."

"Sure we can, darling. I've just showed you." Spence laid the sheets of figures aside and spent the next thirty minutes persuading Cary that the plan was feasible, was doable, just not easy. He didn't want her to go into the enterprise unprepared, to expect a mill to materialize as if by magic. Over cups of ThymeTable's special tea, she gradually accepted his "cautious optimism" that their farm would have a mill. He had saved his best news for last. "We start in earnest tomorrow," Spence said. "Jon and I want you and Mary to come with us. A guy called yesterday with what sounds like a good possibility."

Cary's eyes sparkled again. She straightened in her chair. "Why didn't you tell me? Where is it?"

"I wanted to work these figures up first," Spence said. "Maybe I had to convince myself that maybe, maybe, for sure, we could manage." He drained his cup and yawned. "Hard work, this financial stuff. The mill is down in Catawba County. It should take us at least a couple of hours on the interstate, then off on some state roads. We've got an appointment at eleven o'clock, so keep your fingers crossed."

The expedition the following day was disappointing but not a total disaster. The mill was larger than they expected and would require a larger water source than the men had figured was possible, even with a small dam. Then, apparently once potential buyers were on the horizon, were actually walking through the site, the owner got cold feet and decided he would keep the structure after all. "It was my great-great uncle's place," he said. "I don't feel right about it going out of the family. Even if my boy doesn't want it. Not yet."

Cary brushed away the tears that threatened to obscure her vision. Rationally she saw that this mill, though picturesque in its dilapidated way, was not suitable for their farm. The building was postcard lovely, with a family of ducks in residence, paddling serenely on the huge pond. Its tin roof had at some point been painted barn red and reflected beautifully on the water. While the men discussed various aspects of milling and building, she roamed the site with her cameras. She began to wonder if they would ever find the perfect mill for their farm. She understood why the owner suddenly wanted to keep it, and she understood the other factors, too. But would they ever find just the right mill and just the right circumstances? Seeing her downcast expression, their host stopped as he walked with them to their vehicle. "Well," he said slowly, "Never had a reason to go see it, but I've heard there's a mill, Buckner's Mill, up I-77 toward the Virginia line." A grain salesman had told him the owner might want to sell, though he cautioned, "Don't quote me but I've heard he's got to sell, wife's health problems." He looked at his mill. "Tough."

Cary impulsively gave the man a hug as they said goodbye. He rewarded her with a great blush.

"Millers are great romantics," Mary said. "He won't part with that mill, for sure."

As they drove back toward the interstate, they decided not to call then but to try to visit the mill later in the week. Mary patted her friend's shoulder and said, "Cary can't take another disappointment today. Let's go find that barbeque place he recommended."

"I'm okay, Mary. I really am. It's a treat to wander around looking for and at these old mills, even if today was a bummer."

That evening while Spence and Jon went to look in on Rawlston and on the goats, Cary slumped in Mary's study, watching her straighten up the room. Mary said, "For the past two weeks, you realize you haven't mentioned not being pregnant, have not sighed mighty sighs every time we've passed a store selling baby clothes." She continued to replace various books on the shelf she'd been organizing.

"I confess I haven't been completely preoccupied with motherhood lately. Not that we've stopped trying! But I guess it's good for me, this mill project, huh?" Cary sounded surprised at her own attitude. "Q'est sera sera," she sang.

Mary's brow furrowed. "I wonder, what will be...I wonder about Jon. He seems permanently parked here, yet he seems unsettled." She slammed a book down on the desk. "If he's going to stay, at least he could pretend to be content!" With some irritation, she flicked her computer screen on. "I have work to do. Sometimes I look up and there he is, just standing in the doorway as if he's forgotten how to sit somewhere else!"

Cary asked, "Don't you ever talk?"

"No," Mary said. "If we'd ever talked we probably wouldn't be in this predicament. He'd be totally gone from my life or totally in it. " She frowned. "He knows now that I don't need him...and I did need him when Johnny was small. He wasn't around enough then. Now he can't seem to leave."

Cary gave her shoulder a reassuring touch. "You're big guys now. You'll work it out. We've noticed his restlessness or whatever it is. But he certainly is in no hurry to go." They said goodnight, one thinking of the husband waiting for her, the other of the ex-husband always leaving.

The telephone was ringing as Cary entered the house. Spence said, "You get it. I'm in the shower, unavailable."

"Justin is totally unreasonable!" It was Denise. Cary could hear sniffling, with anger behind it. "I told him to get out, I never want to see him again. He's so, so, so..." She began to sob.

Cary murmured and asked and listened, murmured and soothed. She heard Spence take Winchester for a quick walk and then lock up. With an herbal catalog in hand, he headed for their bed. Thirty minutes later, she woke him up. "Denise and Justin are having difficulties. I think they may have split up. She's upset but she's the one who insisted they couldn't get married, not now, she says."

Spence was well aware of Denise's fiery temper and the artistic temperament that fueled it. He yawned, brushed the catalog from the bed, and looked at the clock. After midnight. "I know it's late," Cary said. "But she was upset. I had to listen."

"What's the problem?"

"Justin won't consider the possibility of returning here to live, of maybe practicing in Asheville."

"Come here to live?" Spence's eyes widened. "He seemed concerned about Denise's business," he reminded Cary.

Cary told him that Denise had come to like The Cove, could see herself here, could sell her jewelry through the many fine shops and galleries in and around Asheville. "Denise said she'd had it with the city. She wants him to at least say he'll consider moving here, sometime."

Cary drew the comforter around her shoulders; with a gentle tug, Spence recovered his share and waited for her to go on. While Cary tried to be fair to Justin's point of view, she and Denise had been friends since their college days and she was inclined to sympathize with her desire to live in The Cove. Spence knew better than to be too critical of Denise so he simply pointed out the difficulty of getting established in a medical practice plus the fact that Justin was not particularly a rural type.

"Still, he ought to think about Denise," Cary argued.

"Now, Cary," Spence said with mock severity, "if I insisted we move to...Nebraska or North Dakota, would you leave these mountains?"

"Well, maybe I would if I couldn't prevail on your good sense and better nature to stay here," she said. "Then again, maybe not!" She pulled at the blanket again, and Spence grunted.

In two minutes they were both sound asleep.

Chapter 7 "A Day for Rejoicing:" The Mill Arrives

"It's coming, it's coming," Cary shouted. She had been dividing her time since 4:30 that morning between the coffee pot (the third pot was brewing), the oven (the second cinnamon coffee cake was baking), and the window, where the sky was brightening. Winchester had given up moving with her every step and settled himself in the doorway to the dining room, out of her pacing route but within sight of any crumbs that might fall. Mary and Jon sat at the kitchen table, she with a large cup of coffee, he with an article on building mills spread before him. Johnny had stationed himself down at the main road, eager to lead the trucks into The Cove and direct their parking. Spence had stayed to oversee the final loading of the mill and was driving in with the truckers. When he called early, very early that morning, they had stopped for a hearty breakfast at a Huddle House.

Cary promised the workers lots of fresh coffee, and then her excitement that the mill was actually "on the road" overcame her and she chattered non-stop. Finally, Spence stopped her with a laugh. He said, "Here's Mr. Robinson. I'll let him tell you."

He had handed the phone to the mover who assured her that all was going as planned. "We like to get on the road and through traffic areas before the morning rush hour," Mr. Robinson said. "Otherwise, we get treated to a lot of cussing." She heard him jingle some keys. "We can't always hear it but we know the air's blue when traffic stops for us." He paused. "Grinds to a halt, you might say! But you gotta be careful with this kind of cargo." She agreed, hung up the phone, and tried to settle down to wait.

Turning from the window, Cary yelled, "It's just down the road! I see the lights down at the curve." She opened the door and stared down the road. Hurrying back in to grab her camera, she jumped over Winchester who started to rise. "You stay here, boy," she said. "I can't believe it. It's here, it's coming!" She ran outside.

"Has she been that excited since her wedding day?" Jon asked. But both he and Mary were on their feet, watching the slow movement of vehicles coming up the road. Johnny's truck led the way, followed by Spence's, then a truck with an oscillating flashing orange beam and a sign "Oversized Load" on it. Some yards behind came the truck with the dismantled mill secured with great straps. Behind it a second large flatbed carried the wheel and various pieces of equipment covered with a tarpaulin. A mammoth extended-cab truck with "Robinson Special Transport" in flaming orange on its side concluded the caravan. Lights went on in Alice's house, and Cary saw Rawlston come out on the porch at Justin's house. There would be quite a crew for refreshments. Mary poured the freshly brewed coffee into a large thermos and set about making another pot. Handling such "precious cargo" (so Cary had called it earlier that morning), the workers would need to be alert; she added a couple of extra spoons for strength.

Cary jogged to an advantageous spot to capture the procession on high speed film, then she stood as if mesmerized by the processional. This momentous day had been months in the making. Cary experienced again the thrill that ran through her at her first sight of Buckner Mill. At that moment she knew that this was the mill they'd been seeking: there was no doubt in her mind. It was almost tucked away, as if waiting, bidding its time patiently. The foursome had left the main highway, a twisting two-lane that hugged the mountainside, and driven down a moderately well-kept dirt road. Cary rechecked her directions and they waited. No one came from the two-story farmhouse to greet them, but an old collie shuffled around the corner and wagged its tail at their friendly voices. "Just go on around the road and cross the creek," the owner's nephew and spokesperson had said. "Uncle'll come out if he feels like it. I'll be there 'round three, after the kids get off the bus." The grass around the house had been recently cut; a red lawnmower sat under a shed, but overall the grounds had a carelessly unkempt look. After calling again, knocking on the screen door, and waiting a few moments, they followed the barely visible grassy track from the yard. They could hear a loud stream. The collie started to follow them but then lay down and watched.

"The place just looks old," Mary had murmured. They walked on and waded through surprisingly shallow water, Cary tense with anticipation. They had not been given much description of the mill: "Sturdy on its base," "pretty little thing," and "not run since back in the fifties," and "good solid oak timber." When Cary tried for more information, the nephew shrugged and referred her to the county library. "You might find something in there about its history. We moved back here from Arkansas ten, fifteen year ago, so I can't tell you about it. Uncle T.J.'s not much of a talker."

Rounding a grove of tall firs, they saw the mill. Literally they stopped in their tracks and stared for long minutes at the structure. Abandoned and ignored the building had been, but its tin roof remained firmly in place, the stone foundation looked solid, the windows were unbroken, with plywood nailed over them. The overshot metal wheel had intact buckets, though twigs and leaves filled some. Later they learned that the main stream had been diverted when the highway was re-routed and thus storms had not deposited debris around the foundation; large hemlocks and poplars apparently broke the force of wind. Sitting as it did beside a mere trickle of stream on the south side of the mountain, the mill was protected. "Safe as a hen on her nest," the owner said, when they finally met him. "I took the sign up on the road down years ago and most newcomers buying up the land hereabouts don't know about it. Suits me that way."

For over an hour they walked around the building, Cary exclaiming and photographing, Mary making notes, Jon and Spence pausing to confer about its clean lines, quality and size, inspecting all they could from the outside. Tom Stokes, the man with whom they had dealt, ambled through the creek with the key and took them inside. Cary was sure long before she saw the dusty interior, and even a first glance told them that the machinery seemed intact. "Let's make them an offer even if we don't get inside today," she had whispered to Spence. "Can you tone that glow on your face down a little, Cary?" Jon said. "We got to talk business here." Spence simply hugged her. Mary said, "It's great, but I've got some questions so we don't sound too eager."

Later they went to the house where T.J. Stokes sat in semi-darkness, a half-eaten dinner in its microwave container before him. The nephew had told them the old man was legally blind, hardly got out at all, that his wife was in a nursing home fifteen miles away and he was on the waiting list. "I think he's just give up," Tom Stokes said. Mr. Stokes' air of resignation, almost indifference, seemed to confirm that evaluation. However, he must have liked them, for within thirty minutes, he shook their hands all around and said, "Get together with Tom here and the lawyers. Your offer's fair enough." When Tom walked out to the porch with the men, Mr. Stokes muttered, "They're all just a-waiting on Lucy and me to go. Think I don't know they've had New York folks in here walking the property lines." He grasped Cary's hand a second time. "I'm real glad you'll look after the mill." Cary assured him it would fit perfectly at ThymeTable and would be grinding before long. She invited him to come see for himself when it was ready, instantly regretting her choice of words. "Don't expect me for that, young lady. Me and Lucy's got our own trip to make." Cary realized he couldn't see the tears in her eyes as he turned, fumbling for the backs of chairs to guide him back to his recliner.

Finding and purchasing the Buckner Mill now seemed the easiest part, though by no means simple. They'd made innumerable trips to the bank, consulted with her parents in two visits, Spence's family by phone, talked themselves hoarse in the evenings reviewing all possibilities for failure but coming back to the probability of success. Once or twice, exhausted by the endless decisions and delays, Cary had succumbed to tears–with only Winchester's comforting licks and paws on her chest for sympathy. She tried not to let Spence see her frustration at the delays, but one day he told her he realized she'd stopped quoting poetry at opportune times. "That tells me something, Cary. It's a kind of barometer of your mood."

With a cheerfulness she did not feel, she rallied, with a smile and quoted: "Bright Star, would I were steadfast as thou art." She'd determined not to let him see her impatience and dismay. After all, he was doing most of the work. He didn't need a weepy wife. Buying a mill already operational was a better option than building one from "scratch," and the Buckner Mill seemed perfect, until they consulted the DOT and learned about the highly restrictive regulations regarding transporting a building of the mill's size along state and interstate highways. Vowing not to cry, Cary had gone to the bathroom and pounded the sink with her fists when they learned that the mill could not be transported in its (wheel-less) entirety on the highway because of its size.

It had been Rawlston who suggested they talk with a Mr. Rice over in Tennessee about the possibility of dismantling the mill and transporting it that way. The Museum of Appalachia had, he said, reconstructed a large mill on its property outside Norristown. He'd seen an article in a copy of the *Old Mill News* that Buddy brought him. Soon an interview and a day trip had been arranged. Cary could have stayed at the Museum for several days, so enchanted was she with all the buildings (primarily the mill, of course) and artifacts revealing mountain life in the past centuries. The men were much more focused in their questions about the practicalities of moving a mill. Seeing the Hacker Martin Gristmill in place convinced Spence and Jon that they could deal with dismantling and re-assembling the smaller Buckner Mill.

Always Cary's optimism and delight in the project ultimately overcame her weariness at all the obstacles various agencies threw before them. Online she found books on mills, their construction, operation, maintenance and acquired quite a collection of resources –which she had not yet had time to fully assimilate, much less really enjoy. They had a thick folder of permits and regulations to abide by, of lists, suggestions, requirements; they had the names of commissioners and boards to consult with and ask of. And certainly they had local contractors and specialists in foundations, water control, soil analysis, and on and on. In addition to attending to all the details and taking several trips to the mill site, they had persevered with the herb business. It seemed they alternated between sleeping the bone-weary sleep that came from sixteen-hour days and tossing through the night reviewing what still had not been done, making lists of innumerable tasks. Could the thyme patch be ignored another day? Would delaying the harvest be feasible, given the uncertainty of the weather? Would the restaurant buyers continue to deal with ThymeTable if shipments were delayed? While seeing to the financial arrangements for the mill, they had to assure a harvest to remain solvent. They kept the farm's acreage at the same level rather than opening another two-acre field; and they managed a "season of sorts" in the herb business, not a very profitable season but an acceptable margin. They paid the mortgage with a sigh of relief, but even Winchester seemed to droop with exhaustion.

Cary dashed back into the kitchen, deposited her camera temporarily, and stood beside her friends. "Drink this–it'll calm you down," Mary said, placing a cup of coffee in Cary's hands.

"This is a big day," Mary said. "In a way it's like a wedding, the start of something new."

"And the outcome uncertain," Jon said, wryly. "Like any marriage."

Mary registered his comment but didn't think this was the time to philosophize about unions or disunions. Or the dismantling and rebuilding of a mill or marriage.

"Not so much a marriage, then, as a community project," Jon said. "A family undertaking."

It was truly a family and friends' effort. Even Phillip had assisted, using his suave business acumen and dropping a few names, in easing the financial settlement. His initial reaction was, "My God, what next? Don't tell me you're going to become a miller, Cary! Or would you be a mill-lass or a mill-mess?" But then Phillip, accepting her childlike enthusiasm, had given them several pointers on the business angle, without knowing, as Alecia pointed out, the difference between an oat and a rye, a corn or a wheat. Cary's parents sent a check for ten thousand dollars, which she refused until they convinced her they had "assisted" Phillip in the same way in one of his early business ventures. Phillip would vouch for their statement, and he did so. Cary had secretly decided to place a small bronze plaque in appreciation somewhere in the mill.

Young Buddy Noland had called and arrived one morning, just in time to help Spence and the others stir the cement and pour the foundation for the wheel. The wheel itself would be installed much later. The boy seemed to have an innate sense of working with his hands, an intuitive approach that complemented the 'book learning' of Spence and Jon. Without much ado, he had the cement mixture ready, and while they pondered on how to do this or that, he simply did it–correctly. Later Spence told Cary it was a shame Buddy probably couldn't make a living as a farmer or builder, but at least his skills were being put to use at ThymeTable. Buddy updated them on his great-grandfather Noland's condition. "He sleeps most of the time now, sometimes talks to my great-grandma. She died in 1985. He's staying with my aunt now. We won't put him in a nursing home." Buddy tried a grin. "Don't think a nursing home'd hold him–when he was awake, anyway." Buddy rubbed his hands on his jeans, trying not to look worried. "Mama sent you a thank you note, she said, for the pictures you took of us. Grandpappy put them on his dresser where he can see them. Once in a while he talks about his daddy's mill, but mostly he don't talk at all."

Buddy and Johnny had hit it off at once, comparing notes on their community college courses and anticipated professions. Waiting now while the trucks seemed to inch their way toward the farm, Cary remembered overhearing a bit of their conversation toward the end of a hot, tiring day. Johnny had asked Buddy how long it took to drive from his house to Asheville.

"I can make it easy in less than two hours," Buddy said. "But I don't push the old truck. Got me a Camaro I'm fixing up. Now that thing will flat out run." He'd paused. "It will when I get it fixed."

"Long drive," Johnny said. "Too bad."

"What do you mean?"

"Suzanne, that's my girlfriend, she's at UNC-A, she's got the cutest first cousin," Johnny said. "We could introduce you, but two hours is a heck of a long drive."

Buddy had blushed, something Cary thought had gone out of style among students. "I could make it in about an hour and half, I guess."

Cary didn't hear the rest of the conversation. Buddy had come by several other times throughout the summer to help with the mill site preparation and with the herb farm chores. He now ate goat cheese with gusto but reported that his mother hadn't yet been converted to its taste. Cary, curious, had wondered about the girlfriend but said nothing. However, a couple of months later, her curiosity surfaced and she asked Johnny if he ever saw Buddy except when he came to ThymeTable.

"Yep, saw him and Chrissy last Saturday. We all went to Waynesville's Folk Moot for the day. Chrissy's Suzanne's cousin," he said. Cary tried to look surprised and must have succeeded. Johnny continued, "She's just eighteen and can't settle down on what she wants to do, besides not be a nurse's aide all her life."

"Maybe Buddy's going to school will give her ideas," Cary said.

Johnny shrugged. "I think she's got ideas about him, but maybe not going to school." Then he hurried off to work with the guys. Cary bet they never once asked him a question about his love life.

After much maneuvering, with plenty of yells and hand signals, drivers parked the trucks in strategic places for unloading, and the men trooped into the kitchen, being introduced by Spence and welcomed by the women.

"Time is money," a beefy and jovial Mr. Robinson announced to his crew. "So let's make it snappy. We're not hungry, ma'am, but that coffee will hit the spot. We want to be unloaded and on the road in a couple hours." He accepted a mug of coffee, shook his head no to offers of cream or sugar, reconsidered, and said yes to a chunk of coffee cake. He ate standing up and, thus encouraged, his crew hustled back at the trucks in less than fifteen minutes.

"Time is money," one of the younger guys muttered, wiping imaginary sweat from his forehead and winking at Mary. "Good cake, Ma'am."

"They certainly earn their money," Cary said, as the young men quickly began uncovering the trucks and were soon creating heaps of boards, where Spence indicated and Mr. Robinson directed. She and Mary spent the next two hours standing, mostly watching Mr. Robinson's crew. Occasionally Spence and Jon stepped forward to help hoist a beam or balance a shaft. Mr. Robinson usually waved their offers of help aside. "Insurance. Liability issues. We can't afford to have even a broke toe. Watch it, there, Andy." He dodged the piece of metal one of his workers swung toward him without spilling a drop of his coffee. The crew worked with an efficiency belied by their shouts, banter, and a few curses.

Alice and Rawlston joined them before daylight. Both seemed alert and intensely interested in all the activity.

"Is this the first time they've hauled a mill–" Rawlston said.

"Piece-mill?" Alice finished.

Cary slapped her hand to her forehead. "You're doing it again!"

"Can't help it," Alice said.

"Some genetic mutation links our language–" Rawlston started. He blinked and said loudly, "Is that the hopper they're unloading?"

Nodding, Cary edged closer to watch the men lift the large box-like contraption from the second truck. After the purchase and before the transporting was arranged, Cary and Mary had spent several hours inside the mill, wiping window sills and sweeping away surface cobwebs, dust, and layer after layer of oily dirt. Much deep scrubbing would still have to be done, but the pieces were superficially clean. She heard Rawlston pointing out different items from the mill and thought how knowledgeable he sounded. She'd have to do a lot of homework to speak with as much assurance about spindles, shoes, and chutes. The millstones themselves had been brought to the farm already, and Cary knew much about French buhrs, grooves, patterns, and tools for maintaining the stones. She had even read that millstones of North Carolina quartzite and granite were documented as early as the 1800s, but she still didn't know whether to spell the term for the stone used to make millstones: buhr or burr.

"I wish you luck with the project," Mr. Robinson said, accepting a final cup of coffee. He shook hands with Spence and Jon. He glanced at and then pocketed his check with a satisfied smile. "See you boys back at the office," he called as he waved his drivers away. "Just a minute, ma'am," he said. "Got something for you." He went to his pickup truck and returned dragging a heavy burlap bag. "I had one of the guys use a metal detector, last thing before we left the Stokes' place. Who knows, maybe there's a nut or bolt in here you can use." With a somewhat sheepish grin, he hoisted the bag onto a stack of boards.

"Hey, Merry Christmas! Cary," Jon exclaimed. They gathered around to peer into the bag. Cary went to the man and gave him a hug, though she could hardly reach around him.

"This is wonderful. Wow, we'll have fun going through it, identifying everything. Just getting the mill here...oh, thank you so much!" She hugged him again. Spence slapped him on the shoulder and the men walked toward his vehicle.

At the end of the day, Cary sank into a rocking chair on the porch and surveyed the piles of beams, boards, belts and pulleys, iron shafts, and "lord-knows-what-all." That's what their neighbor, Mrs. Alison, called the heaps of material. Cary could have kissed her when she said matter of factly, "It's a day for rejoicing." Looking at the organized jumble and at the burlap bag, Cary smiled. She intended to photograph every aspect of this project and to record the progress in her journal daily. She and Mary continued to toss around the idea of a pamphlet or booklet on the project, provided Mary did the technical writing and let Cary do the "fun stuff," the photography.

They would eat in an hour or so. Spence had gone inside to shower and shave. Now he came through the door and handed her a cup of chilled tea and placed a plate of cookies on the railing. Neighbors had dropped by throughout the day, many of them bearing baked goods or other offerings such as deviled eggs, potato salad, cider. They didn't feel right just looking without providing sustenance for those who worked. Long after Mr. Robinson rubbed his hands in satisfaction, pronounced his job finished, shook hands all around, accepted goat cheese and coffee cake as well as the final payment, and left with his crew, Jon and Spence had continued to work. They had sorted and organized the numbered boards, inspected items, moved and moved again the equipment, so that when the reassembling began, they'd know where everything was.

Spence lowered himself into a rocker next to Cary. She had never seen him so exhausted. "I've discovered muscles my body didn't know it had," he said. He stretched his legs out before him and sipped his tea with a weary thirst.

"We're eating with Mary tonight," Cary said. She took his free hand. "No regrets? You look tired."

"No regrets. And I am tired. It's going to take some time, Cary, to get this mill going. You do know that?" He managed a teasing grin. "I want this mill and I want it now!" He was reminding her of what they now called her "seduction" scene when she had declared, "I want you and I want you now."

"I know, honey. I'll try to be patient." Cary sighed with pleasure and anticipation. "We can offer tours and classes for children. It can be like an interpretative center," she said. "Lots, most kids have no idea about how their bread is made. They think milk originates in cartons and that bread automatically comes wrapped in plastic."

"Well, my darling, it isn't ground with an overshot water wheel for power, these days," Spence said. "But I know what you mean. We already have a ready-made zoo and garden--we have the goats and the herbs and even those cows up in the upper pasture–you know those pesky creatures." They laughed, remembering that a cow's head had poked in to comfort Cary when she was lodged in the rocks, needing rescue. She had not realized that a lack of patience was one of her traits until she saw that herbs took infinite patience–and photography, snapping quickly as she usually did, could not always be rushed. She had learned but not completely to take the seasons, the upside, the downside of farm life, in stride. In personal matters, she also liked quick resolutions.

She said, "Rawlston told Mary who told me that his sister's still in Florida–after all these months. One of the nieces had a hospital stay and VeEmma remained to help out. He says he has no idea when she'll return, maybe not in the winter months."

"It seems a long time for him to leave his place," Spence said, with a yawn. "But it's his business, not ours. Justin's happy to have someone in the house."

"Do you notice he doesn't like to leave The Cove?"

"Justin?"

"No, I mean Rawlston. How many times has he been into town, two or three in all this time." Cary ate another cookie, looking slightly guilty. "I better not spoil my appetite or Mary will be cross with me."

When Spence said nothing, she went on, "And sometimes he seems suddenly, strangely, uh, articulate, don't you think?"

"Honey, have I had time to think about the man? He's stronger than he was, his color is good. He and Alice talk a lot. He's a big help there. Just leave it." Spence clearly didn't want to be bothered with any discussion of Justin's tenant, now their friend. He was surveying the "mill" before them, perhaps wondering just what in the world they'd committed to.

Cary thought of their own recent tenant and smiled to herself.

During the summer, they had rented Rosemary Cottage for three months to a youngish professor, Howie Landreau, who would begin teaching in the fall at the local university. In exchange for a reduced rent, Spence enlisted his help with preparing the mill site. Howie readily agreed to give the farm at least twenty hours of manual labor each week, However, he had found that manual labor involved a spade, a scythe, a mattock, involved what he deemed "sweat equity," in the sun and in humid afternoons. He kept his evenings free to explore Asheville's downtown scene. For the first three weeks, he managed to get very little work accomplished, so that when Spence, tired from his own day in the greenhouses or fields, investigated, he shook his head in disgust. Spence was used to hiring and supervising young men who earned their wages, who followed instructions, who took pride in doing a job well–or who, finding they didn't like the herb business, quit with mutual good will.

Cary and Spence had been sitting then (as now) on the wide front porch, saying very little, and a comfortable silence had fallen between them as the dusk turned to darkness. Spence heaved a great sigh and Cary said, "A penny for your thoughts. No, make that a piece of Mrs. Alison's buttermilk pie and some coffee."

Spence said, "Howie said he put in three hours today but I can't see that any dirt's been moved and the weeds look more trampled than mowed."

Seeing the dismay bordering on irritation in her husband's face and realizing that this was one more problem he didn't want to deal with, she determined that he didn't have to deal with it. "Let me handle it," she said, an idea already forming in her head.

"Nah, I'll talk to him–again. I should have looked at his hands when–before–I signed the lease. He's never done a hard day's work in his life." He turned his own palms up and Cary kissed the scratch on one hand, the blister on the other.

"He said he'd worked the apple orchards," Cary remembered. "But you're right. His hands were soft."

Spence grunted. "He has raised some blisters and he's got a patch of poison ivy, he showed me, on his ankle. Though I warned him to wear boots when he's clearing."

He noticed the small smile on Cary's face. "What do you have in mind to get Howie working?"

"Blackmail," she had answered, going in to slice the pie and turn on the coffee maker.

Cary called Johnny the next morning, and Johnny called Suzanne. In the afternoon while Howie sprawled in the shade of the trees near the mill site, Johnny drove up. Cary joined them with cold lemonade and peanut butter cookies. They talked idly of various topics, and then Johnny said, "Suzanne's real excited. She got Dr. Zennor to be her senior thesis advisor. He's tough, she says, but he sees to it that his advisees get the job done."

"Suzanne's never been a slacker," Cary said, noting that Howie had become more alert.

"Right," Johnny said, "but it's easy to let things drift, especially since she's also working at The Hop. Dr. Z will keep her hopping–and not serving ice cream!" Johnny looked pleased with his clever verbiage. "She says he's the same with his department. No slacking there, either."

"And it's one of the best in the university, by reputation," Cary said. She glanced at Howie. "Come to think of it, he's your department head, isn't he? I can't remember," here she crossed her fingers, "if you're political science or history."

"Yes, he hired me. Seems a nice enough guy, sharp, publishes a lot." Howie looked at the palms of his hands as if speculating on their worth.

"Hey, I'll tell Suzanne!" Johnny said. With a sort of worldliness, he announced, "It never hurts to have connections. Maybe he could come out to ThymeTable, see the work you're doing this summer, see you outside the classroom. Maybe Mom would...no, not with her cooking. Maybe you could invite him to dinner, Cary."

Cary swept her hand toward the work site. "With all this to do, no way am I cooking for Suzanne's advisor." She seemed to reconsider. "When the mill's here, maybe, when there isn't so much work to do." She hoped she and Johnny weren't overdoing the emphasis on "work."

Howie's eyes had narrowed a bit, Cary thought, and he seemed to be thinking. "Yeah," he said. "Maybe later. When there's more to see." He turned to place his glass on the tray and pick up another cookie. "How often does your girlfriend see him?"

"Oh, she's in his office all the time, seems like," Johnny said. "She's excited about her project, something about marginalized groups and the media presentation. I don't understand it but she's really into it." He stood and announced, "Gotta go, got work to do. Suzanne doesn't cut me much slack."

Smiling, Cary said, "Bring her out soon, Johnny. We'll have grilled veggies, something simple." Cary wondered that Johnny and Suzanne seemed in no rush to marry. They'd been dating as long as she'd been at Thyme-Table. Maybe Jon's wandering ways had influenced his son. When she'd hinted as much, Mary had shrugged and said Suzanne had decreed no marriage until both of them finished school.

She looked down the road, ignoring Howie's morose frown. "I see Spence and the two Bryson boys coming in. They'll want lemonade."

When Spence had first brought the husky, broad-shouldered boys to the farm, Cary hadn't believed the introduction, and she grinned now as she saw them: Troy and Hector. Troy, the older by a year, was named for his great-uncle on his mother's side. He said, "When a schoolteacher heard my name she asked Mom if she'd read Homer." She hadn't but she did. Hector had added shyly, "Mama read *The Iliad* before she had me and I'm stuck with Hector. Well, it could have been Homer." He'd reddened but obviously the boys were used to people, some people anyway, needing an explanation for their names.

As Johnny stepped into his truck he winked broadly at Cary and she gave him a thumbs up. Howie had put his cap on and taken his shirt off, picked up a mattock, and seemed to be perusing the work site with renewed interest.

Cary was relieved that Howie had lived up to his end of the bargain; by the end of the summer he had callouses on his palms and a glow of pride on his tanned face when he shook hands and said goodby, with promises to come see the mill later. She was especially relieved when Suzanne reported that she really had chosen to work with Dr. Zennor–and that she'd said only good things about his newly-hired associate instructor.

Cary and Spence sipped their tea and looked where their mill would be erected. The wheel, covered with waterproof plastic (somehow that amused Cary) had been placed some yards beyond the site, out of the way. There were already scars and there would be more to the landscape occurring as the mill progressed. But she could see the mill in her mind, surrounded by bushes and flowers in abundance: old fashioned lilacs, forsythia, perhaps a rose garden to the side. A bell clanged, and they both jumped slightly, called out of their thoughts by Mary's announcement of supper on the table. Jon had found a large hand bell at an antique-junk yard on one of their forays through the countryside looking for mills. He enjoyed using it to summon the friends to dinner or to a meeting.

"Ah, what a great day," Cary said, pretending to aid Spence in rising from the chair. She looked over his shoulder toward where their mill pond would be. "I want to plant a lot of daffodils," she said. "'A host of golden daffodils...'"

"'Fluttering and dancing in the breeze,'" Spence said, returning her embrace. "Ah, daffodils will likely be the least of our problems with the dam and pond."

"We can do it," Cary said.

"So we can and you shall have them! And right now, I'm hungry."

Chapter 8 "A Labor of Love" Old Traphill Mill

In the following weeks work on their mill seemed interminably slow to Cary. Delays occurred, workers couldn't make it, obstacles prevented anything being done quickly. To maintain her sanity and sense of perspective, Cary continued to photograph several old mills in the western part of the state. Occasionally she went alone, and Spence joined her twice; he enjoyed the excursions but it was difficult to take an entire day away from the farm and the mill. Thus, she with Mary, when she was ahead of her deadlines, saw mills in various states of decrepitude, restoration, and isolation. One or two they found were treated with devotion. Such was the Old Traphill Mill, now operating as a bed and breakfast resort, in Wilkes County.

Cary read about the mill in *The Old Mill News* and emailed for an appointment. They visited with Kenny Campbell, one of the owners, a transplanted Californian who had wanted a lifestyle change and couldn't resist the lure of the old mill situated beside the sloping rock that provided a constant soothing flow of water. "Except when it's a torrent," he said. His rueful expression indicated that he accepted the storms that blew down trees and brought a rush of muddy water with the same equanimity he accepted the hard work involved in operating the mill structure and site for guests. On the banks of the stream he and his partner had created their idyllic site, complete with geese, ducks, a flamboyant rooster, sleek horses pastured across the stream, aviaries, even emus.

The women accepted glasses of cold water and sat on one of the decks while Kenny released the water from the millpond into the flume and the wooden wheel began its turning. As usual, the rhythmic creaking of the wheel brought smiles to the women's faces, and they were beaming when their host rejoined them. The wheel, he laughingly explained, had been built by his father, using the pattern of the previous wheel, which had broken apart when, inexperienced, he had opened the sluice and allowed too much water to hit the wheel. "It began spinning more and more wildly," he said, "and then flew into two big pieces."

As they walked through the guest rooms, noting the two sets of stones retained in what was now a raised sitting area, Mary grinned. "What do you think, Cary, would you want to run a b&b at ThymeTable?"

"It's a fantastic undertaking," Cary said, "but I don't think so. Much as I like to bake, all this housekeeping would do me in." She gazed at the array of collectibles, antiques, chairs, pottery, and cabinets full of dishware, and shook her head admiringly to Kenny. "Just the dusting would occupy a day!"

He grinned and said, "It's a labor of love." Then he opened the trapdoor in the middle of the great room and allowed them to descend into the basement area where huge wooden beams and large iron gears and pipes lay. "But we know we can't operate the mill, can't grind again. That would take more expertise and reworking of machinery than we can manage," he said. "We're happy to offer hospitality–and happy to have left the rat race!"

"We could stay here the rest of the day," Cary said, "but we want to find another mill in Elkin and maybe have time to swing by Murray's Mill in Catawba on the way home."

They left with promises to return and Kenny's promise to visit ThymeTable when he could get away during the "off season."

"Lunch first," Mary said and turned the car toward Sparta, a few miles away. They were the last patrons seated at the Sparta Restaurant before it closed its lunch service. With their vegetable plates, they ordered cornbread, which turned out to be corn fritters.

"Fried on top of the stove," the waitress told them. Both women ordered a second fritter and Cary said, "I can see us–okay, me–making these at ThymeTable's Mill one of these days."

"Always thinking, aren't you?" Mary bit into the fritter. "But you're right. These are delicious and easy to make, I bet."

While Cary paid their bill, Mary talked to the cook who assured her that the fritters were delicious and a snap to make. She had no specific recipe but told Mary the ingredients, basic to any cornbread. "And, you can add anything you want to–to spiff it up. Cheese, hot peppers, even pineapple."

After driving around for a hour or so and being unsuccessful in finding another mill, the women decided to give up "milling around" for the day and get home before dark.

The next morning, as Cary sat, with Winchester snuggled at her feet, making notes of their expedition, Mary came in. Looking both bleary-eyed and somewhat sheepish, she plopped into a chair. Cary gave her tea, asked what was happening, and said, "What's that in your hand?"

Mary handed her the sheet of paper and said, "My excursion into poetry. Believe me, writing technical documents is easier." She studiously sipped her tea, trying not to look as Cary read quickly, looked up at her friend, then down again at the sheet of paper.

"Oh, I like it, Mary." Cary reread the poem. "We can get Suzanne to do it in calligraphy and frame it–for the mill. Would you mind?"

"Oh, no, you don't. Poems are private." Mary slumped into a chair. "But this one just came out after our ramble-around yesterday. Apparently I'm more caught up in this mill project than I realized."

She looked out the window as Cary read the poem aloud:

Silent sentinels
Stark reminders
Pieces of time
They are
Great-grandpas caught
heavy-footed in cemented blocks
Their youth gone.

Memorials now encrusted
by a stream's side
weighted circles rusted

they wait to be trucked away
by eager seekers of the past
wait to be swept away
by rushing waters

Pieces of the then
Lasting into the now.

"Are we 'seekers of the past,' then?" Cary asked. "I don't know yet exactly why I am so attracted to, so attached to, old mills." She picked up a pencil, tapped it on the table. "I only know I am."

"Be glad you aren't captivated by old covered bridges," Mary said. She retrieved the poem and tucked it into a pocket. A shift in her expression told Cary she wasn't ready to talk about her poem or even about mills. "Or we'd be headed north to New England–"

"Or west to Iowa!" Cary shook her head and laughed. "James Waller and Clint Eastwood–watch out."

"A woman photographer, hmm," Mary said. "It wouldn't be quite the same, would it? A lonely man on an isolated farm–"

"Well, Spence was on this farm," Cary pointed out. "Not exactly lonely, though. And, I stayed." She tossed the pencil aside, an amused expression on her face. "So ThymeTable Farm doesn't echo *The Bridges of Madison County*."

The two women discussed the popular novel that, some years before, had found a surprisingly large readership among men as well as women. Cary remembered the male students, security crew, and at least one faculty member who would admit to it, talking about the book, men she mistakenly assumed weren't readers of what was labeled "a woman's book." She mused, "For awhile there, it seemed everybody was taking sides–a real moral issue. What should the hero have done? What should the wife have done? What price happiness? Who was right, who was wrong? Even which was better, the book or the movie?"

Mary set her cup down and announced bluntly, "Everybody's looking for a soul mate– and it's a lucky person who finds one." A look of irritation flickered across her face.

"You're thinking of Jon?"

"When we were young–and oh so foolish–yes," Mary admitted, "I thought he was it, my soulmate. But then I found I was the "settle in and enjoy where you are" type and he was something else–the eternal wanderer." She sang, almost under her breath, "Oh, he was born the next of kin, the next of kin to the wayward wind..." She shrugged and hummed a few more bars.

"Always searching for something else? Some other place?" Cary said. "He's never quite found it, not like Kenny found the Old Traphill Mill."

"Place, yes," Mary said, "but I was thinking of person as well. Jon certainly hasn't been celibate while he's gone, I know that. And I've had a few lovers, none of whom I ultimately wanted to support. Don't look so curious. There's been no one in some years." She stopped, then went on, "I have to be fair, though. Jon hasn't asked about any lover in my life. He apparently never did, even when we were younger, expect me to wait for him."

"And you haven't, have you? Not really?"

"No. I'm here, though. Steady, stable. Good old Mary. Sometimes I think I should close the door in his face when he comes back after months, or years."

This was as close as Mary had ever come to revealing that she wasn't, if not happy with, at least satisfied with the relationship that had developed over the years with Jon.

Cary said, "I always assumed that you liked Jon to return–and then liked it when he left."

"I thought I did," Mary said. "Lately, though, he's not showing any signs of leaving." Her cheeks reddened and her freckles reminded Cary of an Anne of Green Gables grown up and middle-aged. "We're sharing the same bed now." Mary chuckled a little. "His pants are on the bedpost, ye gads. I guess I am wondering if I want him around from now on. Granted, he doesn't interfere with my work. He spends a lot of time out of doors, up with Rawlston, or just tramping around."

"What does Johnny think?" Cary paid attention to the relationship between father and son and thought she understood it. Johnny surely felt he'd been abandoned, left to the exclusive care of his mother; his loyalty was to her, not to his itinerant father. Yet the two conversed as friends, each careful not to raise issues that would damage the status quo. "He seems okay with Jon, with life itself," Cary answered her own question. "He's a son anyone would be proud of."

"And I am," responded Mary. "He doesn't want to see me hurt, I know that. And," she raised her chin with some defiance, "I won't be."

Cary covered her friend's hand with her own two. As much as she liked Jon, his humor, his generosity, his gentleness, his unfailing courtesy, Cary could not pretend to understand him. She said as much to Mary who shrugged and said, "He marches to a different drummer." She paused to reflect, then said, "Sometimes we're in sync, sometimes not."

Cary said, "I think Jon must need you, need this place right now."

"Maybe so," Mary conceded, "but he's certainly not saying so–or saying why. If I hint at wanting to know his intentions or his reasons he starts with the sweet talk, teasing me. But then, I could never get a straight answer from him." She set her cup down with resolution. "Okay, do you really like my poem?"

The two Bryson boys and Buddy sprawled on piles of lumber and on the ground, all heads pointed toward Rawlston who was apparently entertaining them. Cary, with a jug of cold lemonade in one hand and a bag containing homemade sugar cookies and store bought chips in the other, stopped to listen.

"There was this old farmer out where we live," Rawlston said, blinking, "that always growed the best field of corn in the valley. Ever year it was the same...high grade corn. Why, his crop was so good he sold seed to that store but never once did he buy local seed. When his neighbors admired his fine crop, he swore it was 'cause he bought just certified seed. 'Never buy anything but certified seed,' he'd say. That's the secret." Rawlston paused, pushed the brim of his cap farther back, looked serious.

"Yeah," Buddy said. "So he always bought certified seed. Sounds right to me."

"Never anything but certified. Ever year down to the feed store, demanding certified. Got so the other farmers started calling him 'Old Certified' and a-teasing him about it, but he swore by that certified seed."

The boys were half-way grinning now, waiting, and Rawlston paused again.

"Last spring, down he went to the store, bought him-hisself some high priced certified seed when the others round him was buying regular. He opened up that sack of seed–certified and shipped-in seed–and what did he find in the sack but his old Barlow knife, been missing since last spring."

The boys were chortling and Rawlston was looking proud of himself, so Cary thought it must be a masculine joke she didn't appreciate. She walked up to them and put down the snacks. Buddy slapped his leg and said, "Reckon we'll call you Old Certified from now on."

"Or Old Perfection," Hector said. "He don't let us get away with nothing."

"Do you want this mill to be lopsided because you didn't use enough nails or don't take the time to use a level?" Rawlston held out a paper cup for Buddy to fill with lemonade. "Ten more minutes, boys."

Cary could see that Rawlston enjoyed being the "boss man" in Spence's absence. She also realized that what Spence had said of himself was true: he was no carpenter. He could and did deal with daily repairs around the farm, but long-term carpentry projects simply weren't his forte. He didn't mind holding boards, driving nails, being a general apprentice, but his expertise lay with growing things, not building things. They felt fortunate that Rawlston had a knack for supervising. He enjoyed the company of the boys who treated him with both respect and good humor. He quietly insisted that the site be left clean and unlittered at the end of each work session, even had one of the boys sweep after some sawing. Actually, Rawlston himself had picked up the old broom and started to sweep when Buddy took it from him and finished the job. Cary noticed one day that Troy Bryson was smoking, and Rawlston coughed and frowned. Since then she'd seen no cigarettes on the site. The boy went to his truck during breaks and lunch and smoked there, leaning against the vehicle, depositing the cigarette butts in the truck's ashtray.

That evening, feeling a little lonesome with Spence gone for the night, Cary walked over to visit with Alice. She found Jon and Mary there, along with Rawlston, and a lively exchange underway.

"Politics, smalaticks," Alice declared, "that Ronald Reagan was a good-looking man. Agnes liked Tyrone Power better but I tried to see every movie Reagan was in."

"A waste of a good actor, then," put in Jon, with a wicked grin. "Now, me, I don't see how he could have given up Jane Wyman–"

"Or movies for the government. Lordy," Alice said, "What's the world coming to!" She tossed her head to show Jon she knew what he was up to, and she'd say no more. Her friends had long known the sisters' background and knew now her attitude. But sometimes Jon tried to manipulate them into a political discussion. Alice and Agnes had in their youth and decades beyond been active in liberal politics in the inner city; they had volunteered at the precinct, had distributed flyers for their candidates, had spoken at rallies, and had ultimately become disillusioned with what they could accomplish. They had vowed, once they "escaped" to the mountains of western North Carolina, to leave the active battlefield of politics behind. Not that they didn't keep up with the news. And if pushed or if they had so desired they could have summarized policies and promises perhaps more clearly than some candidates would have liked. They remained liberals and faithfully voted in every primary and national election. "Our hearts will always be liberal," once said Agnes, and "our tongues silent," finished Alice.

Rawlston said, "Alice and I were just talking about seeing *The Good Earth*, back in 1937 or '38, maybe 1940. Now that was a movie to remember, but we drew a blank on who was in it. Oh, Paul, Paul something, Paul Muni, that's who it was!" He blinked in astonishment. "Can't remember what he looked like, though, just Chinese."

Alice's eyes lit up. "That's right, a very credible Chinese man. Now who was the woman?" She turned to Cary. "We can recall a lot about a movie we saw over sixty years ago but not what we've seen in the past ten years."

Rawlston rubbed his hand over his white beard. He had given up shaving entirely.

"Haven't seen a movie in the past ten years," Rawlston said. "Was it Eleanor Powell?"

"Louise Rainer," Cary supplied. "She played in *The Good Earth*, and was great."

Rawlston and Alice stared at her. "How can you remember–?" said Rawlston.

"What was old before you were even born?" finished Alice.

"Video," Cary pretended to preen at her knowledge. "College classics series."

"Hey, you can be our consultant when our memories fail," Alice said. "It's nice, though, to have Rawlston here to talk to. Sister and I could spend hours trying to remember something and cover a thousand other topics, even forgetting what we'd started out to remember." Cary realized that Alice was beginning to speak of Agnes more easily, more naturally than she had since her death. Her voice still took on a wistfulness and a certain vagueness at times when she remembered some words or behavior of Agnes, but she was not as hesitant to mention her.

"I'm glad," Cary said. "Here's one for you. Who played opposite Frances Farmer in *Exclusive*? I'll give you a clue–"

"No, wait, let's see." Rawlston closed his eyes and screwed up his mouth in a parody of concentration. "I give up. Don't have a clue, even about the movie. Was there such a movie? Did you make it up, young lady?"

"Nope, he played the older man in the film about India, where the young missionary daughter fell in love–"

"Fred MacMurray!" Alice fairly crowed the answer. She playfully slapped at Rawlston's arm. "A dreamboat, that one."

"*The Rains of Ranchipur*." Cary pretended to swoon. "I thought then I'd surely fall in love with an older man, preferably one with a problem that I could save him from."

"But along came Spence," Mary semi-sang.

"And you saved him from Darla's evil clutches," Jon said.

"No," Cary said. "Give him credit. He saved himself." She yawned a little and stretched. "But you can bet I'm glad I saw that ad for Rosemary Cottage! Glad I stepped on the thyme patch."

Rawlston blinked a couple of times and said, “As the oldest man here, I’ve got a problem you can help me with.” He held out his hand, blue veined, brown-splotched, but tan from the sun “That’s why I came over here, Alice, and then I clear forgot.”

Cary straightened up. “What?”

“Got a splinter there, in the palm.” He turned his hand over for Cary’s inspection. “I came to see if Alice could dig it out, but we got sidetracked on movies,” he said, “and then you all showed up.”

“I’ll get some alcohol and a needle.” Alice extended her hand and Jon helped her to her feet. She peered at Rawlston’s hand. “That’ll fester if we don’t get it out.” She went from the room, returning quickly with her supplies.

She sat next to Rawlston and took his hand. She swabbed the needle in alcohol and then asked Jon to strike a match so the heat would further sterilize it. When she bent over Rawlston’s palm, her own hand was shaking visibly.

“I can do it,” Cary said.

“I guess you’d better.” Alice relinquished the needle. “I don’t want to dig a hole...”

“Don’t incapacitate the working man, you mean,” Rawlston said. He sucked in his breath, and soon they were admiring the adroitness with which Cary extracted the tiny sliver of wood. Alice wanted to put a band-aid on the hand, but Rawlston and Jon shook their heads at such a precaution and sighed. “Women,” drawled Rawlston.

“Women,” echoed Jon.

“Men!” returned Cary, Alice, and Mary in the same breath.

“Back to that movie, remember that awful flood scene?” Cary said.

“What movie?” Alice asked.

Walking down the road later with Mary and Jon, Winchester at her heels, Cary said, “I love these soft evenings when we just sit around and talk.”

"Or doze," Mary said, nudging Jon, who had a habit of drifting off while the conversation flowed around him. Jon tweaked her long braid.

"Spence will be back tomorrow," Cary said. "He's over in Belvidere, Tennessee, talking to John Lovett who has a huge mill there. He's lining up a master carpenter and a millwright to come to ThymeTable to set the stones in place."

"A lot of work has gone on in these past months," Jon said. "And this is one man who's exhausted. I swear, though, I think Rawlston's livelier now than when he got here."

"It's a miracle that everything has been as smooth as it has," Mary said. "Just some bruises and scratches and a splinter or two."

"So far, so good." Cary said goodnight and went inside. Their bed looked too large and empty for one person. She missed Spence and expected to toss and turn, but was soon asleep and dreaming of sheep bells tinkling just over the hillside.

Not the ringing but Winchester's paws on her chest awoke her. Spence was on his cell phone. "Honey, I'm only two hours from home."

"I'm wide awake," she mumbled. "Where are those darn sheep?"

Chapter 9 *"Truth in a Jefferson Cup"*

Alecia swooped into the warm kitchen just when Cary was in no mood to see anyone, especially anyone as sleekly groomed and elegantly dressed as her sister-in-law. In her haste, Cary had overfilled the cobbler pans and now the oven was a mess. She was a mess, hot, filthy, irritated at herself, the strawberry rhubarb cobblers, the world. Even Winchester seemed too much underfoot, though he had prudently retired to the doorway into the dining room. Glancing up she saw Phillip heading for the mill where Spence was studying the boards with the same intensity that she did her photography and herb magazines. She wiped her hair from her eyes, groaned, and stood up. The sticky goo would be difficult to clean after it hardened even more, but she'd be darned if she stayed on her knees another minute. She drew off the rubber gloves and greeted Alecia. They didn't shake hands, but Cary noted Alecia's perfectly manicured nails, painted a glossy subdued burgundy while her own unpolished nails were chipped and rough, the result of working with mill boards and strong cleansers. "Ugh," she said, sticking out her hands for Alecia's perusal. No need to pretend to an elegance she certainly did not possess.

Alecia smiled, a halfway pitying smile mixed with admiration. "The hands of a mill owner?" she said. "How's it coming?" Cary could sense the question was merely obligatory. Alecia was now beaming, eager to tell her news, whatever it was–a new golf course development underway on the coast, a new swimming pool? No, that was old news.

Cary automatically turned the stove on and filled the tea kettle. She had concocted a new mixture of mint and cinnamon tea and she knew she could trust Alecia to be quite honest about its taste. Her sister-in-law had a discriminating palate and would be up-front about the balance of flavors. She told Alecia what she was doing.

"Oh, okay," Alecia said. "We'll have it–and then we'll call the guys in and celebrate with champagne. It's in the cooler in the car."

"Celebrate what? Champagne sounds major," Cary washed up at the sink and splashed her face, no makeup on today, to cool her ebbing frustration.

"First, tea and crumpets," Alecia said. "Phillip and Spence will be awhile. I hope Phillip doesn't get his trousers dirty. We're going on to dinner in Hendersonville."

"Not to worry," Cary said. "Spence probably won't allow him to touch anything. It's all numbered and tabbed and more or less in order. The exterior work is almost complete." She set out cups and saucers, no mug for Alecia, and found cookies in the jar. Thank goodness for Mrs. Allison down the road. She was a virtual cookie machine.

Alecia sipped delicately, pronounced the tea quite delicious, suggested just a tiny bit more cinnamon. "The mint should prevail," she said, "and does, but more cinnamon would be an unexpected touch. That's what will be remembered about the taste. I'll have another half cup, please." It was the ultimate compliment and Cary smiled, thinking how well Alecia looked. She always looked great, but today there was something more, a kind of light in her eyes.

They called the men in. Phillip poured the champagne; Alecia even produced chilled flutes. Cary didn't mind. She could have provided wedding gift crystal, but this was clearly Alecia and Phillip's day. They sat in the cooler living room and raised their glasses, Cary and Spence with expectant questioning gazes.

"We're going to have a baby," Alecia said.

"We're pregnant," Phillip confirmed.

Stunned, Cary and Spence clinked glasses, exclaimed, "Wow" and "Great news!" and drank the bubbly. There was a flurry of talk, when, how long had they known, who else knew... with Phillip and Alecia glowing and interrupting each other constantly.

Cary burst into tears, set her champagne down, and rushed from the room. Spence held up his hand to prevent Alecia from following. "It's just a shock. She's been hoping, wanting a baby a long time. No, leave her alone for a few minutes. I'll go talk to her."

"We should have called first," Phillip said. He looked surprised at his sister's response. "Alecia wanted to call but I said no, let's just drop in. We thought you'd be home..." He trailed off.

"We're certainly here," Spence said. "The mill keeps us tied up here, and I can't neglect the business." Though both his and Winchester's eyes moved toward the bedroom where Cary had fled, Spence sipped the expensive champagne with appreciation. "Not that I'm complaining, even if my bones do. But Cary needs a break. Except for the mill, I don't think she's done any photography lately."

"She could visit Mom and Dad for awhile," Phillip said. "They'd love to have her. They're tickled about..." He stopped, glanced at Alecia.

"Hey," Spence said, swallowing the last of his champagne, "you don't have to not talk about your baby. You know Cary is happy for you. She's going to be an aunt. She's tired, though, and she's quit talking about getting pregnant. Maybe thinking she'd jinxed the possibility with all her talk." He stood up. "I'll go see how she is."

Shortly Cary rejoined them, her face scrubbed, lipstick applied, her eyes clear, her voice under control. She went immediately to Alecia, hugged her, and did the same to Phillip. "It's wonderful. Fantastic, but you can't be far along," she said, eying Alecia's flat stomach. Well, she noted, almost flat.

When Phillip broached the possibility of a trip to Barrymore, their hometown, Cary protested that she was needed at ThymeTable and couldn't, wouldn't leave Spence. She was so adamant that Spence broke the tension by interrupting, "Yeah, who'd cook for me?" At his forlorn expression and the surprised expressions of Phillip and Alecia, Cary had to giggle. They knew Spence was quite a cook himself and that the two of them shared kitchen responsibilities. Whoever got there first, had an inspiration or plan for dinner, or was extremely hungry, prepared the meal.

"Are you going to cook for Alecia now, brother dear?" she asked. "Gosh, a new Randall in the family. It's great." And her eyes and voice told them how sincere she was. She sat on the sofa and Winchester at once padded over, looked up inquiringly, then jumped up beside her, and laid his head on her lap.

"Well," Phillip said. "Alecia's already starting to crave exotic things, like tapioca pudding with mandarin oranges or mangos. Did you know you can buy tapioca pudding already made?" He looked so naive they had to laugh.

"It will be a change for us," Alecia said. She suddenly looked vulnerable. "Scary, too."

"Let's go see the mill," Phillip said, "while Alecia can still waddle!" He extended his hand to his wife, who was still almost runway model thin. Cary tried to visualize her "waddling" and simply could not.

"Progress seems slow," Spence said. "I'll be an uncle before the thing's finished." As they walked to the site, he continued, "Rawlston has been a tremendous help. He's especially good with figures, does the calculations, ratios, things like that, things I don't want to do. He's a storehouse of information. You'd think he'd studied with a millwright, but he says not."

"He calls it common-farmer sense," Cary said.

"Not herb-farmer sense," Spence said. "And when I've been gone for the day or busy, and some of the local guys are helping out, he's turned supervisor. Quiet, never raises his voice, but he gets things done." Spence shook his head in admiration.

"He's certainly been staying on," Phillip observed. "Must not have much family."

"His sister's still in Florida. He reports that she calls or he calls her. Got himself a phone card. Family trouble down there is keeping her occupied." Spence held his hand to Alecia and she carefully mounted the three temporary steps into the mill. Cary had drawn plans for a porch to be added. They had talked at great length about whether such an addition would somehow destroy the purity of the original building. However, they finally agreed that almost every mill they'd seen had been modified or changed to some extent by various owners. And for the mill to be functional when groups of visitors arrived, more space–thus a wraparound porch on two sides–was essential.

"That's where the hopper goes," Cary pointed. "And over there's where the driveshaft and the belts will be. The new belts haven't come in yet. They had to be special ordered from Canada." In the next hour, Phillip and Alecia stepped over tools, sat on a pile of boards, nodded at explanations, asked about equipment, exclaimed over the job of re-assembling and pronounced themselves proud to be "family" to such an undertaking.

"I had my doubts," Phillip said, "but now I can see it will happen."

"You will have permanent electricity out here, won't you?" Alecia pointed to heavy duty extension cords. A temporary pole had been erected some yards away.

Cary grinned. "In time. We want the power lines to be underground, though."

"Actually," Spence said, "there'll be a back-up system so we can power the wheel by electricity if we need to, and we'll probably need to. We can't depend on the water supply until we have a real mill pond." He ran his hand through his dark hair, now growing over his collar. "And that may be a couple of years or more away."

"Do I see some gray in that hair that wasn't there before?" teased Alecia.

"I'm not telling," Spence said. "But I wouldn't be surprised."

"He's not had time for a hair cut recently." Cary ran her fingers through his hair. "Longer hair suits you–and not a bit of gray is showing–yet."

Phillip brushed his pants. "We have to get going." He turned to his sister. "You really should visit the parents. Mom worries about you. She says she can hear the stress in your voice." He hugged Cary. "Surely Spence can spare you for a few days."

Cary saw the quick glance that passed between her husband and brother. They had probably talked of her bouts of despondency when alone at the mill. She promised she'd think about a visit.

After their departure, Cary and Spence stood with arms around each other's waist and looked at their mill. Then Cary sighed. "Alecia will produce the first 'next generation' of Randalls."

"And we'll produce our own Bradfords," Spence said. Gently he pointed out that, after all, their marriage lagged some six or seven years behind Phillip's and that Alecia, in her mid-thirties, had surely been thinking of a child even if she'd said nothing about it.

Cary's innate sense of fairness took over. "You're right, they should have 'first dibs,' but darn!"

Spence took her in his arms. "So you'll trust us to work on the mill without you for a week or so? I promise we won't install the wheel without you."

"You better not!" Cary thought for a few minutes. Visions of her old room in the two-story brick Georgian home, of the serene English garden in the back, of their elderly cook who in later years had come "just to talk" as they sat under the lilac bushes rushed through her, leaving a pang of homesickness. "I could take my photos and start sorting and arranging them. Mary has an outline draft of the process up to now. It might be good to be away from the scene–to get some perspective. I'll call Denise and go visit her, too, while I'm in Virginia."

"That's my Cary," Spence said.

"It's the second time Spence and I have been apart overnight since we married," Cary said to Denise. "When he went to oversee taking down the mill, he was gone overnight, but then I was up so late and up so early it was hardly a night." In a long pink tee shirt, Cary looked more like a college sophomore than a young married woman who would be a candidate for the Junior League if her mother had her way. She wiggled her toes in the new rabbit-ear bedroom shoes her mother had insisted on buying when she saw the "disgraceful" condition of the ones Cary padded about the house in. When she'd left Barrymore to spend the summer at Rosemary Cottage, her mother gave her the fluffy slippers with the floppy ears as a kind of comfort wear–and Cary just couldn't toss them. Her mother could and had, after finding exact replacements. Lounging on the tangerine-orange sofa in the living room at Denise's condo, Cary gazed around the peach-colored walls. Denise could do amazing tricks with color and make it all work. She set her cup of hot chocolate on the small table and picked up the slice of mango-jalapeno bread Denise placed beside the cup. She said, "This year you're into food colors, right?"

"Right. The bathroom's called key lime and the accents are blueberry."

Cary rolled her eyes and Denise declared, "I'm not kidding. Those are the colors."

They laughed and then Denise said, "This is my first attempt at this weird combination for this sweet bread." She took a tentative bite. "I may have to try a second time. It's my own recipe. You know, making bread has a lot in common with designing jewelry."

"Trial and error, you mean?" Cary was still holding the slice, waiting her friend's judgement. "Dare I taste it?"

Denise giggled. "I meant, it can be a highly creative endeavor...and a risk. Hmm."

"Definitely not a breakfast bread," Cary sputtered, having come upon a hot pepper. "It might need a little, uh, refining, my friend." She took one more small bite to be sure, then wiped her hands on a napkin. "Want some advice? Add some applesauce, maybe a touch of cinnamon."

"Old pro that you are!" Denise sipped her chocolate. "You're right. I'll work on it."

"Poor Justin," Cary said. "I bet he has to finish the loaf–and like it."

Both women smiled. Denise shrugged. "Actually, he will finish it. I don't think the man even knows what he eats half the time. He is obsessed with work. I thought after medical school things would be easier, we'd have more time together. Shows how much I know."

After a moment, Denise pushed the bread aside and returned to Cary's earlier comment. "So did you sleep last night okay? Back in your own room? Did your mother tuck you in? Did you feel like a kid again?" Denise had always been intensely interested in Cary's family life. She had been raised by an aunt, her parents having been killed in an accident when she was seven. The aunt was dutiful but hardly warm and motherly, and Denise spent much more time in childcare centers, schools, camps, and after-school centers than in the cramped apartment of her mother's sister. The day after high school, she moved out and soon the aunt, perhaps fearful Denise might return, penniless and needy, had moved to New Mexico. Now they exchanged cards at holidays. Denise told Cary that now her aunt, having seen to her "obligations," had joined a cooperative housing movement and was studying watercolors in the desert.

"Barrymore was great, just more traffic and more cute shops lining Main Street," Cary said. "And my room, well, Mom had not changed one thing. I felt sixteen again. And she did tuck me in–and bought me these." She wiggled her toes in the new bright pink bunny slippers and propped two pillows behind her head. "So the first thing we did, after visiting a few people, was to head for the mall. My cute room with its frills has now been transformed. Well, it's still in the process. Plain old cream-colored walls."

"Food again!" Denise interrupted.

Cary nodded. "Mom is turning it into a sewing room, complete with a new sewing machine that cost more than my first car! She's getting quite good at making fantastic quilted jackets and quilts. She placed third with one of her elegant quilts in the local Heritage Fair back in the spring and now she's hooked."

"Good for her," Denise said. "But you never felt, did you, that she'd been denying herself things and hobbies because of you? I never sensed that."

"No, no," Cary said. "Mom's never laid a guilt–or a quilt–trip on me!" She reflected for a few moments while Denise took the tray to the small kitchen and returned with two slices of a bread that smelled of oatmeal and chocolate. "But, now that I think of it, Mom always put us and Dad first. Given a choice between meeting her friends or her book club and seeing Phillip or me play in the band or something, we knew she'd be there for us. I guess mothers are like that. Now, though, Denise, you'd be amazed at the 'stuff' she's buying for herself, her hobby. I love it."

"And your dad?"

"He thinks it's great. He's so proud of her quilting. He wants her to do a quilt as a wall hanging for the bank president's office. She's thinking about it, but I think she wants to keep her quilting separate from his business."

"Smart woman."

"She's like a lot of women her age," Cary said. "When we went visiting, I noticed a difference somehow. These women are 'doing their own thing'–and most of them are happily married, like my mother. There's a wave of independence sweeping through them." She sipped her chocolate and absently picked up another slice of bread. "We talked like friends, more than like mother-daughter. Not quite like you and me, of course. But like women–equals."

After the two analyzed the attitudes they saw developing among women, young and older, Cary said, "I do miss

Spence, and we talk every day–all three days I've been gone–but this time away has been good for me. I was getting too uptight about things. And Spence probably needed the time apart, too. Of course, he sounds so mournful, telling me what he and Winchester are doing. The man can cook, but he seems to be eating out of cans–"

"You know Mary and Alice keep him in food," interrupted Denise, sounding somewhat impatient with what she must have considered Cary's non-problem.

"Of course, but he manages to sound hungry and lonesome."

"Justin eats to fuel his body," Denise sighed. "I might as well not even bother. But, heck, I'm enjoying baking for myself, for itself, not for Justin's self!" She finished a slice of bread and licked her fingers delicately. "Interesting taste, huh?"

"Interesting," Cary agreed. "Really quite good." She studied her hands around her cup and a silence fell. Denise did not seem inclined to talk about Justin and Cary's thoughts were miles away. Finally she released a long sigh. "I saw Lanny today," she said, "before I came here."

"What? Why didn't you tell me? What happened? Wait–not another word. I'll get them!" Denise jumped up and hurried to the cupboard in the kitchen. Cary smiled a little and waited. During their college years they had developed a ritual they called their Jefferson Cup time. When one or the other realized a major revelation was about to occur, she dashed for the two pewter Jefferson cups and a bottle of wine. No matter how important the revelation was, how "itchy" one was to relate the episode, it waited for the solemn pouring of the wine. It was understood that absolute honesty ("Truth in a Jefferson Cup") would prevail once they began their "Jefferson Cup Time," no blustering, no pretense, no coyness.

Now Denise poured, not the cheap wine of their college days but a smooth Cabernet Savinguon. They touched cups and took the first sip, the pewter cool to their lips. Once Denise had held the cup at arm's length and mused that the coolness of the rim of the cup cooled their intensity, gave them an objectivity, mediated their anger, despair, or whatever emotion called forth the cups.

A second long sip followed and then they settled again into comfortable positions for listening and talking. "I never thought I'd see him," Cary began. Then she sat straighter and said, "No, I wondered if I might, but I didn't say anything to Spence. After all, the odds were against my seeing him in the short time I'd be in Barrymore. I'd convinced myself...so seeing him in front of Andrews Pharmacy really threw me." She wiggled into another position and plumped a cushion.

"I'm surprised he's still living there," Denise said. "I assumed he was gone, picking on somebody else." Her voice started as indignant, ended more quietly.

"He worked somewhere in Staunton for a couple of years. Anyway, Mom had gone into the drugstore to pick up a prescription. I was looking in the dress store a couple of stores down. You know it?"

Denise inclined her head. "We bought dresses there years ago. Daniels Fashions?"

"It's Sylvia's Styles now." She sipped again. "I want to get this right," she said.

"No hurry."

Cary described Lanny: bulkier than she remembered, his striped green shirt tight against his chest, his black pants tight. His hair was cut shorter than she remembered it, actually a nice scissored cut that somehow didn't mesh with his swagger and attitude. It was difficult to describe his appearance to Denise because she'd been less aware of it than of her instant physical reaction to seeing him. "I went all watery, watery but heavy too. I started to steady myself, to touch the brick at the corner of the store. I reached out but then I didn't touch it." She'd looked at him, a lover who'd never loved her, a domineering arrogant personality who expected submissiveness and sweetness, a man who in that instance, the first time she'd seen him since she had come to ThymeTable, looked, she said, "exactly like a thug."

"A thug?" Denise repeated.

"Exactly. I actually thought the word." Cary frowned. "He was with a girl, a petite girl with black hair, dark eyes. She was holding on to his hand. The minute he saw me, he turned red in the face and he muttered something to her. She looked surprised and then she turned and went into the store. She looked back at him, just as he and I stopped in front of each other." Cary shook herself, an exaggerated shiver. "She started to turn back toward him but he looked at her and she darted inside. That dark look of his." She tried to imitate the look.

Denise said, "You okay?"

"Yes, I am. I really am. We were this close," Cary spread her arms wide, "and I looked at him, really stared. And it was like a revelation. What a jerk he was. I stiffened my back and said hello. And he answered, kind of shrugged without really shrugging, as if who is this creature. But, Denise, I could see fear in his eyes, a sort of cornered look."

"Has Phillip threatened him or something?" Denise pantomimed shooting a pistol.

"Not that I know of. He just looked angry and cornered–not a very pretty sight." She tried to laugh. "He said, 'Hey, I hear you're married now,' and I smiled, oh so sweetly and said yes and even stuck out my hand with the diamond. Oh, that felt good."

Denise gave her the high sign. "You go, girl!" and they raised their cups.

The rest of the encounter, she told Denise, lasted less than five minutes as a few shoppers flowed around them on the sidewalk. Lanny now worked for a grocery distribution company, had gotten out of the restaurant business. He implied that her family had spread rumors that caused his business to fall off. He liked the more regular hours and didn't miss the hot grill or the customers.

"Rumors!" snorted Denise.

Lanny had surveyed Cary as if she were herself a grocery item and said, "You're looking good. Guess married life must agree with you," and Cary had again smiled sweetly and said, "It does." Then he scowled and mumbled that he had work to do and she'd smiled again. She thought for a moment that he wanted her to say something, to accuse him, to berate him, or even to speak openly of their past relationship but they stood there, pretending to be polite.

Cary gulped the last of her wine. "You'd be proud of me, Denise. When he started to turn to go in the store, I said, 'Lanny, you're a real loser. You take care. Bye.' and I strolled, yes, strolled around him. If I'd turned I bet I'd have seen fire coming out his mouth, but I wasn't about to look interested." Her eyes sparkled. "And my legs weren't watery any more. I don't ever need to see him–or even think about him–again."

"Then what? Didn't he say anything?"

"Not a word. He must have gone into the store. And I went on down the street to Mother's Deli and sat down and just grinned like a cat."

"Well, I've heard more exciting encounters, Cary. Couldn't you have slapped him or kicked him or something?" Denise poured more wine and they giggled. Then she asked, "Are you sure that you don't–and I'm coming to despise this word, don't need more 'closure'?"

"I'm glad I saw him–and I never need to see him again. What I ever saw in him to begin with is beyond me. I felt just a coldness toward him, not rage. I really should have thanked him–I wouldn't have met Spence without his giving me cause to leave my comfort zone." Cary knew Denise would have liked to hear that she hit, kicked, or at least spit on Lanny, that she had reminded him of his brutal push, the other bruises he had inflicted. She had felt an immense relief after seeing him, an indifference; she didn't want to give him the pleasure of responding in any way that could call forth explanations, apologies, excuses, or denial. When she walked away she was free of Lanny forever; he was a non-entity. She tried to explain this to Denise. Half an hour later, Denise said, "Well, someone ought to tell that girl. Warn her."

"Yes," Cary said. "And I did do that. Mom said I should and I thought so too. I talked to her the next day. In Barrymore it wasn't difficult to learn her name. I called and told her who I was. She thought I was a current girlfriend so she wasn't happy to talk with me at first." Cary leaned her head back on the sofa. It had been a long Jefferson Cup time. "And she said Lanny'd never hurt her...but then she admitted she was frightened by his rages. I don't know what she'll do."

"You've done all you can," Denise said. "Chances are she will look at him differently and then–"

"He'll know I told her and he'll move on to another girl, another potential victim," Cary said.

"You can't follow him around and warn every girl he dates–or put an ad in the paper." Denise yawned. "Come on, let's put these cups away." She put her arm around her friend's shoulder as they went to the kitchen. "I'm proud of you–but I'd have kicked him in the you-know-where."

The following morning, over scrambled eggs and toast, Denise propped her chin on her elbow and announced, "I might as well tell you, Cary, well, I told you on the phone. I'm getting fed up." She rolled her eyes toward their breakfasts. "Yep, fed up with Justin these days. He works too hard, that's one thing." She broke her toast into smaller pieces. "And he doesn't seem at all interested in anything I do, or make, or even say." She looked at Cary. "And you know, I can't stand that–because I say a lot."

"Oh, are you overreacting? His practice–"

"I sometimes don't give a damn about his practice," Denise said flatly. "And he doesn't even seem to notice that. He's got to be the perfect doctor, the one who never says no to being on call anytime the others, the older guys, want to go play golf or something." Her voice was bitter. "I'm not a happy camper," she said. "Right now I can't imagine being married to him. I am not sure I even want to stay around."

"I didn't realize you were so out of sync," Cary said. "I know you've postponed getting married, but, truly, Denny, I think he loves you. He seems proud of you."

"He is proud of me. He likes showing me off to his doctor friends." Denise poured another cup of coffee. "I am not going to be a trophy wife." She started to say something else but hesitated. She stirred the coffee.

"Come on," Cary said. "Spit it out. Have you actually broken up?" She saw that the small diamond still glittered on her friend's hand so that must not be the case.

"I'm thinking seriously of moving, of saying 'to hell' with all this. I'm thinking of moving to The Cove." Denise frowned as if in anger. "I can design anywhere," she announced with some defiance. "I have some big names who want to see what I've done before it goes on the market. I don't need Justin!"

Cary sat bolt upright. This she hadn't expected. Denise in Rosemary Cottage. Great friends they were, but Denise next door? Her college experience had taught her that Denise was a "high maintenance" friend who expected a friend's undivided attention whenever a crisis occurred and her life was a series of crises. Her startled gaping seemed to irritate Denise.

"What's wrong? You think I can't live in the country? You think I'm kidding?"

"I, I think you ought to think about it," Cary said, almost stuttering. "Have you told Justin you might leave Virginia?"

"No, not yet," Denise said grimly. "I told him I loved The Cove and could live there–that was when we were driving back after seeing Alice. He laughed, he actually snorted. He thinks I'm a city girl."

"Well..."

"I am, but it all seems so serene around there. All of you seem so happy, so content...and I'm, I'm just not." Two large tears rolled dramatically down her cheeks. She reached for a tissue. "Maybe I'm envious, Cary. You and Spence just seem to fit. And Justin and I, lately, we fight. No, not really.

He doesn't have time to fight, and he doesn't take me seriously when I try to tell him I am frustrated and unhappy. Darn." She tried a wan smile. "Don't look so worried about me, Cary. I'm okay. Just mad at Justin too much of the time."

Cary went over and sat beside Denise, gave her a quick hug. "You sound tired, for sure. And I don't want to sound motherly. It's a big step, Denise. You can design anywhere but your business is here. And Justin, well, you need to talk..." Cary trailed off, aware that the course of true love didn't always get changed by talk. She and Spence had certainly talked, but often at odds. Counseling was not her strong suit, but she could listen. She hugged her friend again and said, "We've got all day. Talk."

The telephone rang. Denise shook her head. "It might be Spence," Cary said.

"Let's see," Denise said.

"Hi, Denise, this is Justin. If you're there, please pick up. I'll be working late tonight, doubling for a guy at the emergency room." There was a pause, then, "I'll call you tomorrow."

"See," Denise said. "Not even 'I love you.'"

Hours later, after shopping, having lunch, then touring Denise's studio, they were back on the sofa with glasses of iced tea and a jar of peanuts. The two friends had not moved much beyond what Denise had already said. Cary realized that Denise viewed western North Carolina as a sort of rustic paradise where the sun always shone and no one ever got tired or short-tempered. And she'd assumed Justin and Denise were perfectly matched in terms of ambition and energy, that their love affair ran smoothly as a newly-paved superhighway, that they knew where they were going and would get there easily and quickly. Another lesson in growing up, she realized.

Chapter 10 "In Good Hands"

Even before it was fully re-assembled, Cary liked to wander around the mill's interior, touching its weathered walls, running her hand over the uneven doorframes, or sitting on the floor; once the major construction was complete, Cary went to the mill at some point every day. She chose a time when she hoped to be alone, uninterrupted, free to sit quietly and think or not think. Sometimes she went in the early morning, after Winchester's walk, and while Spence showered or slept later than his usual seven o'clock; occasionally she found a free half hour during the day. Her daylight visits, she soon realized, were too often interrupted by Rawlston wandering through, Mary poking her head in, one of the workers or neighbors just dropping by. She discovered she could best find total solitude at dusk or soon afterwards, and her friends, if they saw her headed for the mill, honored her desire for the peacefulness she found within its walls.

Suzanne asked innocently, "Do you meditate there?" and offered to give her a mat and demonstrate some yoga positions she'd learned recently that would assist in meditating effectively. Rawlston nodded sagely and used the words "haven" and "sanctuary." Denise described her technique for "centering" herself when she was under stress. Knowing simply that she was drawn to it, Cary preferred not to elaborate on reasons for her mill time or even to give a name, a label, to the time she spent at the mill alone.

"It's all those things," she said to Spence one day, "and not precisely any of them." She told him about her pleasure in being in the mill, after she snapped at him when he came in looking for a piece of equipment. "Sorry for snarling at you," she apologized.

Rushed and surprised at her abruptness, he had snapped back, "I don't have hours to look for this drill part. Put a sign on the door if nobody can come in!" Cary had, in fact, made a "Do not disturb" sign and tacked it to the door on her next visit; however, the sign itself disturbed her and left her unsettled and grumpy. She crumpled it and tossed it into the trash.

Had she been forced to label her time in the mill, Cary would have called it her "emptying" time. Among the odors of old wood, old grain, old oil, the slight but distinct mustiness of time that scrubbing had not eradicated, and the scent of newly-sawn boards and fresh oil from the chainsaw, and varnish, Cary could temporarily lose herself; she could let go of the minor "frets and furies" of the day. In the silence of the mill, a myriad of daily gnat-like irritations fell away as if a soothing hand brushed them aside, as if a rumpled cloth were left smooth. The mill's walls muffled, if not totally obliterated, the noises that were a constant on the farm: Winchester's barks, a car down the road, a goat bleating, a lawnmower or an unwieldy fan in one of the greenhouses. Cary gave herself up to the silence.

"When I was five years old, I was allowed to ride my pony Stewart over to my grandfather's mill," a woman's voice said, with a strangely lilting Scottish tone. "I loved this mill. I used to sit on my pony on the road and watch all the men working or waiting. There was a lot of waiting. They wouldn't let me come in when all the machinery was moving. Grandfather didn't have time to watch me and he didn't trust anyone else to see that I didn't touch something dangerous."

"Dangerous?" Cary wasn't sure if she'd spoken aloud.

"Oh, it was fascinating–I would see a wagon load of corn come in, pulled by a mule or a team of oxen, and then hours later the farmer would tote his big bags of cornmeal out to his wagon. I climbed off my little pony one day and clambered up on a mule. It didn't like it one bit and started braying and stomping its feet and turning its head with its big yellow teeth back at me. I was scared. The farmer came running out and jerked me off. He'd like to have spanked me, but he knew my grandda wouldn't like that. He just set me down so hard on the ground my teeth clattered and then he spit sideways. Grandfather came out and said to him, 'Let's sample some goods,' and they ambled off. The belts and pulleys...I guess he didn't want me around them. I tried to figure out how it all worked when the mill was shut down, and Grandda explained it over and over to me."

Cary dreamed on, entering the world of the speaker. "This old mill has seen a lot of living. One time old man Jenkins mis-stepped, that's what my grandda said, but he told Grandma that young Zach Boyllet somehow hooked the rope that carried the grain up to the upper floor onto his overalls and up he started, squalling, 'Get me down, get me down.' He could've been badly hurt but two men ran up there. One of them cut his galluses loose and he dropped to the floor. His overalls dropped to the floor too and there he stood with a big red patch on his longjohns. I guess he was grateful... the man saved his life. Didn't save his pride. They called him Patch from then on–the rest of his life. I don't think he liked the mill after that, always sent one of his boys."

Cary had drifted into the dream and said, "If he was an old man...."

"Oh, he lived another twenty years, long enough to see Zach marry...Sarranda, and have three boys."

The speaker lowered her eyes modestly and smoothed her dark hair, coiled in plaits around her head.

"Sarranda, that's a pretty name, unusual."

The woman smiled sweetly. "That's me. Sarranda Hensley Boyllet, named for my grandmothers. That Zach, he was a good husband but a real cut up, a prankster." She turned aside and her voice took on a leaden, flat quality. "They said he kept the soldier boys at Camp Chase laughing with the sly pranks he pulled on the Yankee guards. Zach was a real cut-up."

Her voice ebbed and Cary wasn't sure she heard the next words.

"But the jokes didn't help when the fever came. One of his buddies came by after the peace and told me and the boys Zach tried to smile even when he coughed and spit up half his lungs, seems like, he tried to smile. He's buried somewheres up there in Ohio, maybe around Columbus."

"Did you, did you live near the mill? Did you own it?"

"It was lost to my cousin who inherited it when Grandda passed and my daddy drowned, lost after the war, everything was lost. I was lost."

"Lost?" Cary waited for what seemed minutes, aware of a tightness in her own chest, as the woman put a hand to her bosom and then went on.

"All during those awful days when the fightin' was going on and even when deserters came through and took our food, cramming their pockets with turnips and cabbage leaves, I never give up. I didn't give up till my youngest, my Josiah, named after Grandda, was taken sick and no daddy, no doctors....no medicine..."

The voice was full of pain and so faint Cary barely made it out.

"No help. He died without any shoes for his feet. We always managed shoes for our boys every year but not then. A deserter picked up his old brogans, they was too tight for Josiah. He'd outgrown them in the three years and more since Zach left; we kept them, me thinking when Zach came back I'd not be too old for another child and... but the man just took them, said his young'un could wear them. I didn't begrudge him, thinking he had a boy at home. My Joe, he died without shoes. We buried him in his socks. It was a cold February. The men dug the hard frozen ground. His little body could have stayed in the back room, cold as it was, but they dug the frozen ground. There weren't no able bodied men around here then. I hated to see them diggin', frail, white-haired as they was, in the cold." She shuddered. "I couldn't stand to see him go into that cold ground with just his old socks on. But I couldn't bear him being in that cold back room either. The church women, seven of them, stayed with us for days on end, going home to milk, if they had a cow still and to collect eggs, if they had a hen left. It was a barren time. For a spell I thought I might lose my mind, but they was the other two boys, Fredrick and Larsen, and they had to be comforted. Cold comfort though it was. In the spring just when the dogwoods bloomed, Larsen left home, fourteen years old he went to Kentucky and then on a boat down the big river. We never heard from him after two short letters, one saying he was hooking up with a band of men headin' west and one from a jail in Depot, Wyoming. He was sixteen the day he wrote it, in jail for disturbing the peace, whatever that meant. Sixteen."

Cary felt faint with apprehension. She asked, "What happened to the other son?"

"I used to come to the new mill, for solace maybe, for something, for remembering the old days when Grandda was here, covered with meal dust, his eyebrows frosty and his boots white like snow. My cousin didn't want a woman in black wandering in or around his mill. It caught fire during the war, folks blamed the outliers–strong-built as it was and far from the main road. Cousin rebuilt and he thought he'd lose his customers if a sorrowful widder-woman hung around. So I started coming at dark. He locked the door, of course, and some nights he left his old hound here to bark and warn him if anybody came around. Old Blue, though, he was partial to me and never barked once, after I brought him a piece of fatback I stole from the Macks' house."

The stream of words halted for a moment. Cary didn't move, hardly breathed. The woman sighed and continued. "Then Fredrick went to work for the Macks, taking on the chores and duties of the son they lost. Seems like after his brother left, he gave up on me and made hisself into a young Mack. He rode their mule to see me once in a while, took to going to church regular. By then he was a big strapping boy, smart and shrewd too. When he told me they wanted to officially adopt him, make him their own boy, I stayed in this mill all night and prayed about it, cried my eyes out, and, I admit, cursed God and the devil and the United States government for taking, one way or another, all my boys, my menfolk. Then I said no, I can't write my name to a paper that'll give you away. I believe that's when he really left me. His eyes got sleety cold. His fist clenched up and if I'd been a man he'd of hit me. But he looked at me without a whit of feeling except pure coldness and he walked away. They'd said they'd make him their heir and he wanted that farm. He wanted more than the cabin that was falling to pieces around me, more than the few acres Zach had cleared. It was growing up in brush anyway."

Cary wasn't sure if she asked a question; the woman seemed to fade for a moment. Then she continued. "The next year I told him, standing on the front porch of the Macks' white house, that I was going to Charlotte. I was going to keep house for a woman who wrote the postmaster about needing a woman, 'a clean, upright woman who could be trusted.' Standing there in a store-bought shirt, he nodded, looking way older than his years. He put some money in my hand and I took it, not wanting to get to Mrs. Whitney's dirt poor, I took it and I thanked him. He said, 'Mama, I couldn't never make up for, for my brothers. You expected too much. I wanted to be more than the son who didn't die.' Some of the cold shrewdness had gone from his eyes. They regarded me with almost warmth, with a mite of compassion, I guess you'd say. 'I hope you like your job,' he said. I handed him a paper, the deed to the land me and Zach had worked. I knew I'd never set foot on it again. He looked surprised and he took it and stuck it in his pocket. That was the last time I saw the boy. He lived with the Macks and was, I think, a better son to them than he'd have been to me, and they heired him the property twenty years later when they both died of the flu. Me, I grew to like the comfort of Mrs. Whitney's home, liked my little bedroom and later she gave me two rooms of my own, even with a bathroom. We well suited each other.

You might say I became a city woman, even. Her children, she had four girls, provided for her and for me. Their daddy had been something in the insurance business. She called me her mountain woman, but I left the mountains and turned my back on them. My heart was sealed up tighter than a miser's purse, and I never looked at another man nor encouraged one to look at me."

Cary's chest had tightened in sympathy and sorrow. It seemed the woman, Sarranda, placed her hand on her shoulder. "On my way to the highway to get a ride to town and catch the train down the mountain, I stopped once more at the mill. Cousin was there and like the rest of them then, seeing as how I was leaving, he was kind and pressed a gold coin into my hand. They was glad to see me go. I sensed it. A grieving woman don't help people get on with their lives, I reckon. And they had to move on, bury the dead, so to speak, survive as best they could. T'weren't long, I heard, before the mill changed hands again. Cousin went to work in the new general store a Yankee soldier come back to build and supply. I quit dreamin' about the cabin and the mill after a few years, settled in right good in that fine brick house on a shady street, filled out from skin and bones. Ate well and regular."

Cary's subconscious noted that as the woman talked her vocabulary and grammar shifted a bit, overriding her city-acquired correctness. She asked, "What happened finally?"

"What happened to all of us, just more peacefully, more quiet-like than the way Zach or Josiah, my little Joe, went."

"Do you, have you," Cary started again, "will you keep visiting the mill?"

"I think not. It's in your hands now. I won't need to look after it. I will rest now...the mill is in your hands."

"The mill is in my hands, she said," Cary repeated to Spence.

She, with a start, had looked at her watch, realized how dark it was. She had stayed so long in her dusk trip to the mill that Spence would be wondering where she was. Maybe he thought she'd just fallen asleep. Maybe she had. Shaking her head, almost dazed, she hurried to the farmhouse.

Cary was shaky, her cheeks flushed as she entered the kitchen. Winchester bounded to meet her, and Spence's worried frown was replaced with concern. After a quick, "Hey, Hey, what's wrong?" Spence guided her to a chair and threw an afghan over her. Winchester jumped into her lap, and Spence made her some tea, put the cookie jar close at hand. He sat across from her and covered her cold hands with his own.

When he asked quietly but firmly, "What is it? Did something scare you up there? A snake or something? A ghost?" she focused her eyes on the steaming tea and blurted out the story.

Now she said again, "Sarranda said, 'The mill is in your hands.' and then she was gone. And the mill was icy cold."

"Honey, you must have fallen asleep, been dreaming." Spence held her hand, looked into her eyes.

"I honestly don't know. She was...the visit was so clear, so clear at the time I'm sure I could sketch her face." She described the black-frocked woman, who metamorphosed into a slightly stooped figure in a dark outfit covered with a white apron. "And her hair toward the end had become white and thin at the last when she, uh, when she disappeared."

Cary pushed her camomile tea away, folded her arms before her, and put her head down on the table. With the telling of the incident, her heart had calmed; her face had lost its flush of agitation. But the dream, the vision, the atmosphere the visitor brought to the mill did not totally evaporate in the serenity of her familiar kitchen. She had a husband at her side, looking concerned and tender, a dog now at her feet, his nose on her toes. She had the twenty-first century around her. She lifted her head and gazed at all the kitchen gadgets and equipment, most of which Sarranda could not have imagined. She was here and now, yet the aura of the woman who had seemingly lost all and yet survived was strong enough that Cary shook her head as if to clear it.

"Okay?" Spence moved behind her and began to massage her shoulders. "I'll make an omelet, my special omelet in a few minutes. Whatever it was--"

"It was so real, Spence. I'd know the woman if I saw her on the street."

"Something not likely to happen," he said. "Whatever it was, dream, apparition, your imagination, whatever–it wasn't frightening?"

"No, it, she was like a friend, no, an acquaintance who needed to tell me something." Cary leaned back into Spence's hands. "She was entrusting the mill to me, to us."

"Sort of passing on her memories, her experience with it?" Spence said. "Do you...expect to, uh, see her, experience her again?"

Cary's smile was timorous. "I wouldn't mind at all. She survived...more than I could ever imagine and I'd like to know more of her story. But do I expect to see her again?" She hesitated, thinking. "No, I don't. Maybe it somehow helps that the mill has been moved away from the place of all her losses. Maybe her spirit can now really be at peace."

Spence stood and began collecting eggs and milk from the refrigerator. Cary sat, watching him. Then she said, "I feel immature, silly. I know how lucky I am...baby or not."

His hands occupied with a skillet and a cheese grater, Spence nodded. "Lucky, for sure."

Later after they'd devoured the mushroom omelet and half a loaf of Mrs. Alison's molasses bread, Cary seemed her old self. "I think if we don't treat that mill right, and you don't treat me right--" She suddenly grinned. "Sarranda will reappear!"

"Then have no fear," Spence said. "You're both in good hands."

Chapter 11 "The Course of True Love"

"Oops, Pardon me!" Cary stopped so abruptly that Winchester, at her heels, bumped his nose into her calf. She'd knocked on the front door of Mary's house and heard no answer. The door was open; Mary must be working at her office. Cary carried a warm apple pie, delivered only a few minutes ago by Mrs. Alison's nephew, a birthday treat for Mary, compliments of their neighbor.

Jon and Mary didn't break apart from an embarrassing or compromising position. They were, in fact, sitting upright in the bright kitchen, staring into each other's eyes, holding hands across the table like thirteen-year olds. Cary later told Mary, "It was the glow–the absolute glow–that radiated from you two that stopped me in my tracks!"

"Come on in, Cary, and Winchester, stay away from that garbage bag." Mary laughed at her friend's expression. She disengaged her hand, stood up, and took the pie, wrapped in a red checked towel. "Sorry about the garbage, but Jon's announcement took me so by surprise that I just dropped it there." While Mary's office was often cluttered and stacked with papers, books, file folders, her kitchen stayed in pristine condition, evidence, as she said, that seldom did anything creative come out of it.

Jon pushed his chair back from the table. His eyes sparkled and his grin stretched wide. "Should I leave you girls alone?" His fingers put quotation marks around the word "girls" so they wouldn't take offence. "I'll go check on Alice. She was sorting books and albums this morning. I can help with the wrapping or packaging if she's going to send material back to her hometown."

"No, stay," Mary said. She turned to Cary. "Sit down and we'll tell you all about it."

"All about what? You two look like cats who've discovered the cream pitcher." Cary picked up the plastic garbage bag and set it outside the kitchen door, beyond Winchester's sniffing. "Now, settle down, Winnie, you can't be hungry." She plopped into a chair. "Mrs. Alison says she can't remember when your birthday is but it's sometime this month, so she sent the pie." She looked at Jon and Mary, who were once again smiling widely at each other. "So what's going on?"

"We're getting married again," Jon said.

"We're renewing our vows," Mary said, in the same instant.

"Wow!" Cary's mouth dropped open. She looked first to one, then to the other. "Which one–or both?"

"You know I've been unhappy, well, dissatisfied," Mary said, "with Jon these past weeks. He's been moping around here, like his mind was somewhere else half the time. I thought he wanted to leave and didn't have the money or the energy to go." She smirked a bit. "Although occasionally I knew he had some energy!"

Jon actually blushed. "Hey, Mary, you don't have to tell all–at least not while I'm in the room!" He ducked his head a little, then stood and headed for the refrigerator. He took his time pouring a glass of cranberry juice while the two women watched him. Cary's head swirled with questions. Marriage? Vows? Total commitment? Mary and Jon? It was the very last thing she expected to hear.

"And when I tried to talk to him, he skirted the issue and finally I just stopped talking–and maybe started sulking, a little," Mary said.

"A little, my foot," Jon said. "This woman has ignored me mostly and generally given me the impression she wanted me out of here, the sooner the better."

"That's your interpretation!" Mary protested, but she was smiling.

"Well, Jon," Cary said, "you have stayed quite a while. We thought it was the mill that interested you. Didn't we, Mary?"

"Darn it, Cary," Mary said, "he's asked me to renew our vows." Tears sprang into her eyes. "He wants to stay–permanently."

"My roving days are over," Jon decreed. Then he held up a hand. "I know I may have said that before..."

"No, in all fairness, you never did," Mary responded. "You implied and I inferred, but you never actually said those words."

"I'm saying it again, in front of witnesses," Jon said, touching Cary's shoulder and nodding toward Winchester. "My roving days are over."

Cary had placed her hand on Mary's on the table. Now she gave it a little shake. "So you're making it legal, again?"

"Well," Jon started. He took a sip of juice. "It's never been un-legal exactly."

"Weren't you divorced all those years ago? I thought you told me, Mary–"

"I definitely thought so," Mary said. "But–"

"But it didn't happen," Jon confessed. "I told her I'd gotten the divorce and just never got around to sending the papers."

"I was so busy when Johnny was little," Mary interrupted, "that gradually I forgot I'd never actually received any formal documents. Alimony was never an issue with us. He sent money."

"When I had it," Jon said.

"Young and foolish, that was me. I guess if I'd ever found somebody else I wanted to marry–don't look so cocky, Jon–I'd have insisted, but the years rolled along and our divorce seemed a fact." She frowned slightly at Jon. "In fact, you even told me a specific date, November 18!"

"It seemed like a good idea at the time, when you finally asked." Jon managed a weak grin. "Being specific makes something more believable, doesn't it?" His face became serious. "Something deep inside me kept me from getting a divorce, Mary. As I said, before the pie came," he went on, "I would have done it if you'd ever told me you wanted to marry again. But when I left–and left–and left–I couldn't do it. And this time, I just can't leave."

Cary gazed at Jon and saw a man committed, in love, and liking it. She sensed behind his words, serious as they were, a certain mixture of sadness for the years he'd missed with Mary and an understanding of himself that told him that, in all those earlier years he wasn't as capable of the certainty of love as he now was. She must have been staring because he broke into a chuckle.

"Ah, Cary, you're thinking 'love at their age' aren't you? Listen, kid," he chuckled again, "this is seasoned love. Aged in the barrel, so to speak. Mellowed out."

"Whatever," Mary flicked an imaginary crumb from the table. "If you keep going with that line of thinking, it's going to go from aged to rotten!"

"The woman keeps me honest," Jon said. "So I proposed again."

"It took more than just a 'will you marry me' to convince me," Mary said. "We've been sitting here almost three hours, talking."

"And grinning," Jon said. "I even offered to get down on my knees, but she was afraid I couldn't get up again." He patted his ample stomach.

"I wanted to be sure your proposal wasn't a desperation move." Mary glanced at Cary. "That he wasn't proposing because he had no place else to go, or needed a nurse, was sick or something." She hesitated and then continued, "I'd certainly not send him away if that–either one–was the case, but it'd be different. I had to know for sure, for sure and certain this time."

"I'm healthy as a horse," Jon told Cary. Certainly in the past weeks, working outside with the Grayson goats and with Spence on the mill site, Jon had turned tan. He hadn't lost his girth and still looked impish, reinforcing Cary's first impression of him as a jolly leprechaun.

"And eats like one," Mary said.

"But I don't expect you to fill up the trough," he said. "Mary says I have to make myself useful around here, beyond getting my own meals if she's busy."

"And you have been useful," Cary said. "You've been at the mill–"

"Spence and I talked yesterday," Jon said, with a smug expression, "not about me and Mary, but I'm to be the miller–or the miller's assistant, to you, Cary, if you agree. I've already found a place to go for a couple of weeks in a sort of apprenticeship. Falls Mill over in middle Tennessee, where Spence went months ago. It will be a challenge, but I'm a quick learner. Besides, just listening to Rawlston and working on the mill, I've learned a lot."

For a few minutes they talked about the mill and Jon's "apprenticeship" and all the tasks associated with actually grinding cornmeal. Then, over a fresh pot of coffee and the apple pie, they returned to the topic of Jon and Mary's relationship.

"We thought about a double ceremony, with Johnny and Suzanne, but we don't want to put them on the spot." Mary took Jon's hand, once again. "They aren't in a big hurry, apparently, to marry, and besides, they deserve a ceremony all to themselves–if and when. And speaking as a mother, I hope it's when!"

"It's too soon for Spence and me to renew our vows, isn't it?" Cary asked. "It's only a couple of years..."

"But who's counting?" Mary finished. She looked directly at Cary. "I know you are counting..."

Cary became thoughtful. "Remember Old Traphill Mill? On the wall there was a small plaque: 'You can't change the past but you can ruin the present by worrying about the future.'" She bent to stroke Winchester. "I've quit ruining our present. A baby will be wonderful, but right now is wonderful, too, even with the stress of the mill and the farm and thinking of Alice's health and everything."

"Right. *Carpe diem*. Snatch the day." Jon took a final huge bit of pie, wiped his lips, and kissed the top of Mary's head. "I'm leaving now so you two can further discuss the situation. You'll find me with Alice and her creatures until around dinner time."

"Take the rest of the pie with you," Mary told him. "On my birthday we'll celebrate in town."

He wrapped the pie in foil and planted kisses on the cheeks of both women. Declaiming with a flourish, "Old time is still a-flying," he closed the door.

"He knows me pretty well," Mary said. "I do need to talk to you and rehash it all again."

"That's what friends are for." Arm in arm, the two women went into the living room. Mary picked up a stack of papers, settled them on a worktable, and plumped up cushions on the worn sofa. As they each found her favorite spot, Cary said, "Ah, this beats sitting behind a desk from nine to five. But I do need to run into town later this afternoon. I'm working with Mark in the darkroom from four until six. But now, tell me all of it–I've got at least an hour and a half before I take the guys an afternoon snack."

As the women talked, unconsciously they were aware of the sounds that meant work on the mill was resuming. There had been a long break (Cary bet Rawlston had the boys sweeping or measuring) while Buddy went to town to purchase a certain size bolt that Rawlston decreed was absolutely essential. Unable to distinguish actual words, they now heard the hammering, the shifting of materials, masculine voices raised in question or command, the clank of metal dropped. Thus both became instantly aware of a change in the noise–an abrupt silence and then a louder commotion, excited yells, running. They jumped to their feet, saw a cluster of bodies hovering above something or someone on the ground. They ran to the door and then to Mary's van.

Rawlston met their vehicle when they pulled into the parking area. "It's Buddy. He fell off the ladder. EMS is on the way. But," he assured the women, his voice shaky, "it's just his leg, we think. He's conscious so it's not a concussion."

Buddy's face contorted in a grimace of pain when he raised his shoulders as they rushed toward him. He was pale and his left leg was twisted oddly. He struggled to halfway sit up, but lapsed back when Mary said, "Lie quietly." She bent over the boy while Cary put her hand to his forehead, why, she wasn't sure. His skin was clammy to her touch.

They could see no bones protruding through the worn denim jeans. "Don't move," Cary repeated Mary's admonition. "I wonder if we should cut your pants leg? They do that on ER. Is that blood?" She felt a moment of queasiness.

"Just my hand," Buddy said. "I musta scraped it on something. No problem." He flexed his fingers tentatively.

Mary picked up his hand and saw that he was right. It was mostly skinned but one deep cut on his palm bled profusely. She whipped out a white handkerchief and loosely wrapped the hand. Cary wondered if Mary always carried a man's handkerchief or if she'd intuitively known that day to tuck one in her pocket.

"To keep sawdust out of it," Mary told them. Cary knelt beside Buddy, as the Bryson boys and Rawlston moved away, allowing the women the role of comforters. One of the boys flung a light jacket over Buddy. They hovered about, uncertain what to do or say, studying the road for the rescue squad. Jon, who arrived just behind the women, checked Buddy's blue eyes with the expertise of a medical authority and agreed there seemed to be no concussion.

"His head's harder than his leg," Troy Bryson quipped.

Buddy grimaced. "Yeah, you told me, Rawlston, not to try to reach that upper beam from that ladder before I went up. Damn, I should listen better."

"You'll be okay," the old man said. He blinked. "Nobody's fault."

"Here they come," Jon said, as they heard the siren of the EMS vehicle.

Within minutes the efficient young technicians rushed in, assessed Buddy's condition, transferred him to a stretcher and maneuvered him into their vehicle. He was sweating but articulate. "Tell Mama I'm okay. Call Chrissy."

"We'll do it," Jon said. "And we'll be along to see you shortly."

"We're going now," declared Troy and his brother Hector nodded. "We'll see you there." He winked at the EMS driver, an attractive blond woman. "We may beat you there."

"Stay out of my way," the driver said, and the brothers shrugged.

"I'll bring chocolates," Cary promised, feeling inadequate and useless. She hugged the boys, ignoring their red faces. They waited for the EMS vehicle to pull away, and the next moment they were tearing down the driveway, spewing gravel.

"There'll be some paperwork," Mary said. "I'll take some notes on exactly what happened and how, in case there's a question of liability." She picked up a looseleaf notebook from a workbench to the side. She had gotten in the habit of coming down, taking notes on the construction, often leaving the notebook if she had no time to transcribe her notes that day. She looked around. "First I'll draw a sketch."

"It looks like the boy simply tried to reach too far for that beam and toppled," Jon said and they nodded. The ground was level, the ladder sturdy. The workplace was free of clutter and debris, something Spence expected and Rawlston insisted on.

"Where's Rawlston?" Cary looked around. "I hope he doesn't think we–or they–blame him."

"No, the boys are all over eighteen, not children." Jon shook his head. "I didn't see him while the rescue squad was here. He must have slipped away in the excitement of their coming. Maybe he went to tell Alice what happened."

"Strange," Mary commented. "Well, I'll talk to him later." She finished jotting down notes as to time, persons on the scene, equipment.

"I'll go make the calls," Cary said, "and meet you all at the hospital. I'll go on to my meeting from there if everything's okay."

"I'll see if Rawlston wants to go," Jon said. "Hope he's not feeling bad, not sick or something."

Later that evening the friends ate take-out Chinese food back at ThymeTable. Drained from the waiting, the anxiety about Buddy, the conversations with his mother, his assorted cousins, and Chrissy, they semi-slumped around the table. Buddy would be on crutches, but walking in no time. The break was a clean one, and the doctors reported they expected no problems. Buddy's mother assured them their family's insurance would cover the medical expenses–or most of them. Spence announced that the farm's insurance would kick in, and they greeted that news with sighs of relief. Buddy himself had worried about the hospital expense, hoping it wouldn't interfere with the work at the mill.

"The hardest thing for the hospital is going to be keeping Chrissy at bay," Mary drawled. She flipped her hands wildly in exaggerated imitation. "That girl is the most hysterical thing. I'm glad we had a boy!" Jon nodded.

"Buddy had promised to take Chrissy over to The Stomping Ground in Maggie Valley," Cary said. "And you can't do a lot of stomping in a cast."

"Buddy was embarrassed when Chrissy couldn't keep her hands off him–" Mary began.

"When his mother was there," Cary said. "I doubt he's embarrassed when they're alone."

Jon laughed. "You'd think you were the mother of a teenager already."

Cary shrugged and asked, "Are you sure Rawlston's okay?"

"He's fine, just tired." Spence rubbed Cary's shoulders. "He said he hates hospitals, gets weak when he goes in one. His wife's death, he said. He's with Alice, giving her the news I gave him about Buddy's condition."

"And Buddy says he's going to be the old guy's assistant as soon as he can get out here and prop his leg up," Jon told them. "He wants to help give the orders."

"Meanwhile, Johnny will take time off from the garage to come out and work after his classes. The schedule won't get too far behind," Spence said with a grin directed at Cary. "I know you're worried about that."

"You did a terrific job while I was gone," Cary said. "My absence didn't hold up the work at all. Darn, I thought I was indispensable."

"It may have even speeded up," Jon said. "We didn't stop nearly as often for cookies and lemonade."

"Life is never dull around here," Spence declared later that month. He shed his jacket with its light dusting of November snow and washed his hands at the kitchen sink. "Denise's things are now in Rosemary, finally. That woman has more stuff...and the place was already furnished."

Cary looked up from the mess around her on the table. She was teaching herself to hand-tint black and white photographs and had before her one of her pictures of the Francis Mill. Earlier that day she had thrown up her hands and left Denise to the task of directing Spence and Jon in emptying the rental trailer, carrying in box after box of materials, hangers of clothes, plastic containers of jewelry supplies. Denise's managerial mood definitely surfaced. When she told Cary too many times that she was in the way, Cary finally snapped back, "Then I'm out of here. I promised Tanna I'd try to finish the photograph–and it's harder than I thought."

"For goodness' sakes, you've been working on that forever." Denise was short tempered, surrounded by her belongings and clutter and, Cary thought, probably wondering if she'd done the right thing in giving Justin an ultimatum and then packing up and leaving when he didn't seem to believe she'd do it.

Rosemary Cottage had been unoccupied after Howie's departure at the end of summer, and thus Cary, even with misgivings, couldn't see how they could refuse to rent to her friend. Denise had toyed with the idea of moving in to Justin's house, sharing the quarters with Rawlston.

"Justin flatly refused to consider it," Denise had stormed, relaying to Cary her request of Justin and his response. "He said absolutely not, if I insisted on moving here, leaving him, as he put it, then he wasn't going to provide a house for me. I'd even have paid rent, darn it."

Peace-loving Cary tried to point out that Justin had reason and emotion on his side. Why should he assume responsibility for providing living quarters when he neither wanted Denise to leave Richmond nor believed she'd be content away from the city? Denise, angry at her landlord, angry at Justin, even angry at a client who had presumed to die without finalizing a contract for an expensive necklace, had called Cary and the next week drove into The Cove, pulling a small rental trailer packed with her belongings. She'd left the surplus in a rented storage unit near her former apartment. A couple of days later, Cary admitted to Spence that she found herself resenting the time Denise's move was taking from her own endeavors.

"I don't want to be in the middle," she told Spence. "Between Justin and Denise. I understand he can't just move at her whim," she paused, mentally rejecting Mary's term, "quim," and then continued, "You can't pull out of a practice when your fiance demands it." She ran her fingers through her hair. "But to be fair to Denise, he acts like he doesn't think she even has a right to talk about where they will live, and it's their future, not just his."

"Darling," Spence said. "This is a tug of war, of wills, between the two of them. She is used to being totally independent, even domineering–" He reached across the table and put his fingers to her lips, forestalling her retort. "Yes, usually controlling any relationship she's in. She is in the process of learning–or not learning–the art of compromise. If both, notice I said both, of them don't learn to give a little, then Lord help them when or if they ever do marry."

"I guess you're right." She looked pensive. "As you-know-who once said, 'The course of true love never did run smooth.'" Cary bit her lip. "But do you think I compromise too much? I mean, sometimes I wonder if I'm too passive." She smiled then. "But then I think, no, I'm just happy."

"Well, you're hardly passive. Who insisted on French toast this morning? Who declared we would not go see that blood and guts movie last week?" Spence's eyes sparkled. "Who really runs this place? And who is responsible for that mill out there!" He got up and came around the table, bent and enveloped her in a hug, kissing her neck and nibbling on her ear.

"And who decided the rose-colored comforter had to go and that Winchester couldn't sleep in the bedroom?" True, the flowery print hadn't done a thing for their bedroom, and true, the beagle was happy in his kitchen bed, but still.

"Just one little quirk after another," Spence acknowledged. "That's marriage. And, Honey, you're good at it. Keeping me on my toes, but not stomping on them!" He looked into the refrigerator. "Nothing but healthy stuff in here," he announced. "I miss all those cookies and brownies you kept the crew supplied with this summer." He took a container of yogurt from the shelf and found a spoon.

"I'll make a double batch this evening, for tomorrow's work day," Cary said. "But first I want to finish this project." The Bryson boys and Buddy had promised to put in eight or nine hours at the mill the following day. Buddy hobbled about on crutches, but he insisted on helping out, "sub-bossing" he called it, relaying and clarifying Rawlston's requests and orders. The recent rains prevented work on the outside, but they could do some painting, finish a counter, put up shelves, and complete a dozen other minor alterations and tasks.

"I have a list," Cary said. Spence threw up his hands in mock surrender. She and her daily list had kept them all somewhat organized in the confusing first days of the mill's reassembling, and they all respected it, even if much remained at sunset to be shifted to the next day's list. Even when no work was in progress, not a day passed that Cary did not spend some time at the mill; often she simply walked in and sat quietly, alone or in the company of whoever happened to drop by. She took her books with her and studied them to be sure nothing was being overlooked: the corn shellers, the sifters, the bolters, the scourers. Who ever would have guessed that "simple" technology had so many components, all to be identified, learned about, defined? Jon kidded her about absorbing the atmosphere of the mill in its former days, asked her if she'd been visited by the spirits of its previous owners. She merely smiled and ignored his good-natured comments.

"Rawlston is feeling better today," Spence said. "His cough is gone. No temperature. He credits Alice's herbal remedies. She's been plying him with echinacea and goldenseal."

"And her attention," Cary said.

"The attention of a good woman never hurts when a man's sickly," Spence said.

"And vice versa," Cary replied. "You were so good when I was laid up after you rescued me from the mountain. All that time I was in bed..."

"Well, my motives weren't exactly pure," Spence teased. "I was hoping to be invited to join you!"

They were laughing when Jon knocked briefly and pushed open the door. "That Denise is on a tear. It wears me out trying to follow her instructions." He flopped into a chair. "She could run an entire hospital!"

"She's angry because Justin hasn't yet called," Cary said.

"It's only been a couple of days," Jon growled. "I just hope she doesn't decide to return in a few days. Mary was smart to stay clear of helping." He sighed mightily. "Lordy, do you have some tea for a tired man?"

"Sure," Cary and Spence said at the same time. Spence filled the kettle while Cary, in turn, checked out the contents of the fridge.

"I'll make some cheese sandwiches," she said. "An afternoon snack for working men."

Chapter 12 "A Phantom of Delight"

It was two days after Christmas and two hours after a large mid-afternoon meal at ThymeTable created, by Cary's decree, entirely of leftovers. Three inches of new snow covered the ground and the air was still and calm, the sun low and weak. Cary looked around the cluttered living room where, according to their age and disposition, her friends sat quietly or sprawled in satiated contentment. Spence wore a soft moss green plaid shirt that Mrs. Randall declared made him look like a "gentleman farmer." In fact, everyone had arrived in new garments. Both Jon and his son sported new jeans and new boots; Mary looked quite elegant in Cary's gift of a suede vest to complement her long beige skirt. Alice and Rawlston delighted in the hoots of approval for their matching woolen toboggans and earmuffs from Johnny and Suzanne, who insisted they model them for Cary to photograph. She herself wore a striking pendant created by Denise that Spence had commissioned during the summer–a gristmill in a swirl of gold wire and glowing glass. It was simply wonderful to be back at ThymeTable, ahead of a new predicted snowfall.

Their holidays had been complicated by family obligations and expectations. Because of the busy summer and autumn, Spence had not been to see his family in Oklahoma, so, leaving Winchester with Mary and Jon, Spence and Cary flew out on December 20 to visit for two days. Then, back at ThymeTable they'd stopped only to pick up Winchester, do laundry, repack, and say quick hellos and goodbyes before driving to Virginia. Cary had promised her dad that she would wake up in Barrymore to her mother's traditional eggnog pancakes on Christmas morning. It was the only "gift" her mother wanted, he told her.

"It was a perfect day, Mom," Cary said. "I loved it, loved it all." They sat in what her mother persisted in calling The Florida room, with its three walls of glass. Over the wide lawn, Cary glimpsed a streak of red. "There's a cardinal," she said. "A bright red, a male."

"But?" Mrs. Randall was no fool. And birds weren't her concern at the moment. She sensed her daughter's restlessness even as the family gatherings had comforted with the routines of her youth. After the eggnog pancakes and a decent interval of resting afterwards around the highly decorated tree, Cary and Phillip built a tiny snowman, actually a baby snowboy, in the sparse Christmas Day snowfall. They knew that only in a few years did the weather allow enough snow for their tradition. They let Spence help to scoop enough snow for their efforts but wouldn't allow him or Alecia to help with the construction of the plump round-faced snow child. When they surveyed their masterpiece, only then were spouses permitted to add the final touch: tiny blue mittens in recognition of the fact that in the new year there would be a baby boy Randall. Alecia, large and occasionally clumsy, positively glowed, and Phillip beamed and called her beautiful a dozen times a day.

"But, I miss ThymeTable and the mill. We've been gone a week." She rubbed Winchester's back with her foot. He sported a new red collar to which her dad had attached a small bell. The dog wasn't quite sure he liked the tinkling sound whenever he moved. "You understand, don't you, Mom?" She wanted her mother to want them there but not to insist, to enjoy their company but not demand it. And her mother didn't disappoint her.

"I remember when David and I were first married. His mother expected all her sons and their wives and children–eighteen of us around two huge tables–to be at their house all day Christmas, and we were. It took some real negotiating to strike a compromise in the next years between his mother's iron will and my mother's gentle persuasion." She shook her head. "And some battles between David and me, too. Somewhere along the way, I must have told myself we wouldn't hold the reins so tightly on you two." She hesitated and tucked a strand of her white hair back into place, "and we haven't, have we? We would love to have you–as long as you'd like to stay."

"But you have that cruise booked in early January," Cary said, her tone playful. The Caribbean cruise was Phillip and Alecia's gift to the Randalls–and a first for them.

"Before the baby's due," her mother agreed. "I do understand about wanting to be at your place, Cary. I'm going to pack up some ham and turkey in the ice cooler, and sweet potato casserole, corn." She went to the second refrigerator in the laundry room.

Grinning, Cary continued the enumeration. "And squash casserole from Aunt Mercy, lemon pie from the preacher's wife, pound cake, rum balls." She laughed. "Pack it all up, Mom, and we'll have a party when we get home and call it 'Mom's–the Aftermath.'"

"Your dad and I could never finish all this food," Ruthlene said, "and Phillip and Alecia will take very little."

"She's got her mother's leftovers," Cary said. She smiled as her mother picked up various items in the pantry and refrigerator, inspected each one, returned some, and placed others on the table.

"Goodness, here's a fruitcake we didn't even put on the table, sent over by my garden club president when she knew you all were coming."

"Knowing I love fruitcake–a rarity, according to all the jokes about it," Cary said. Then to tease her mother, "I bet somebody gave it to Mrs. Delamore last Christmas!"

"Cary," her mother reprimanded her, then giggled. "No, it's homemade." She peered at the cake. "And she put the date on it. She makes a few dozen of these, starting right after Thanksgiving, for the board members of her various organizations." She continued to rummage in the refrigerator. “Make a list of all these things, Cary, or we’ll forget them in the rush.”

Cary dutifully wrote down all the dishes her mother called out to her, enough to fill a large cooler and a couple of bags. “And don’t forget to empty the candy dishes,” her mother said. At Cary’s protesting glance she added, “Those guys will be over to check on the mill. They’ll eat it all.” Cary had to agree and listed: “candy and nuts.”

Now, “Mom’s Aftermath” feast had been a huge success, supplemented unnecessarily by additions brought by Mary and Alice.

In the quietness, broken only by a log breaking in the fireplace and long, contented sighs, Cary reflected on the peacefulness of the day, the glory of good friends, the love she felt in the room. She touched Spence’s knee lightly. He covered her hand with his and mouthed silently, “I love you.”

“I wonder how Denise and Justin are getting along,” Cary mused aloud. Her friend had been determined to remain in Rosemary Cottage during the holidays, declaring she needed no one. She certainly didn’t need Justin, who would be working three times as hard so the senior physicians in the practice could be with their families.

He’d said as much, Denise told Cary, imitating Justin’s voice: “After all, I’m not married, don’t have children and grandchildren obligations. I volunteered to be available.”

Denise had scowled, but her face changed when Cary murmured, “Well, he’s right. You could change that, Denise...just get married and have a bunch of children.”

Her voice had caught on her own words. Denise declared, “I absolutely refuse to even consider having a baby before you do, Cary! Why, I depend on you to show me the way...when, if I get married.” They continued to pore over the photographs Cary had taken of the mill’s progress and those of mills she and Mary had visited. A few moments later, Denise admitted, “I know he’s being nice about working the holidays. I guess I want him to resent the time away from me–"

"Does he argue about the time you spend on your jewelry business?" Cary asked in the silence.

"Never a word. Maybe that bothers me, too. I'll stay here and work on the commissions I have for that Chicago store. No, I won't be lonely. I'll be busy." Denise grinned. "Just leave me some of your special barley soup and I'll survive."

However, when Spence and Cary returned to The Cove, they found that Denise had gone to Virginia on Christmas day, leaving a note for her "landlords," as she delighted in calling the Bradfords. Her note said: "Something is breaking... I need a doctor–and I know where one is working. Bye." Denise had drawn a tiny heart above the word, 'breaking.' Cary had not called, sure that when Denise was ready she would tell her what happened. Still she wondered.

A slight rustling on the sofa called her attention to Alice who was struggling to sit more upright while Rawlston settled a cushion behind her back. Alice's small frame did not mesh well with the overstuffed sofa, but it was her favorite spot once she settled into its plumpness. Now she cleared her throat and said, "This is as good a time as any to make our announcement."

Pulled from their collective thoughts, everyone turned toward her. Cary felt a wave of apprehension sweep over her. Alice wasn't sick? She wasn't moving? The woman's flushed face and smiling eyes revealed that her news couldn't be bad. Cary waited. They all waited.

"Well," said Jon after a few seconds.

"Rawlston and I–" She glanced at the man who sat beside her. He nodded encouragement. Like a student she took a deep breath, and then said firmly, "Rawlston and I are going to get married."

"Whoa," said Johnny at the same time Suzanne said, "Wow!"

The others sat in surprised silence for three seconds before erupting in questions, congratulations, exclamations, hugs and handshakes.

The elderly duo seemed almost as dazed as their friends. Rawlston grasped Alice's hand and held on. Mary went to the kitchen and returned with a pitcher of her special cold Russian tea. "I know we can't hold another bite," she said, handing out small glasses, "but we can surely find room for a toast." She poured tea for all of them, and they raised their glasses and congratulated the couple once again.

"It's for the best," Alice said, somewhat primly. Yet a beautiful smile accompanied her words.

"Sure, and you'll be doing it purely for economical reasons." Jon imitated the tone of what he assumed would be an Irish father. "And sure, we'll all be admiring you for such level-headed thinking!"

They chuckled at his theatrical brogue, and Cary said, "And sure, 'tis the case, indeed." Cary and Spence had not been surprised when in early December Rawlston said he wouldn't be joining his sister in Florida for the holidays. He felt, he said, more at home where he was than where he'd been going. He'd added, "I can't leave this mill unfinished." Cary had smiled and nodded, though they both knew very little work would be done in December and January.

Cary winked at Rawlston. "You couldn't leave the mill unfinished, huh?" He blinked and grinned. With his neatly trimmed white beard and tanned brow, he hardly resembled the pale man Johnny had brought to the farm months before.

Following the initial wave of good will, a veritable lava flow of questions enveloped Alice and Rawlston. They glanced at each other with smiles that straightened out, only to reappear. Would they live in Alice's house? Would they live in The Cove? What about Rawlston's family? Was marriage really the best solution, if, as Mary said, "you want to live together? Doesn't marriage work against people on Social Security?"

Sounding very much like a father questioning a son, Johnny demanded, "How long has this been going on?"

"Are you going to get a shotgun?" Jon quipped, and the boy looked abashed.

"Ah, well, we–" Rawlston began.

"It's not–" Alice said.

"Tell us all," Cary said softly, and the others settled back.

"We considered, we thought about," Alice hesitated briefly as if aware that her listeners couldn't believe they had even considered the possibility that Mary had mentioned, "about not marrying, just living together. But–"

"Our generation's views about that aside," inserted Rawlston, smiling at Alice.

"We want to get married." Alice glanced around the room at their Christmas faces. "For all the obvious reasons."

"Love," Rawlston said quietly. He looked at Alice. "'She was a phantom of delight,'" he began. Then he turned to Cary. "You've got us all thinking and quoting poetry."

He continued the narrative when Alice beamed at him. "And I, we, looked into the options. I asked a buddy I met in town to check on the social security thing–not wanting to bother you folks yet–and he looked it all up on his computer."

"Verified by that nice librarian who volunteers at the Harvest House," Alice said.

"Essentially," Rawlston said, with another blink, "the financial factor wasn't a consideration, didn't make up our minds."

Financial factor, thought Cary who glanced at Spence. This didn't even sound like their Rawlston.

"We'll live in my house–our house," Alice said. "It's plenty big enough. Rawlston wants a dog of his own." She smiled. "The goats can't keep his feet warm." She glanced at Winchester who had retreated to the coolness of the doorway. "And Winnie's not around enough."

"When will you, uh, tie the knot?" Johnny asked, then blushed as if embarrassed at his choice of words, if not the question itself.

Suzanne frowned at him. "That's not our business," she said.

"Sorry," Johnny muttered, with a quick glance at his parents.

"Uh, well," began Rawlston. "Well, there may be some things to clear up first, but we were thinking of the spring, sometime." He blinked rapidly and ran his hand over his beard.

Alice looked at Jon and Mary. "We even thought about a, well, a kind of double ceremony with you two. Or, if that doesn't work," she paused and bit at a fingernail, "of course, we can find a judge in town or a wedding chapel. We don't want to impose–"

"Or cause any extra trouble," Rawlston said.

Again, exclamations and disclaimers erupted. Mary went to Alice and bent to kiss the top of the older woman's head and then her cheek. "We'd be honored," she said, "to share the day with you."

Jon waited until Mary moved away and then he pulled Alice to her feet and whirled her around, so that Rawlston and Cary, nearest to them, dodged to avoid her tiny flying feet. At once everybody stood and shook hands with Rawlston and Alice, hugged them, and congratulated them all over again. "Gads, the place is going to dissolve in tears," Jon joked.

"Let's have a great gala," Cary said. "When the mill is ready–"

"If ever!" Spence said.

"When the mill is ready–or almost ready–in the spring, let's do it all at once! Jon and Mary can re-commit. You two can commit, and we'll celebrate our commitment to the mill!" She looked at Alice and Rawlston and then at Spence who was grinning widely. "Yes, that's what we'll do!"

"Get a sheet of paper for her list," Spence said. His tone was joking but Suzanne dashed to the back of the room and ripped a sheet of paper from a notebook. She thrust it into Cary's hands, and Rawlston leaned forward with a ballpoint pen.

"First things first," Mary said. "A sip of champagne. I know there's one bottle on ice."

A collective groan, punctuated with "I'm so full" and "I can't hold another thing," was immediately followed with a chorus of "yes, why not, bring it on, I'll get the glasses."

With a satisfied sigh, Spence placed the last glasses on the shelf and folded the drying cloth. "What a day." He yawned. "Now if Johnny and Suzanne decide to get married at the same time–"

"They won't," Cary assured him. "Suzanne wants a big wedding in her church, with at least six bridesmaids. She's told me her plans. Two of her girlfriends are recently married and she has absolutely forbidden them to get pregnant and spoil the effect!"

"I wouldn't have expected that of her," Spence said. "A huge wedding seems at odds with her very practical and level-headed nature."

"Different strokes for different girls. Her mother and father simply went to South Carolina one evening and came home married. I think she's doing the big wedding for her mother, partly–but not only." Cary leaned against the sink. "She wondered if I wanted to be the official photographer, but I said no, I'd take lots of candid shots but formal weddings need a real wedding photographer. She was relieved, I think."

"You'll be the official photographer at the double deal this spring," her husband said.

"And glad to be. I'm so excited, Spence. Who would ever have thought it–Alice and Rawlston!" She wrapped her arms about him. "This Cove creates romance. It's in the air."

"Rawlston looked a little worried, didn't you think? And he seemed reluctant to talk about his sister in Florida–is the woman ever coming back?–or his family, at all."

"Maybe he's embarrassed to tell them. You know, at his age." Cary held up a hand. "I mean, families can be that way. Even Johnny at first thought what his parents are doing was silly. He got over it in a hurry after Mary had a talk with him. Anyway, I did notice Rawlston's reticence and vagueness. Well, we'll surely meet his family at the big double deal."

"It's actually a triple deal," Spence said. "The mill is a player, too." Almost automatically he looked out the window toward the silhouette of the building against the sky. Though they had not sited the mill with the view from the kitchen window in mind, both he and Cary were glad they could see it plainly from their kitchen. The twenty-four foot wheel was in place, though not yet attached to a source of water or electricity. Surprisingly, erecting the wheel had been relatively easy, once the crane, John Lovett as consultant, and a crew of workers arrived. Now she had to wait, probably several months, for it to actually turn.

"It's been a long day, but let's go look at the drawings for the landscaping again," Cary said. "I'm thinking a stone path might work better than just a mulched one from the side parking lot." She saw his expression. "Don't roll your eyes like that. We can surely find a stone mason to do the actual work."

"My miller, my love." Spence studied the drawings and then nodded. "You're right," he said as he turned and whistled slightly. Winchester opened his eyes, got to his feet, stretching mightily. "Come on, boy, time for your walk." He kissed Cary. "Be back in a minute or two."

"I'll do a rough sketch," Cary said. She had thought of trying to find old millstones to pave a path but discarded that notion as being almost impossible (no one wanted to give up millstones even if a few could be found) to execute as well as being, to her mind, somehow "demeaning" to the stones themselves. Upon reflection, Cary concluded that millstones weren't meant to be stepping stones, but to be working stones, turning, not lying idle under countless footsteps. Of course, each time she saw a millstone in someone's yard or elsewhere on their property, she promptly inquired about purchasing it, so she knew how attached most persons were to their artifact from the past. Most could tell a story about how they came to have the stone: a great-great grandfather's mill, a cousin's gift to someone's mother after he saw his mill and hopes wash away in the great flood of 1916, the only reminder of a long ago uncle; a very few had simply found the stone or stones when they bought the property but they intended to keep them there. So far, she hadn't met a single owner willing to part with a single millstone.

Chapter 13 "All's Right with the World"

The month of January provided a lull in outdoor activity at ThymeTable. Two snows of four and six inches each turned the countryside into a glittery winter showcase. Cary and Spence spent much time reviewing the needs of the herb fields and planning for various festival and fair exhibits, and some time looking out the windows at the snow, falling, fallen.

"Darling, we can't ignore our rosemary and thyme and dill and everything," Spence said. He flung his arms toward the fields and greenhouses. "Our bread and butter, as it were."

Cary embraced him. "Look there's a cardinal–I saw one at Barrymore." She nestled under his arm. "I love ThymeTable. It has to come first. But the mill, oh, I can't wait to see the wheel turning."

"We can't count on that until at least this fall, my impatient one, maybe not even then. We'll be lucky to get the flume constructed by then. Spence spoke with the reality of a man of business who had become a man of the land. His realistic appraisal of promises by commerce and nature sometimes was at odds with Cary's expectations of instant results. She had come to appreciate, however, that deadlines weren't necessarily binding and that the winds, rain, and sunshine did not march in tandem with her "to do" list. "It's not been a year since we started the mill project," her husband reminded her. "Everything has moved faster than most people expected."

"I know," she said with resignation. "How many people have quoted to me that 'the mills grind slowly but surely'?"

"Sometime this new year, we'll see the wheel turning," Spence promised. "Even if I have to rig up an electric motor and leave the belts unconnected, so the stones don't turn."

"Oh, no," Cary exclaimed. Then she reconsidered. "Well, maybe just to see it going."

He laughed. "It will happen, but not for the gala you'd hoped for."

"Have I been that obvious? I had hoped to tie in our mill with the Francis Mill restoration workshop in July, but..." She didn't finish the sentence and sounded forlorn.

"We can aim toward having almost everything ready by then," Spence said, "except the water source. When you factor in the environmental concern, the safety concern with an earthen dam, some county regulations, to say nothing of the weather, as Mrs. Alison says, 'Don't count your chickens until they're hatched.'"

Cary looked at him and saw that even with his awareness of all that had to be done, he was cautiously optimistic the wheel would be turning by fall.

"We'll have a picnic, then, in the summer and invite the Workshop people over. They'll need a day of rest." After a moment, she went on. "But I don't think our couples want to wait for the mill's grand opening–when we really start grinding."

"Your impatience is contagious," Spence said. "Let's sit down and see what we can come up with and talk to them. Maybe an Open House before we're ready to grind."

For the rest of the morning, while Cary's huge pot of soup simmered and filled the house with earthy, root vegetables and oniony odors, they looked at dates and compiled lists. She had to return to Barrymore to celebrate her parents' fortieth anniversary and again for the birth of baby Randall, plus, they were committed to at least three herbal fairs.

At dinner, with Mary, Jon, Alice, and Rawlston, they fine-tuned their plans. Cary at first proposed that the wedding be held outdoors, an afternoon lawn party, and she would have invited a great number of friends. "Half the county," Spence commented. However, both couples wanted relatively few at their combined nuptials/renewal ceremony.

"We're shy," Alice said.

"Let's have it in the mill," Mary suggested. "That way, we can plan for an earlier time of day."

"Yes," piped up Alice. "I'm wearing dainty silk slippers and don't want to get them wet in the dew."

"Silk slippers," gasped Cary. She was accustomed to seeing Alice in sturdy, comfortable work boots and socks.

Alice lightly touched Rawlston's hand. "He has ordered them for me, light blue they are," she said. "And I'll wear Agnes's lovely shawl." Her lips quivered a bit. "She never did wear it after we left the city. An admirer gave it to her."

"It goes perfectly with your blue frock," Rawlston said. "You'll be the loveliest bride there."

"The only real bride," Mary said. "Remember, we're married and have been, lo, these years!" She and Jon exchanged proud glances.

"I guess if Alice is dressing up so fine, you'll have to abandon your usual pants and sweatshirts," Jon said to his wife. He feigned dodging Mary's thump on his head. "Not that you don't look great in them!"

"I've already decided what to wear. You're not the only one, Alice, to get out the finery. I'm wearing a long skirt with that Indian top. It's peach and beige."

"Gads." Spence glanced at Cary. "Then, it's suit and tie for me–or tux?"

After a few minutes of clothes talk, Jon said, "So, say a 10 o'clock ceremony?"

"Yes, then we could have an Open House starting at noon." Cary looked at her notes. "That will give us time to set things up without rushing."

"Can you get dressed by then?" Rawlston asked Cary with a twinkle in his eyes.

"I can, indeed! For weddings and picture taking, I can get up very early."

"What about your family, Rawlston?" Spence rose to pour tea while Cary removed the soup bowls and cleared the table for dessert.

"Well," Rawlston coughed and blinked. "Well, since Alice has no family except all of you, I, uh, we thought I'd stand alone–"

"Not invite your sister? Your nieces?" Cary placed a buttermilk pie on the table. "Are you sure?"

"It's, it's uh, for the best–"

"And I'm fine with it," Alice said. "Meeting his family is something I don't mind delaying." She picked up the serving spatula and busied herself with slicing the pie, not meeting their eyes.

For a few seconds, no one spoke.

"It's your wedding," Spence said. "Your decision."

Cary tackled her pie. "Isn't this fun! I'm making a list of our select invitees." She savored a bite of pie. "This is Mrs. Alison's recipe. But I made it. Yum yum." The others pronounced the pie excellent and Jon attempted to sneak a forkful from Alice's plate. She never finished a rich dessert and always offered it to Jon, but not until she was ready. Playfully she batted his fork away.

Cary smiled at the exchange and went on, "Alecia and Phillip will have their baby before then."

Mary said, "And next year at this time I bet you'll be pregnant."

"I'd put money on it," Rawlston agreed.

"Want to start a pot?" Jon asked. Aware of Cary's disappointment, as a group they seemed determined not to let her "pine about it," as Alice had said one day.

"I'm in," Alice announced. "And I will be a god-grandmother, if I may!"

Cary's eyes misted but she leaned over and hugged Alice. "You may, for sure! And Rawlston can be god-grandfather."

"Taking bets, taking bets," sang Jon as Spence kissed Cary resoundingly.

In that lighthearted moment, Cary felt sure, without a doubt, that she would be pregnant within months, maybe not by the mill's Open House but surely by the time the water rushed over the wheel and the grindstones turned. She burst into laughter, startling them, and then they joined her. "God's in his heaven and all's right with the world," Alice proclaimed.

Rawlston glanced at her with a question in his eyes, Cary noted, and the slightest shake of her head answered him. In the merriment Cary thought no more of it. "Robert Browning," she said.

After further listing and note-taking, Spence cleared the table so that Cary could spread out her mill photos and solicit their help in choosing the best. She and Mary reported on their progress–though Mary declared they were under no deadlines–on the book the two were collaborating on: the story of reassembling the mill. She rummaged in her shoulder bag, her portable briefcase, and showed the thickening packet of pages. "I never thought of me as an author," she said, "but it's been," she paused, "a pleasure to put this together. There is still a lot to do."

Cary nodded. "A lot of technical terms to become more authoritative about. Sometimes I have just said 'the whatyamaycallit' or the 'doodad,' knowing I can rely on experts later to straighten us out."

"I can just hear Rawlston say to one of the boys, 'Hand me that thingamagig, right next to the whatyamaycallit.'" Jon snorted, got choked for a moment and had them all laughing.

"Well, we haven't always wanted to interrupt you guys as you work with those things," Cary said. "I promise I'll look up everything–or ask someone."

"It's a great start–and it will definitely need a good content editor." Mary picked up the manuscript just as Spence lay it down. "First, of course, we would want you three–" she nodded to the men, "to read it for the facts, though I've taken notes and so has Cary when possible, but we likely have missed something."

"Then we'll find an editor–without the bias you all might have," Cary said.

"I knew you were busy," Jon said, "but I didn't know you were this far along with the project. No wonder I was underfoot." His tone was full of admiration and Mary's face lit up.

"Now you know why you'll have to do a lot of the cooking!" she retorted.

"Hey, this is a great picture of Rawlston directing the installation of the gears and pulleys," Spence said.

More discussion followed about the merits of the photographs, the chapter titles, possible editors, all the pre-publication details. Mary recommended Neweyesediting.com, a local partnership that did both hardcopy and online editing, fiction and technical material.

"Getting late," Jon grunted. He looked at Mary and she nodded.

Alice shifted in her chair, and Cary was immediately stung that they'd kept her at the dining room table so long. "Oh, Alice, I should have moved us to more comfortable chairs."

"Nonsense," Alice said. "These old bones have sat longer on harder chairs at far more tedious faculty meetings. Granted, that was a long time ago."

As they started to rise, she motioned them back. "This is probably as good a time as any..."

Everyone settled back with questioning looks.

Rawlston leaned toward Alice; their shoulders touched.

"Don't look so worried, Cary, dear," Alice said. "I'm not sick–"

"But," Rawlston prompted when she paused.

"But I am tired." She took a deep breath. "It's time for me to retire a second time, to give up the goats or at least, the business." She sighed and turned to Rawlston, "You tell them, please."

"We want to travel, and we can't burden you all with the goat business. Oh, we both love the little creatures and we want them to stay here in The Cove, if possible."

"It really can't be a total shock," Alice said, seeing consternation on their surprised faces. There were slow nods of confirmation and understanding around the table.

"And a couple of cheese shops have found other sources that can produce more volume."

"Dummies!" Mary exploded. "After all these years you've–"

"And I've sensed," Alice held up her hand to forestall other disclaimers, "that they may wonder about my ability to continue on the same degree of, shall we say, production, even sanitation. Johnny reported that one buyer had the audacity to ask about my age and about my eyesight!"

"We want to travel," Rawlston repeated.

Alice smiled. "It has been decades since I've been out of this state, do you realize that? While I can, we are going–going wherever we want to!"

Her voice was girlish in the declaration but then she said quietly, "I only wish Agnes and I had taken that trip to Peru way back when, when we could have climbed Machu Picchu, but we were committed to our goats." She spoke more firmly. "And I recognize the work is getting harder. My legs don't always have the 'git up and go' to do what has to be done, and my arms ache."

In an instant her friends surrounded her and assured her they thought the decision was for the best. They adjourned to the living room for more talking about where they might travel, the great advantages of tour groups, when and whether Alice would attempt to sell the business with its well-established name. To that Rawlston said, "We have some expectations along those lines but haven't broached it to anyone yet."

Mary said, “Hey, Alice, let’s put together a recipe book for your cheese dishes!”

“That could be our next project,” exclaimed Cary. “After the mill book.”

The elderly woman beamed. “After we travel,” she said.

The women nodded enthusiastically. “I’d take the photos, you know that,” Cary said.

“A swan song for your goats,” Jon said. “Hey, you can call it ‘Goat Song.’”

Mary threw up her hands in despair, even as Cary put her finger to her lips, seeming to consider the title.

“I think that’s a wonderful thought, you two, and I thank you.” Alice stood and Rawlston took her arm protectively. “Now, I am a little tired. All this talking...reminds me of school teaching!”

“Time for all of us to turn in,” Jon said. “We got a lot decided.”

“ThymeTable is buzzing–under the snow,” Cary said. “Like all those crocuses ready to burst through.” She showed them to the door and then she and Spence bundled up to take the patient Winchester for his stroll.

They, of course, walked up to the mill and admired its profile against the sky and the snow. Cary handed the leash to Spence and without a word fell backwards into the snow, startling the beagle who barked excitedly at the sudden movement. Cary laughed and began to rotate her arms in the snow. “Snow angels!” she cried. “I’m making a snow angel.” She stood up, stepped away a short distance, and again fell backwards, giggling.

Spence gazed and grinned at her. “I could never do that,” he admitted. He led Winchester in a giant circle around the two angel forms, and then extended his hand to help Cary to her feet. He dusted the snow from her back and shoulders and they looked at her creations. Spence turned to her, “Did you make a wish? Did you invoke the spirit of the mill?”

“If I did,” Cary said, with a wide smile, understanding his question, “we’ll have two.”

"Crazy woman," Spence grabbed her hand and they ran back to the house. Winchester ploughed a snow furrow beside them.

Chapter 14 "Bringing in the May"

Brilliant sunlight graced the first Saturday in May at the appointed hour. The inside of the mill also shone, so clean had it been scrubbed, brushed, and swept.

The previous day Buddy, Chrissy, Hector and Troy had outdone themselves in finding greenery, and Chrissy and Suzanne spent hours that evening arranging evergreen branches, lots of ivy, and quite a bit of white azaleas, studded with yellow roses. Buddy turned up with branches of late dogwood, from a tree he'd found uprooted by bulldozers at a new house site. Others added an assortment of favorite weeds and mosses. Yellow ribbons and white bows added color and the overwhelming motif was freshness.

Rawlston had stood before the dogwood as the girls fussed with it as if he were studying their art. He touched the bark. "Kind of like alligator skin, isn't it?" He turned to Chrissy who had just finished listening to her employer on the cell phone and seemed on the point of tears. "Come on, smile," he said. "Maybe your boss will find somebody to work for you." The younger girl had been told she must come into work at least until noon the next day, the day of the wedding. She'd protested and pouted, to no avail.

"Nobody looks that close at the bark," Suzanne said pertly, trying to ignore Chrissy's glumness. "It's the blossoms that shine."

Silently they surveyed the array of pottery and copper containers. "Signifying new beginnings," suddenly pronounced Chrissy, smiling bravely. When not artfully arranging the offerings of the woods, Chrissy had clung vine-like to Buddy's arm. Both Suzanne and Rawlston looked surprised at her words.

"There's more to you than meets the eye, young lady," Rawlston said gallantly, "and there's a lot of beauty that meets the eye."

Chrissy giggled and rushed off to help Buddy and Johnny set up the chairs.

Cary had caught Rawlston's eye and grinned, causing him to redden. She hummed "Here comes the bride," just as Spence entered the mill and the four young people dashed out. She couldn't refrain from quoting Robert Herrick: "'There's not a budding boy or girl this day/But is got up, and gone to bring in May'...let me see, then 'Come, let us go, while we are in our prime,/And take the harmless folly of the time.'"

"Not to be outdone," Spence said, "'Gather ye rose-buds while ye may,/Old Time is still a-flying.' I can't remember the rest of it, something about 'then be not coy, but use your time...'"

"'And while ye may, go marry.' And that we did, my love."

"Looks like they will, too." Spence nodded toward the open doorway. Chrissy had leapt on Buddy's back and he ran around the mill's exterior, whooping. Her exuberance had returned.

The chairs were arranged in a two-sided semi-circle with an aisle between them, and from Alice's house Spence and Jon had carried a small beautifully polished mahogany table. On it Cary placed a vase of ivy and a variety of herbs from their greenhouses: thyme, of course, basil, lavender, whatever she thought contributed to the collection. Mary pronounced it "perfect" and then Cary added dried milkweed seed pods. Mary said, "More perfect. Stop while you're ahead."

Mary surveyed the room. "This mill has seen a lot in its time. Wonder if this is its first wedding?" She wandered across to make yet another adjustment to her contribution of azaleas.

A very slight breeze stirred the flowers and brought Sarranda to Cary's mind. For her the mill, except for her childhood visits there, had not signified happiness; for her, it represented loss and sorrow. Certainly she had not witnessed a wedding in it. But now, Cary breathed silently, now, Sarranda, it's a happy place. A happy place. Sarranda would surely be pleased with the events of this day.

"Hey, are you coming along?" Mary called. "You look a thousand miles away."

"Just a century and a half away," Cary said. She had not told Mary, or anyone except Spence, of her one "visit" from Sarranda. In some strange way she knew Sarranda was her friend alone.

Cars began to arrive, and soon the guests began to find seats in the mill. The minister from the Unitarian Church appeared in an exquisitely embroidered robe, green on white. "Very herbal," she whispered to Winchester, who was, for the morning, consigned to the kitchen. She had stopped at the farmhouse to don her vestments and to have a quick solitary coffee. Rawlston had shyly requested that the ceremony be kept as private as possible. Cary anticipated fewer than fifty guests: their cove neighbors, the Alisons, and a few others plus Mark, the photographer, and his wife and the Graysons' oldest long-time goat cheese customers were there. Howie Landreau brought a lovely girl. Tanna and husband Tim slipped in beside Buddy, his mother, and the Bryson boys. Justin and Suzanne arrived with a flurry in his Jag, followed by Cary's parents, Phillip and Alecia and the baby, David Daniel. Alecia, slender and beautiful, graciously allowed Davey's grandmother, Ruthlene, to carry him, but she hovered nearby. At the last moment, Kenny Campbell from Old Traphill Mill hurried in, followed by Jack and Leslie Dellinger (all of whom had come quite a distance), and Cary gave them a small wave. Although she had promised a quick light brunch after the service, almost everyone arrived with some sort of food and drink, which was placed behind the counter temporarily. More people would arrive for the mill's Open House at noon, so Cary was sure all the dishes would be devoured.

Each couple graciously asked the other to "go first," and finally the evening before, Spence tossed a coin to decide the issue. Mary had contemplated letting her hair down, and she and Cary and Suzanne conferred while she brushed the long gray strands. Suzanne had wound it around Mary's head in an elegant coif that was, they decreed, "totally not Mary." And somehow loose hair didn't suit the quietly efficient, often grave, woman. They voted for its being re-plaited into its usual single braid; then Suzanne, clucking as a mother hen might, drew a few tendrils to fall gently to the side of Mary's face for a softening, "bride-like" effect. Since Jon and Mary had written their own vows for their first wedding, this time they elected to follow a fairly standard re-committal ceremony. Johnny walked somberly in front of them to the minister and stepped to one side, blushing as if he were the groom. Mary and Jon looked the picture of not totally reformed hippies: he wore loose trousers of handwoven material with a slightly darker linen shirt with blousey sleeves and a laced front. Mary's flowing gown of soft peach and beige was complemented by heavy beads Jon had brought years before from a South American trip. No one could doubt they were free spirits, very much now bound by love. Suzanne wanted Johnny to wear his one suit, but upon seeing their attire, she decreed that khaki pants with a white shirt and tie would be more appropriate. They were a most attractive family unit, Jon shifting from foot to foot throughout, Mary solemn and serene.

The minister joined their hands and said, "Jon, repeat after me," and she recited a short re- commitment statement. Jon, pausing occasionally, intoned: "I receive you, Mary, as a precious gift. Today as I stand before you, I wholeheartedly (he moved their entwined hands to his heart) recommit myself to you. I vow to love you, treasure you above all else, encourage you, and," here he inserted his own words, "to live with you," before continuing, "I am your partner for life and promise always to honor, cherish, and care for you."

Through her own moist eyes, Cary saw Mrs. Alison dab at her tears and Mary bite her lip while gazing at Jon. Soon, Mary murmured the same words, looking as innocent and as much in awe of what she was saying as surely she had decades before. Without faltering, she also inserted "and to live with you" and raised their hands to her breast.

Their declarations were clear and audible. At the conclusion tears rimmed Jon's eyes when they kissed. Since many of the onlookers knew their story–that Mary had assumed she was a divorcee all these years--a splattering of applause broke out with the minister's final declaration.

Alice, small, just slightly stooped, looked both vibrant and timid. Her face shone, and her hair gleamed white in the sunlight that entered through the mill's doorway. The interior of the mill was dim except for the sunlight; white candles nestled among the greenery on the counter added a romantic aura. Rawlston, in a well-fitting gray suit with a blue tie, stood in the doorway. She placed her hand on his arm, and they walked toward the minister and Cary and Spence. A quiet "ooooooh" rippled through the onlookers. They made a sophisticated couple. Cary's smile trembled. They certainly didn't match a stereotypical image of a goat farmer and a Yancey County farmer. So much for labels, Cary thought. They moved slowly but with confidence, smiling as they reached the altar-table. They had pored over several versions of the marriage ceremony and had chosen wording, they told Cary, that reflected their situation.

Alice turned to Rawlston and in a low tone spoke her vows: short and direct. "I Alice Grayson will love you, honor you, care for you in sickness and in health." With a twinkle, she said in a lower voice, "Just don't expect me to obey you." She raised her voice again after the appreciative ripple of humor died down, and Rawlston shook his head as if to say 'I'd never do that.' "Knowing what I know of you and trusting what I do not yet know, I welcome the chance to grow older (she emphasized the word, with a shy grin) with you, to cherish you, only you. I forsake all others..for as long as we both shall live."

With courtly deliberation, Rawlston raised her hand to his lips. He looked into her eyes, blinked, cleared his throat and said. "I," –he coughed again–"I promise to honor you, to forsake all others, to be true and faithful, to love you beyond all measure...and never to expect obedience in any form." He beamed at her and went on with words similar to hers.

They then turned to the minister who continued the ceremony before pronouncing them husband and wife. "You may now proclaim your union with a kiss," she said.

Alice and Rawlston, however, stood looking at each other, making no move, a certain expectancy in the air. Cary saw Alice nod slightly and grip his hand. A hushed silence prevailed. For an instant, Cary felt faint. Surely nothing had been amiss. Why didn't they move? What kept them from the next step? Was the marriage official without a kiss?

Rawlston stepped to the minister who waited with a puzzled expression and whispered in her ear. She looked at Alice who nodded and murmured an assent. The minister bent to speak to Rawlston again and he said something. Spence glanced at Cary, a slight frown of confusion on his face. In the silence they all heard a car pull into the parking lot and a door slam, then another. Tearing her gaze from the bride and groom to look over the audience, Cary could think of no one who should be arriving for the wedding. Surely it was too early for Open House arrivals? What was going on?

The minister took Alice's small hand, joined it to Rawlston's and said clearly: "I now pronounce you husband and wife, Mr. and Mrs. Raleigh Jordonson."

The wedding attendees broke into an excited buzz, turning in bewilderment and surprise to each other, even as Alice and Rawlston, now Raleigh, kissed briefly and she leaned against him.

Cary and Spence moved to hug the couple, Cary slightly dazed. Suzanne had promised to play a tape as a processional, but Suzanne was gazing out the door, then was moving toward it. They heard raised voices. Johnny had risen from where he sat on the back row and tried to close the door of the mill, but two people pushed him aside.

"This is a farce," a hefty, angry woman shouted. "Stop it!" She stormed toward the front, flapping her arms as if scattering chicken feed.

Alice, startled, cowered beside her husband. Then she straightened and gripped his arm. For an instant, Cary thought that neither seemed totally dumbfounded–as certainly the onlookers were. Cary and Spence both stepped in front of the older couple.

Spence said, "Stay right there. You're trespassing. This is a private ceremony on private property!" He held up his arm, and Cary, without thinking, did the same. Realizing they looked like traffic wardens, she dropped her arm but kept her feet planted firmly.

The large woman hesitated and the younger one caught up with her. Several men and women were on their feet, protective, ready to block their further progress.

"You've brainwashed him! You're keeping him here under false pretenses. We've called the police. They're on their way here. You'll all be arrested. You'll see, you'll never get away with it!" Her voice grew hoarse, and she put a hand to her bosom, as if to ward off an attack. The younger woman placed her hand on the other's elbow, but the heavy one shook it off, and took a deep breath. "You thought you'd get away with it, kidnaping him, I bet you thought you could keep him up here–up here in this, this holler, taking every cent he's got, hiding him back here in this–this place!"

The silence that greeted this outburst was absolute, until a crow's raucous cry on the hillside beyond the mill broke the stillness. The "caw" seemed to give everyone, now standing, permission to shift a bit, to glance about. Johnny and Jon stood almost at attention, ready to prevent further disruption, waiting for some signal from those at the mahogany table-altar.

"Mama," the younger woman said, quietly. "Calm down. Your blood pressure...."

"Edith," Rawlston-Raleigh said, matter-of-factly, "and Lenora."

Oh, my god, thought Cary, he's married already. Oh, Alice, how could he? But Alice's face told her this was no abandoned wife and daughter storming in. There was no horrified expression there, but a determined glint in her eyes, a glint that softened as she turned her gaze from the large woman to Rawlston-Raleigh. Though the thought had been fleeting, Cary was ashamed of herself. Raleigh (Cary told herself to get used to this new name) would not deceive them, not deceive Alice in that way. But clearly, some deception was in the air.

"I won't say 'welcome to The Cove,' Edith," Raleigh said. Cary noticed he didn't blink once and his voice, always soft, had a touch of steel in it. "And certainly, you're not welcome at this ceremony–"

"Ceremony, my foot! Who are you fooling, Raleigh Jordanson? Do they know where you belong? I'll have the lot of you brought up on charges–"

Spence motioned to Buddy who had quietly moved closer to the aisle. In a normal voice, calm and unthreatening, he said, "Call your law enforcement instructor, Buddy. See if he can get over here or can send somebody." He turned to the two women. "Madam, I suggest you reconsider your statements and that we finish this, this confrontation elsewhere."

"Don't you talk to my mother like that," the younger woman said, her eyes blazing. She pointed to Raleigh. "It's him you ought to be thinking about. We've got our rights–"

"You have no right to come in here, to invade this gathering," Cary stated. She took Spence's hand. "Whatever the situation may be, it will not be resolved in this," she paused, "this disrespectful way." She felt her face growing hot in outrage. While staring at the women, she saw from the corner of her eye, her mother Ruthlene smile broadly and give her a thumbs up signal. A smile tugged at her lips. If it weren't so humiliating for Rawlston–Raleigh, the scene would be ludicrous, even comic. But 'kidnaping,' 'charges,' 'taking every cent'?

Raleigh broke the clasp of Spence and Cary's hands to step between them. He swept the group of neighbors and friends with a look, then addressed them. "Folks, this is Edith, my niece, and her daughter, Lenora–" He knew the effect of the dramatic pause. "On my mother's side." Everyone smiled or grinned. "From up in northern Virginia." He seemed to run out of anything more to say and glanced toward Spence.

The minister spoke just as Spence turned toward her. "Our official business is concluded. Let's welcome Mr. and Mrs. Raleigh Jordanson." She stumbled a bit over the last name, having jotted it down quickly when the groom divulged it. In a lower voice, she said, "We'll get the marriage certificate signed right away."

The congregation broke into scattered applause and cheers. Jon and his son stepped to the two women, and each one took an elbow. Motioning others aside, they firmly escorted them to a couple of chairs where Lenora jerked her arm from Johnny's grasp and helped her mother to sit. Edith was breathing heavily, and the daughter took an inhaler from her purse and insisted her mother use it. "You haven't heard the end of this," she muttered. She took a notepad from her purse and began to fan Edith.

Jon and Johnny stood in the aisle near the woman, with Mary hovering nearby, her smile telling them she approved their behavior. Others flowed forward to congratulate Alice and Raleigh, to embrace, to hug or to shake hands. No one asked the obvious questions, questions that hung in the air. Perhaps they sensed that in time the mystery would be resolved and the questions answered. For now they could have been wedding guests anywhere, rejoicing in the happiness of the couples. The glowering women muttered to each other and sent stormy frowns toward the front of the room, where they were ignored or unnoticed.

After a few minutes Mary announced over the buzz in the mill, "If all of you want to go over to the farm, we'll have the refreshments there. Give us a few minutes, though, to put the coffee and tea on." She conferred with Mrs. Alison and Cary's mother who nodded and headed for the door. They would see that all was in order for the buffet, knowing that some things had to be settled before the Jordansons and Bradfords could join them. With a quick glance around, Mary asked, "Can we do anything else here, Spence?"

Cary answered for him. "They'll see to everything. If you and Jon would stay here..." She turned to Spence who nodded in agreement. People obligingly began moving toward the door, creating a small island around the two women, glancing at or ignoring them completely.

Buddy dodged around the departing guests and announced, "Mr. Warren's alerted the deputy who is on standby. He'll come if we call. Says he's no more than five minutes away."

"Thanks. Everything's under control here–"

"Ha," exclaimed Lenora.

After they signed the papers the minister placed before them, Raleigh led Alice to a chair across the aisle from Edith and Lenora. Alice's eyes had a sparkle that she didn't attempt to hide. In fact, Cary saw that she was making an effort not to grin outright at the women. Edith shoved the inhaler back into her purse and Lenora stood defiantly, scowling at the small group that now converged on them.

"Let's all sit down," Spence said. He indicated that Buddy should keep an eye on the door to insure privacy. The boy answered smartly, "Yes, sir."

"You thought you'd get away with it, didn't you?" Edith almost hissed.

Raleigh shook his head, whether in pity or disgust, Cary couldn't tell. "No," he said, almost wearily. "You thought you'd get away with it."

"What?" Cary said. "What?" She pinned Raleigh with a look. "Are you an escaped prisoner or something? You're not married to somebody else, are you?"

"My wife died sixteen years ago," Raleigh began. "She was an invalid for years. Lupus. And then she was diagnosed with, with Lou Gehrig's disease." He stumbled over the words, blinked and went on. "Our boys, Timothy and Theodore, twins...well, our boys went to serve in the desert, the Gulf War. They'd enlisted together in the National Guard years before–to support their surfing and smoking habit, they said. Well, both of them came home intact. Physically, at least. But they'd changed–"

Edith made an impatient gesture and interrupted. "You both, LucyAnn especially, spoiled those boys! Surfing–when they should have been working!"

"And Ted definitely had a drug problem after coming home, if not before," Lenora put in with a tone of righteous indignation.

"They're both dead." Edith's bald statement stunned Cary, and Spence jerked his head toward the woman as if he couldn't believe the words.

Raleigh's shoulders sagged a little and he rubbed his beard. "Yes. Forgive me. I'm taking a long time in the telling. The boys never were the same after being in the desert, and they couldn't accept their mother's illness. She was confined to a wheelchair and then it got worse, a lot worse. She couldn't chew, couldn't swallow–"

"They have hospitals for people like that," Edith said. "You should have–"

"Yes, I know what you think I should have done. But the boys and I couldn't put her 'away' like that. They tried, they did all they could to help."

"And their wives left them," Lenora said. "That and them acting like they were still twenty- year-olds. Surfing!"

A silence fell. Raleigh's face had paled.

"I'll tell them, Raleigh." Alice stood up. The look she directed at the two women was so scathing that Cary herself almost flinched. "They were killed in a car accident, coming home from the beach. They had been drinking, yes, maybe more," she said. "It was the anniversary of their mother's death." She took a deep breath. "And Raleigh–"

"I'd been suffering from depression for years, but living, I guess, for Tim and Ted's sake, covering it up, going to work, until I was seventy-two, anyway. When they died in that fiery crash, I lost it. Water, I could have accepted, I think, their death in water. After the desert, they loved the water so, but in fire..."

Cary moved closer to Raleigh, and Alice stood behind his chair, her arms on his shoulders, her hands trembling. Raleigh hunched forward, his face in his hands. "I can deal with it," he said. "I've learned to live with it."

"You don't have to say another word," Cary told him. Her eyes brimmed with tears.

"No," Spence said. "But, what in the hell are these two doing here?"

"They had him committed, got papers declaring him incompetent, even somehow got control of his checking account," Alice said before Raleigh could respond. Her voice had started strong but was weakening, and her hands shook a little. "They told lies to the doctors and acted like they were paying his bills!"

Mary went quickly to a cabinet in the corner and took out a bottle of water. She handed it to Alice. "I remember stashing it there one day. Here, drink this. We really need to get all of us to more comfortable chairs."

"I'm not inviting these women to ThymeTable," declared Cary.

Jon spoke for the first time, his arm around Mary's waist. "No, but we do have guests over there and every one of them curious as cats."

"Rawlston–I mean Raleigh, you broke out, didn't you? You escaped? You don't have a sister in Florida!" Cary had been so wrapped up in the story that she'd forgotten for the moment how Rawlston had appeared at ThymeTable so unexpectedly. She laughed. "I knew something was up. I just knew it!"

Raleigh raised his head at her excitement. "I'm afraid I lied–"

"A sister in Florida? That's a lie, for sure." Edith almost spit out the words. "We're his only living relatives. You can't believe a thing he says."

"I think, ladies, that we'd believe his lies rather than anything you tell us," Spence said. "But, Raleigh, are you–what–an escapee? Should we inform the police? Deputy Marlott is likely still having coffee just down the road. We can settle this." He glanced in the direction of the farm house. "The short version, now. Our guests will be wondering where we are."

"I walked out of Woodburne Hall a couple of days before I got this far," Raleigh said. "I stopped taking most of the medication. I somehow realized I was sedated most of the time. Those months are fuzzy, hazy times. I lost weight, didn't sleep." He stood up abruptly. "I'll tell you all about it–as I've told Alice. But now I'm tired." He regarded his new wife. "Tired but happy, dear."

"Woodburne will sue to recover their expenses in trying to find you," Lenora proclaimed. "And we placed ads and pictures around."

"How did you know he was here?" Spence asked the women, but he looked at Raleigh. "That's why you didn't want to spend a lot of time in town?"

"Why you grew a beard?" Cary said.

"These two went to a lot of trouble to convince some doctors and lawyers, a judge, that I was incapable of taking care of myself, and I didn't think I had a chance of changing their minds. I actually wasn't thinking too clearly then. I realized I had to get out, get away, and since I was so fuzzy and sleepy all the time, nobody paid much attention to me, so that part was easy. I suppose," he said, "that my room is still being paid for."

"Not after the first two months," Edith snapped. She apparently was not ready to admit any semblance of defeat. "You expect us to believe you simply walked into this place and they took you in without knowing anything about you?"

"Yes, I do expect you to believe it, Edith." He took Alice's hand. His voice had the ring of authority. "Let's go over to the house. We're finished here."

Cary stepped to the couple and whispered, "We'll all come back here later, and I'll take pictures. The minister will come with us, I'm sure."

Alice and Raleigh nodded their gratitude and, without another word, the two walked away. Cary saw that Raleigh carefully assisted Alice down the steps of the mill. Cary remembered that her mother had once said of a suicidal friend, "He's a man of sorrows and acquainted with grief." On this happy day, Raleigh had been re-acquainted with, slapped with, his sorrows and grief.

"What is this place?" Lenora sneered, "A home for old folks? What's he paying you?"

Cary's mouth dropped open. Rawlston–Raleigh paying? Raleigh with his two pairs of overalls, his jacket inherited from Agnes, his cheap boots? Alice had, she told Cary, convinced him to delay buying a ring, declaring she didn't want one and would have a hard time fitting one over her knuckles. And they apparently had not planned a trip yet away from The Cove. She smiled. She and Spence had created an elaborate card which they intended to present after the wedding: a "honeymoon cottage" stay in Rosemary. Fresh flowers and a basket of gourmet goodies awaited them. She had Johnny lined up to drive them from the farmhouse reception up to their houses, gather their suitcases and drive them back to the cottage.

Well, that could still happen. But first, they had to get rid of these two creatures who showed little inclination to move. Edith's face was an ugly shade of red, and her curly gray hair was damp. Her shrewd eyes darted from one to the other as if trying to find, shades of the television quiz program, "the weakest link." When her eyes met those of her daughter, she rose haughtily, almost regally, from the chair, adjusted the front of her dress where buttons threatened to pop any moment, and allowed Lenora to take her arm.

Spence spoke up. "Jon, why don't you see these women to their car?" He paused for emphasis. "And let the deputy know they're leaving, would you? Buddy has his number."

The women moved toward the mill's door with Lenora steering her mother as she might steer a sailboat through rough waters. Edith's back was stiff, but when she turned to glare at the remaining couples she stumbled slightly.

"Oh, please don't let her fall on our premises," Cary whispered to Spence. They stood watching until the two descended the steps, Jon at their heels. She muffled a giggle. "Jon looks like he's guiding cows from pasture to pasture."

Spence gave her a reproving glance, ruined by his contained grin.

"Okay, like livestock," Cary retorted to his look.

"Let's go to the party," Mary said. "Who knows what kind of rumors are circulating already!"

They quickly shifted the chairs to the sides of the room, straightened brochures on the counter, and removed the table that had served as an impromptu altar. Cary pronounced the mill ready for the Open House that would follow within the hour.

"Did you see the look on the minister's face?" Cary giggled as they hurried across the path to the farmhouse.

"It was nothing compared to the look on yours," Spence said with a laugh. "A fairly dramatic wedding, I'd say."

Chapter 15 "We Look Before and After"

Guests milled about the light buffet, sampling the smoked turkey, the salmon puffs, and the veggie wraps; with plates in hand they moved around the smiling Alice and Raleigh. A light buzz of conversation filled the air, overlaid with an element of excitement and curiosity. When Jon and Mary, holding hands, swept into the room, followed by Spence and Cary, a momentary lull in the noise level occurred. Then Johnny, after a gentle nudge from Suzanne, stepped toward the center of the room and raised his glass of soda.

"Here's a quick toast to the newly married," he said, looking toward the elderly couple and then toward his parents, "and to the newly committed." His face turned red and his voice deserted him. Everyone who had a drink of any sort raised it and waited as if for more. Johnny, however, seemed suddenly overcome with shyness. He gulped his drink and so did the guests.

Mrs. Alison rescued the boy. She put her arm around his waist and said, "We'll all drink to that. Congratulations, you all. It's a wonderful day for all of us."

A murmur of assent was followed by another sip, and just before people resumed their conversations, Spence spoke. "I know you're all wondering...First of all," he paused dramatically, "the intruders have left the property. Secondly, the groom here," he gestured toward Raleigh and grinned, "henceforth known as Raleigh is legally entitled to marry our Alice. Congratulations, again, you two."

"And he's perfectly safe," Cary put in. "He's just not Mr. Jabbers." Smiles and muted laughter greeted her comment. "That's all we need to know right now. Let's enjoy this food before the mob arrives for the Open House!"

"Hey, the press will be here, right?" It was Hector Bryson who self-consciously smoothed his hair. "We'll go right over and see that everything's shipshape...I mean mill shape."

"Yeah, we've got a lot of labor invested here," said his brother. "I don't want to see a nail out of place."

"You sound just like Rawlston–I mean Raleigh," Buddy said. "Let's hurry up, guys, and be there to greet the press! Reckon WLOS will send a crew?"

Other guests congratulated the couples with toasts, handshakes, and hugs before the party returned to more individual conversations. Alice and Raleigh stood to one side of the buffet, near the fireplace where a small blaze took the nip from the spring day. Jon and Mary, across the room, exchanged hearty laughs and quips with neighbors, some of whom remembered the early days of "communal living" at The Cove. Jon received good natured teasing from some of the longtime community residents who recalled his footloose days. He asserted that his wandering was over. "This rolling stone has stopped rolling, ready to gather some moss," he promised.

A neighbor ran his hand over Jon's thinning hair. "What moss?" and the group laughed.

Before noon, cars filled the side of the road and the few available parking spaces. A small item in the local paper had announced the open house for the public, and Spence and Cary had sent invitations to their herbalist and photography colleagues, and to a list of friends provided by Alice, Mary, and Justin. Raleigh had shaken his head and said, "No one I care to invite." She assumed he meant his Yancey County friends wouldn't want to drive over.

The refreshments for the larger group expected for the Open House were to be outside. Suzanne and two friends dubbed themselves "the caterers," and they moved the buffet table onto the farmhouse porch. They would keep the buffet laden with hot cider, hot tea, iced tea, sodas, and (after the wedding food disappeared) platters of cookies. They would also keep a steady supply of hot popcorn for the children.

As Suzanne placed a cup of tea in Cary's hands, Cary looked toward the mill. Its sign announced its new name: ThymeTable Mill, though Cary still thought of it as the old Buckner Mill. Cary and Denise had designed the sign. Simple lines showed a waterwheel and a sprig of herb that might be thyme. Spence had put it on posts, a temporary solution, until the final design of paths and planting around the site was complete. Johnny promised to learn stone masonry so he could create a suitable base; he went to Madison County once a week to be instructed by Buddy's uncle. He wasn't ready yet to lay the stones, but by the fall he would be. And by then a porch would be constructed around two sides of the building.

Spence hurried toward the mill to greet the arrivals. Cary went to Alice and Raleigh who were beginning to look harried and tired. She could see that they were ready to be rescued from the well-wishers surrounding them. She took Alice's arm, murmuring, "Excuse me," to those nearby.

"Come with me, please," she said. "We have a surprise for you." They smiled and excused themselves from the group. Cary said, "Rosemary Cottage is yours for the night. Flowers. Champagne. Everything's ready...and Johnny will drive you–"

"Oh, Cary, dear," Alice interrupted, looking slightly flustered.

"We've made reservations," Raleigh said.

"At Richmond Hill Inn," Alice finished.

"You're blushing like a newly-wed." Raleigh touched her cheek lightly.

"I'm sure you understand, don't you, Cary?" Alice's blush deepened. "You're not upset?"

"The limo's just pulling in, right on time," Raleigh said, glancing down the road. "We kept our going away a secret–"

"Lots of secrets today," Cary said, pertly. Then, seeing Alice's eyes darken in dismay, she whispered. "Of course, I understand." She stood back and took Alice's hand and Raleigh's hand in her two, surveyed them. "Of course, you want to leave for a day or two." Raleigh and Alice moved with one accord to embrace her, and as she looked over their shoulders she said, "Wow, that's some stretch limo out there. All the guests are staring."

"Our bags are packed," Alice said. "Just inside the door of my house, and," she paused in anticipation.

"The driver knows to go pick them up. He'll be back here in a minute or two," her husband finished.

"Oh my gosh," Cary said, banging her forehead with her fist. "We have to have the formal photographs. How could I forget. Let me grab my camera!" She ran outside and yelled to Spence. "Stop the minister! We'll be there in a minute." Suzanne handed the flustered Cary her camera bag.

Jon and Mary took the elderly couple's arms as they left the farmhouse porch. "Cary would never have forgiven herself if she'd forgotten pictures," Mary said. "Too much excitement, as Mrs. Alison would say, too much flustaration."

The next few minutes were a flurry of activity as more cars arrived, and the gleaming white limo came back down the road and parked. The driver, seeing that small commotion was going on, stood beside the vehicle while some wedding guests wandered out to watch the procession returning to the mill.

Thirty minutes later, everyone having been photographed, wreathed in smiles, Cary and the others ushered Alice and Raleigh toward the vehicle, and the wedding guests mingled with the newcomers, with much gawking and explaining going on. Alice had carried no bouquet down the aisle, but Alecia impulsively grabbed a handful of yellow roses, whisked a light hand towel around them in a knot, and thrust them into her hands. Alice stood for a moment, poised much like a beauty queen, before stepping to the limo, Raleigh's hand at her back. She beamed and gave the flowers a great heave. Suzanne caught them in a well- executed leap. Guests applauded, and with a flourish Raleigh helped his bride into the limo. The smartly uniformed driver shut the door, trotted to the other side, and with a toot of his horn and a slight squeal of tires they were off.

The Open House was scheduled from noon until three; over a hundred persons signed the visitors' book. They would have a write up in the local paper although the television crew had not shown up. Spence told Cary a crew would be there when the wheel started operating. The last of the visitors straggled to their cars around four o'clock, perhaps taking a hint from the "caterers three" who carried empty platters and plates to the kitchen without refilling them, swept the tablecloths away, and folded the tables. Johnny and Buddy tied up garbage bags and lugged them to the back of the house. Just then, Chrissy came speeding up the road. Her part-time job at a nursing home typically left her free when she requested it, but today three other aides were out and her boss offered her an ultimatum: show up or quit. Her mother's frown and her car payment helped her decision. She saw there was little she could do to help. Her bad mood at having to work on this momentous day apparently dissolved with Buddy's long welcoming kiss, and soon she was her buoyant self, exclaiming over Suzanne's lucky catch.

"I would have caught it," Chrissy pronounced, "if I'd been here. Wouldn't I, Buddy?" They grabbed another bag of garbage and with it bumping between them ran to the back of the house.

Suzanne, all of four years older than her cousin Chrissy, grinned. "If she had her way, she'd be married tomorrow. Youth!"

Cary and Spence slumped against the side of the mill. Her face was damp; her lipstick had long since disappeared, her feet hurt and her legs were weak. "I feel great," she said. "Next to our wedding day, this is the absolute best day ever."

She squeezed Spence's hand. "You look worn to a nubbin," she said. "You must have been up since five or six this morning." He had pulled his shirt from his pants and now he used it to wipe his face and hands. "Hard work, this hosting," she said.

Denise and Justin had left off immediately after the open house started, both having heavy work commitments the next day. Cary and Spence sent Phillip, Alecia, a sleepy Davy, and the Randalls back to Asheville to have dinner at Vincenzo's, pleading all the work they had to do and promising to provide breakfast in the morning. Alecia had been adamant. "You'll do no such thing. We'll have breakfast in town and come out later–much later for coffee."

The others nodded, and Phillip said with pride, "She's a regular tyrant now that she's a mother." Cary's face was wistful as she watched Phillip carefully transfer Davy to his car seat. Cary's parents hugged her. Her dad said, "We're so proud of you," and her mother whispered, "The mill is great, but don't you work too hard. See you tomorrow afternoon."

Now Cary said, "I'm glad we'll have time for a sleep-in tomorrow."

"Yep, farming was never this hard. How many times did I explain, or try to explain, how a mill, how it all works? I've just about memorized my spiel, and I hope I got it right!" He had written up a script, with the steps for grinding in numbered sequence, but many questions, Spence admitted, he just could not answer with certainty, not until he had real experience.

"Not to worry, darling. Only a few people here actually knew how corn is ground, and they didn't contradict you. I'm so glad the mill owners came, and, and–everybody."

"Let's lock up and go clean up," Spence said. He yelled into the mill, "Hey, you two newly committed, stop whatever you're doing. It's time to call it a day." He glanced around. The site looked fairly clean; visitors had been careful with their paper trash, taking a cue from Johnny and the Bryson boys who were quick to pick up any litter that touched the ground, but he saw a few scraps. "Or at least, stop for now. I can get back to this later."

They heard chuckles as Jon and Mary emerged. "She's been trying to edit her poem," Jon said, giving Mary's long braid a tweak.

"Well, just change a word or two," Mary pointed out. She had reluctantly allowed her mill poem to be framed and hung. "It needs some help."

"It's perfectly okay," her friend assured her. "Several people commented on it–good comments." When Mary's face still registered uncertainty, Cary went on, "Let it rest awhile. Isn't that what you'd tell a writer? Look at a couple of days from now and see how you feel. I bet you won't change a word."

The four walked to the farmhouse, now swept and restored it to what Suzanne pronounced "its pristine glory." They were lavish in their praise of the girls' hard work. Johnny and Buddy had taken the chairs back to the church fellowship hall and the garbage to the nearest dumpster; they were to meet the girls later. Knowing Suzanne and her "caterers" would take no pay, would even be insulted at its being offered, Cary had earlier that week purchased several movie gift certificates which she pressed into their hands, saying, "These can't be returned. They have to be used. We couldn't have had such a good time without all your help. Please take them."

"Treat your guys, sometime." Spence shooed them toward the door. "And get some rest."

"What about Alice and Rawls–Raleigh?" Chrissy asked, and the girls hesitated on the porch, curious.

"We'll let you know when we know," Cary said. "Here, take all these extra cookies. Now, go on so we can get some rest!"

"We're going to the Orange Peel downtown," Suzanne announced. Spence and Cary groaned in mock horror at their energy level. Jon held up Mary who pretended to sag in exhaustion.

Later, as the two couples sat in ThymeTable's living room, having vast grilled sandwiches that incorporated leftover vegetables and cheeses, they were also wondering about Raleigh's situation. Each admitted to having doubts about the authenticity of his Yancey County identity–not at the beginning but as he occasionally revealed a knowledge and vocabulary at odds with his "persona." But each also admitted to being surprised, if not stunned, at the confrontation and his relatives' behavior and their anger.

"Enough," Spence finally said. "We'll be told what we need to know. Let's leave it for now and just wish him and Alice all the best." They raised their cups of tea and nodded.

"I just hope they will stay on here," Cary said, a mournful note to her voice. She couldn't imagine The Cove without Alice and now without Raleigh.

The others nodded in agreement. Spence teased, "Honey, you have your mill–our mill. Won't that content you?"

"Yeah," Mary added. "What more do you want?"

"You know perfectly well what more do I want!" Cary cast a sexy leer at Spence. Jon and Mary laughed and stood.

"Sex," Jon exclaimed. "It's all women think about!" He winced in pretended pain at Mary's light slap on his shoulder.

"Guess we can take a hint," Mary said.

"Gads." Jon yawned and rubbed his back. "My bones are creaking in all directions. We should have brought the car. I'm not sure I can make it back to our house." He picked up Mary's jacket and settled in around her shoulders.

"You'll make it," Mary assured him, "if I have to carry you."

"Lord forbid," Jon said. "Let's go." He reached down to tousle Cary's hair. "It's not miles to go before I sleep, but I do have promises to keep."

Alice called the following afternoon, after Cary's family had left for Virginia, saying she and Raleigh would return late the next day; he was scheduling an appointment with an attorney in town and she would treat herself to a morning in the luxurious spa at the Grove Park Inn.

"The Spa?" Cary repeated, trying to reconcile the advertisements for lush luxury she'd seen with the practical Alice.

"I'm not too old, young lady," Alice said, as if she could see the expression on Cary's face. "I've had my hair done, and I'm having a pedicure right now."

"Pedicure?" Cary giggled. "I sound like a parrot, don't I? Gosh, will we recognize you when you return? Have you done anything drastic to your hair?" Cary had visions of Alice as a newly blond or a blue-sheened lady.

"You'll recognize me. Wish us luck with the family from...with Raleigh's family, and say hello to my goats for me."

"Let me just put this toe separator here, Madame. That's fine," Cary heard before Alice said, "We'll see you after dinner tomorrow."

Cary stood holding the phone. Alice was definitely having a good time on her honeymoon. Being pampered. Yet the difficulties with Edith and Lenora had to be dealt with. Cary wanted to call back and recommend an attorney, wanted to drive into town to comfort Alice, to bolster Raleigh's resolve. She shook her head. She was being silly. It sounded as if the couple were in need of no help from anyone now. They would have had dinner, but Cary decided she would make a special dessert for them, maybe a blackberry pie. No, too many seeds. She'd make creme brulee, and Spence could use the culinary torch he'd gotten for Christmas. It was still in its box. There had been little time for creative cooking, or any cooking, this spring. She replaced the phone and walked to the window to gaze out. She wondered if she'd ever get tired of seeing the mill. No, she didn't think so. She could hardly wait–though wait she must for a few months–for the wheel to be operational. She smiled just thinking of it. For a brief moment, thinking again of Alice, Cary envied her the spa pampering. She and Spence had been up since before seven, ignoring the mill for a change, working in the greenhouses. Then she saw Spence, his face smudged, carrying trays of seedlings from the greenhouse to the porch, and she thought a good hot shower for both of them was the order of the day. Even if it was midafternoon.

The next evening, around eight o'clock, the white limo delivered the Jordansons, with the driver once again hopping out to open the door and then to set their suitcases on ThymeTable's porch. Cary saw Raleigh shake his hand and slip him a bill from his wallet. The driver bent to kiss Alice's hand, and she patted his shoulder. With a wave, the driver closed the limo door, tooted the horn a couple of times and was gone. Cary, the others right behind her, Winchester in front, rushed out to welcome them. Later, the three couples sat around the kitchen table, the place they always seemed to gather. Almost simultaneously, satisfied sighs indicated the success of the creme brulee and the spicy hot tea. They had talked in generalities about being such tourists in Asheville: playing croquet at Richmond Hill, Alice's spa experience ("Every woman should treat herself once–at least!"), and the trolley ride around the downtown streets.

"You were missed, you know that?" Cary said. "Not even two full days and the place seemed empty and your goats desolate. I wish I had the wedding photos to show you, but maybe in a couple of days. Welcome home."

They'd already drunk to the wedding day, to Jon and Mary's happiness, and to the returning honeymooners, but they raised their cups once again.

"And we await your news," Mary said. "That is, if we're not being overly nosy." She regarded Raleigh. "At least you didn't come back bloody or bruised so they didn't assault you."

"Not physically, but they acted like they wanted to," Alice said. "They were even staying at the Grove Park Inn. If

I'd known that, I might not have tried the spa there. I ran into them in the lobby, but I certainly didn't tell them where I was headed."

"I bet they didn't splurge on a spa treatment either," Cary said.

"Afraid it'd soften them up," quipped Jon.

Mary said, "Go on. Tell us about it. Did you meet with them? Have they left–?"

"Edith has left the building," Jon muttered. Mary rolled her eyes.

Raleigh laid his hand on Alice's wrist. "I met with an attorney, Mr. McDowell, for a couple of hours this morning, told him everything. I'd already called Woodburne. No problem there. I thought Edith might have called them but she hadn't. I'll, we'll have to make a trip up there soon, maybe next week."

Alice nodded.

"Once I get control of my bank accounts again, Woodburne knows they'll be paid," Raleigh said. "Mr. McDowell arranged a loan if we need it to tide us over, though I had and have a little stashed away."

"I should think so," Mary said. "Otherwise, Richmond Hill might have kept you there, washing dishes!"

Raleigh leaned forward, his hands clasped. "I called a friend of mine who called in his credit card number to the Inn. He wondered where I'd been for almost a year. He has certain, shall we say, political connections that should expedite matters."

"Okay, Raleigh," Cary said. "We still don't know–well, you're not a farmer and you're not," she hesitated and smiled, "not depressed. Not now, but who are you?"

"I taught history. First in Pennsylvania's state system. At Mary Baldwin for the last twenty years."

"Professor Jordanson!" Jon said. "I heard you lecture once, let's see, it must have been over twenty years ago. Out in Iowa. You had a full beard then, longer hair."

"Didn't we all?" Raleigh returned.

"The things you remember," Mary chided. "What was the lecture on?"

"Hmm, a possible tie in between the stone circles in the upper U.S. and along the Mississippi, something like that." Jon shook his head. "I just happened to be in town, went with a friend who was into archeology and Native American sites. It's coming back to me now, but I never ever would have made the connection. Hadn't you just written a book?"

"You're to be commended for remembering even the topic," Raleigh said. "A monograph, dry and unexciting." He looked at Mary. "I could have used a good editor who could translate that scholarly material into the interesting topic it really was."

"A teacher. I just knew you weren't a farmer. Your hands gave you away and some other stuff. But you seemed to know a lot about mills," Cary mused. "Have you done research in that area of early U.S. history?"

"Not at all. But I learned quickly once I hooked into Asheville's library system and the internet there. I'm a real fraud when it comes to mills." For a fraud, Raleigh looked proud of his knowledge.

"Tell us what you'll do next?" Spence said. He looked at his watch. It had been a long day, a lot of catching up on work he'd ignored during the pre-wedding days.

"We all need our rest," Alice acknowledged. "The short version, please, Raleigh."

"Edith and Lenora are still in a huff, threatening all kinds of legal action. They accosted us in the lobby–quite loudly–when I went to pick up Alice. They must have been waiting and watching, but I insisted we'd talk only in a lawyer's office. We already had an appointment. They didn't like it, but they came on to his office." He blinked and shook his head. "It wasn't a pleasant meeting. Don't know why I didn't recognize their meanness before or their money-grubbing. Anyway, the lawyer thinks they're all 'sound and fury signifying nothing.' Or very little. He's checking more thoroughly with Virginia laws." Raleigh stopped and looked at Alice, as if for help.

She continued his story. "Mr. McDowell will go through the entire process of Raleigh's being committed and, uh, leaving Woodburne. He'll have to file a petition in district court and appear for a hearing before a judge."

Cary frowned. "It was a judge who committed you, right?"

"Yes, involuntary incompetency it is called. Now I have to demonstrate competency–"

"Which you can easily do," Alice finished, her face glowing.

"Which I'm very hopeful of doing. Marrying you shows how smart I am," Raleigh said. "Any judge can see that!"

"Is the process long and involved?" Mary asked.

"I suppose it depends on the case load, the system, various factors. However, I've given the lawyer names of persons to call, doctors, professors, even a judge or two, who will surely speak for me...now." He rubbed his forehead. "It's difficult for me to recall exactly what happened. I really didn't care at that point. Trust me. Severe depression is no illusion. No doubt Edith can and will produce persons who will document my condition–then. I hope if it becomes necessary, I can ask you," Raleigh looked around the table, "my friends, to testify on my behalf."

"Absolutely," Spence said, amid a chorus of assurances and nods. Cary got up and gave him a hug, kissed his ear. They laughed at his blush.

"Anyway, if the judge determines I seem okay, he'll likely then refer my case to a state agency called Adult Protective Services. They will do even more investigating, interviewing, getting references, and will render a recommendation to the court. The attorney says the judge typically goes with the agency's recommendation."

"Could be a long time, then," Jon commented. "Will you have to establish or re-establish residency in Virginia?"

"Oh, don't say you have to leave here," Cary exclaimed. "No, not now, you have to see the mill operate! We're depending on you."

Alice looked at Raleigh for affirmation. "The hearing has to be in the state where Raleigh's legal residence is–and that's still Virginia." He nodded and she asked, "The mill may be ready by this fall, didn't you say, Spence? I'm sure things will be settled by then, but–"

"We may be traveling by then. If all goes well, and I have confidence it will, I want to take Alice to the south of France."

"Skipping Paris," Alice said, with a flounce of her head. "Paris is where dear Agnes's soldier friend was when he wrote her that farewell letter. It's silly, I know, but at my age, I can indulge my silliness. I just don't want to see the city that, that seduced him, took him away from her."

How much we don't know about each other, Cary thought, seeing the determination on Alice's face. How little we really know. And yet she felt she knew these friends and her husband better than anyone she'd met before coming to ThymeTable. Even Denise.

"Paris be skipped," Jon declared.

"We'll make our home here," Alice went on. "Raleigh doesn't want to return to Virginia to live and this has been my home too long to adjust to anywhere else." She took Cary's hand. "But to be realistic, as we've told you, we will give up the goat business."

"Keeping Mercury," Raleigh said. "That creature is my buddy."

"Of course, we can't let Mercury go," Alice turned to Jon. "Will you and Johnny look after the goats while we're gone?"

"Of course, anytime." He pointed to his chest, with a slight nod toward Mary. "I'm not going anywhere. Nowhere. No nada, no never."

"Ha," returned Mary without a trace of skepticism.

"We'll likely be going to Virginia quite often in the next few months. Raleigh has a house and his car to deal with," Alice said. "That nice limo driver said he'd drive us, in my car, not the limo! He's separated from his wife, wants to get away some. People are so wonderful." She paused, then said, "I hope they're as wonderful in Virginia."

"Oh, they will be. They are," Cary assured her. "If you're anywhere near Barrymore, you should stop and see my family. And Phillip may know just the right people, Raleigh. He seems to know everybody in Virginia."

"It's going to be an adventure," Raleigh said. "Just as being married to this woman is going to be. Who knows what she may get into in France. Stomping grapes, maybe."

"Are there any spas there?" Alice's eyes sparkled. "Ah, we may have to have a jacuzzi installed!"

"The woman is transforming completely!" Raleigh said. "From overalls and work boots to silks and spas." But his eyes said he liked all facets of the woman he'd married.

Chapter 16 "Mellow October"

The trees and shrubbery proclaimed October's visage in colors befitting a clowning king: burgundies and oranges flouncing on the hillsides, yellows out-glowing the russets and browns; golds and reds vying for dominance, while the steady evergreens stood like sentinels guarding an ever-changing color palate. Earlier, Cary had stood on the porch, admiring the scene, until she just had to quote one of her favorite Keats'odes, "To Autumn:" "Season of mists and mellow fruitfulness/Close bosom friend of the maturing sun;/Conspiring with him how to load and bless..." She couldn't remember the next lines, something about "And fill all fruit with ripeness to the core;/To swell the gourd, and plump the hazel shells..." Her radiant smile saluted Keats, and then she had made her morning pilgrimage to the mill.

She found Jon, oily and frowning, making yet another adjustment to the wheel. He assured her that within a few days, it would, he guaranteed it, truly would be capable of grinding the few bags of corn that sat waiting. "Damn," he said. "I intend to get this wheel balanced today. This one last bolt should do it." Cary had hoped the dam would be complete and the water flow through the new race would do the turning. But contractors and inspectors counseled delays and cautions, indicating they did not expect to approve the dam until the following spring. She realized just how naive she'd been about time frames. An increase in patience had certainly been a by-product of getting and setting up the mill. She now accepted the adage: the mills of the gods grind slowly. An electric motor would temporarily turn the grindstones, while the wheel would (as Spence said) "look picturesque" with a small amount of water flowing over it, courtesy of a pipeline from the stream.

They had invited her family to arrive on November 1 to see the first grinding. It had to be in early November. She'd even promised to make cornbread for them. Mrs. Alison had already given her the recipe she used, with the admonition, "Get the iron skillet good and hot, so a water drop dances off it before you pour the batter in." Cornbread she could make, but a few times, Cary and the two men had been at odds. She insisted that somehow they could get water over the wheel whether the wheel itself, at that point, could turn the stones. Feminine determination, plus a few tears, had overcome masculine logic and understanding of mechanics.

Sunlight slashed across Cary's desk, making her computer screen almost impossible to read. No matter. She could draw the curtains in a few minutes when she checked for morning emails.

Now she didn't mind because, in a reflective mood, she spread all kinds of messages, dating from months ago until a couple of hours ago, including emails turned into hard copy, before her. The blank screen mirrored the face of a woman smiling widely. One by one she picked up the bits of paper before her, and one by one she reread them all.

A postcard in Denise's sprawling script in purple ink:

Hi Cary and all who abide near her, Justin and I have only three days here, for his interview and big decision. Who would have thought he would even consider this small hospital in a rural area? Lots of arty types around; Penland School nearby, studios and galleries. Heaven for me–and close enough to you, old college friend. It's a big opportunity and J. is seriously talking. Postmarked Spruce Pine, NC, approximately an hour away. Justin found he enjoyed both the challenges of a small hospital and the challenges of the ice skating arena. Denise already had herself lined up to teach a course at Penland School and her jewelry in the most prestigious gallery/gift shop in town.

Cary grinned and picked up another postcard from much farther away: Provence, France.

Having a wonderful time–delightful young French woman driving us--chateaus, villages, churches. No grape stomping yet. This is Monet's grave. It's beautiful but it's not our Cove. We'll be back before you get this. Alice and Raleigh. And back they were, happy to be together, sad at giving up the goats and cheesemaking, but finding compensation in each other's company and the concerts in Asheville, plus, finally, concluding any connection with the Virginia mental health care system.

An email from Mary dated three weeks earlier:

Trying out my new computer and email server. If you get this, come out and wave! Seriously, as I mentioned this a.m., thank goodness TTable has the mill to keep Jon busy. All this togetherness could get to be much! Let's talk! Let me know if this comes through. M.

Two newspaper clippings:

A wedding announced: *Mr. and Mrs. Edward Lawson announce the marriage of their daughter Chrisanne Lee to Bertrand (Buddy) Noland on September 10, in Gatlinburg, Tennessee. The bride attends Asheville-Buncombe Technical Community College in the AAS nursing program. The groom is employed by CraftMart as a security guard and will complete the requirements for a degree in Criminal Justice at ABTCC in December. The couple resides in Pine Park, Weaverville.*

A death announced: *Franklin Bertrand Noland, age 98, went to be with his Lord on July 22. A native and lifelong resident of Madison County, he was the son of Dewey and Rose Tennant Noland. He was also preceded in death by....* (Cary glanced up, recalling again with fondness the gentle man she'd met at Francis Mill). *A retired tobacco farmer, he is remembered for being one of the last millers in the county. He was a member of Locust Field Baptist Church for over eighty years. He is survived by...*(once again, Cary skipped the formidable list, which ended with *"28 grand-children and 23 great grandchildren."* Cary and Spence had gone to the funeral, where Buddy had been one of the pallbearers. Mr. Noland had outlived most of his contemporaries, but the church could not accommodate the hundreds of people who came to "pay their last respects."

A work of "folk" art :

A large piece of construction paper encased in a plastic sheet held the palm prints–in dark blue fingerpaint–of a child. A smudge had been almost completely removed with a dab of correction fluid. Across the bottom, Alecia had printed: Davy's hands. Age six months.

A letter from High Country Publishers:

Dear Ms. Bradford, We are happy to enclose a copy of our standard publishing contract for your signature. We enjoyed meeting and talking with you and your co-author (a copy is being sent to her as well) about the manuscript, marketing strategies, and our production schedule–and based on your excellent proposal we certainly have high expectations for The Making of a Mill: Amateurs Turning a Wheel. As your proposal and sample chapters illustrated, it likely will require very little line editing, which we find both delightful and highly unusual. The photographs enhance and complement the subject matter greatly. We will be in touch as soon as we receive the contract. Call us if you have any questions. And welcome to High Country.

The last piece of paper was the most recent, a note Spence scribbled that morning while Cary was still in bed. He'd brought her a cup of tea before he drove into town with the Jordansons to finalize the sale of Alice's house to Johnny and Suzanne, still unmarried but planning. For the time being Alice and Raleigh had decided to lease Justin's house, which was smaller and less drafty than Alice's. Raleigh had already installed a dog door.

Sweetest one, See you around lunch time. I know you want to help at the mill but remember what the doctor said– no heavy lifting. Period. Please! Love.

The note was tucked into a book, sent by Cary's parents: *Everything You Need to Know When You're Having Twins.*

Cary heard a rumble and looked out the window. The wheel began to turn.

Old Traphill Mill

Made in the USA
Middletown, DE
01 November 2022

13906186R00117

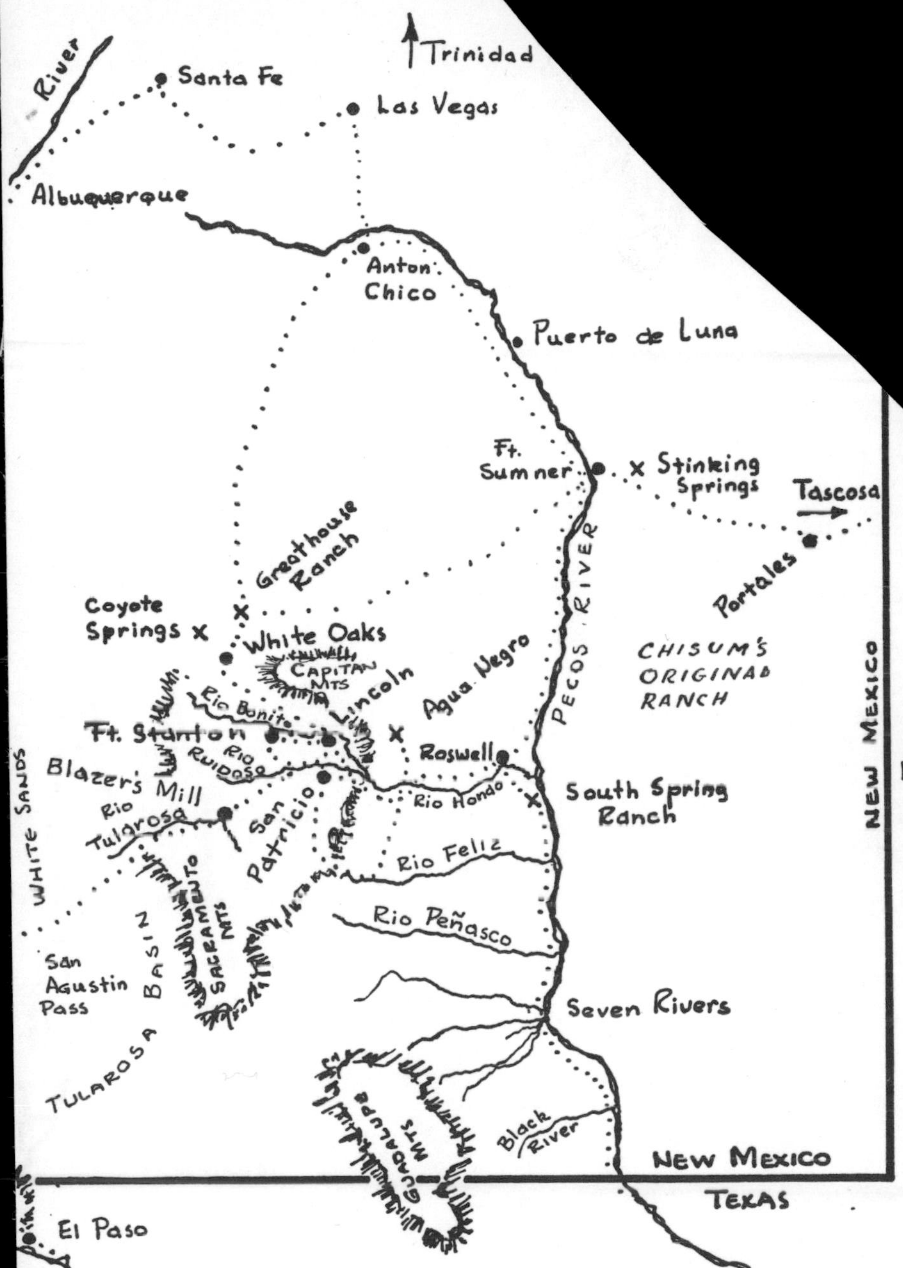

Trinidad
River
Santa Fe
Las Vegas
Albuquerque
Anton Chico
Puerto de Luna
Ft. Sumner
Stinking Springs
Tascosa
Portales
Greathouse Ranch
Coyote Springs
White Oaks
Capitan Mts
Lincoln
Agua Negro
Pecos River
Chisum's Original Ranch
Rio Bonito
Ft. Stanton
Rio Ruidoso
Roswell
Blazer's Mill
Rio Hondo
South Spring Ranch
Rio Tularosa
San Patricio
White Sands
Sacramento Mts
Rio Feliz
Rio Peñasco
San Agustin Pass
Basin
Seven Rivers
Tularosa
Guadalupe Mts
Black River
New Mexico
Texas
El Paso